Eleanor Roosevelt Goes to Prison

Eleanor Roosevelt Goes to Prison

A Missy LeHand Mystery

To Sue

By Kelly Durham and Kathryn Smith

Kathryn Smith

In memory of Dr. Stuart Raper, Janice Howe Raper, and all the physicians, nurses, and physical therapists who cared for polio patients at the Warm Springs Foundation

PROLOGUE

July 1935
Middle Georgia

It was a hundred miles from Greenville, Georgia over to Milledgeville where the state prison farm was located. At the height of summer, every one of those miles was hot, humid, and dusty. If you got behind a logging truck, you'd have to slow down until you could find a straight stretch of road to pass on. In the meantime, you'd limp along at a turtle's pace sucking in the exhaust fumes from the truck and going so slow you couldn't even raise a breeze to cool yourself off.

Wilton Biggs was about to melt by the time he got through Macon and reached Gray. He stopped at a filling station, his wet shirt clinging to his back as he climbed out of the car. He went inside while the boy filled his tank. There was a fan mounted in an upper corner of the little office, wafting the air just enough to keep the flies at bay. Wilton pulled a Coke out of a tub full of ice and bought a pack of peanut butter crackers. He drank the Coke in about three swallows and stuck the bottle back in a wooden rack next to the tub. He paid for his gas and climbed back into his car, a blue Buick, the envy of nearly everybody in Greenville, and turned east on Highway 22. He munched on his dry crackers and enjoyed the coolness of the wind his side-windows channeled onto his face and through his short red hair. *Shoulda got me another Coke*, he thought as he drove along.

By early afternoon, he was shaking hands with the warden of the state prison farm, a Captain Carlson.

"Nice to know you, cap'n," Wilton said.

"Likewise, likewise, Mr. Biggs. It's nice to have a distraction from the riff-raff I have to deal with most of the time." Carlson had come to work that morning wearing khaki pants and shirt that had been painstakingly starched and pressed in the prison laundry, but they were visibly wilting in the sticky heat of the afternoon. The men were sitting in the warden's simple office inside the two-story brick headquarters building of the farm, a sprawling complex that included a brick yard and four thousand acres of agricultural fields where the inmates worked to grow their own food. An electric fan hummed quietly off to the side occasionally ruffling the papers stacked on the warden's wooden desk. "I understand you're in need of a maid," Carlson said.

"A maid who can cook," Wilton said, nodding. "You got some girls that fit that bill?"

Carlson chuckled. "We have inmates eligible for parole to fit most any opportunity, especially for distinguished citizens like yourself."

"Good," Wilton said with a smile, pulling a fat envelope from his back pocket and laying it on the warden's desk.

Carlson eased open his desk drawer and slid the envelope into it with a deft motion. "Now the State of Georgia requires that you provide meaningful employment for its parolees, you understand? Plus, we ask that you provide us with regular reports on the rehabilitation of your parolee."

"Of course."

"You can just send those here to me, say once a month or so." Carlson stood and gestured toward the closed door. "Come on, we'll go see what the matron has selected for you."

Wilton followed the warden outside into a fenced yard and over to a line of sweating, black women in striped dresses who were standing in the sun. Two khaki-clad guards, armed with shotguns and wearing pistols on their belts, stood watch.

"We think one of these gals might suit you, Mr. Biggs."

Wilton walked along the line, his eyes traveling up and down the bodies of the women. Now getting a girl who could cook and clean was the main item on his agenda, but a couple of these girls had additional qualities. The light-skinned girl second from the end was a fine-looking woman, from her facial features to her voluptuous physique. Wilton stopped in front of her.

"You cook, gal?"

"Yes sir."

"What's your best dishes?"

"I bake pretty good, sir. Corn bread, cakes, pies."

Wilton chuckled. *Just what I need, a piece of this, a piece of that.* "What's your name?"

"Nell, sir. Nell Gaines."

"Where you from?"

"Coweta County, sir."

"That right? I live in Greenville, just down the road. What got you into this place?"

She hesitated. "Go on and answer him," the warden ordered.

"I cut my husband. He's trying to hurt me and my chil'ren."

"Got some fire in you, huh? I like that, Nell. How you like to come work for me and my missus over in Greenville?"

"That'd be mighty fine, sir."

Wilton turned toward the warden and nodded. "I think she'll do. How soon can she get ready?"

CHAPTER 1

September 1935
Greenville, Georgia

Nell Gaines rinsed the heavy butcher's knife in the water from the kitchen tap. It didn't matter that it wasn't her knife and that it wasn't her kitchen. Wasn't her carrots that she was cutting but that didn't matter either. What mattered was that Nell had a job cooking for Mr. and Miz Biggs. That was important because Nell also had two children, Enoch who was seven and Delilah who was five, and she was their sole support since their daddy ran off following the altercation that landed her in prison. And while she had two children, one thing Nell didn't have was a man around the house, if you wanted to call the tarpaper shack they shared with her mother a house. Oh, sure, it wasn't much but it kept the rain off their heads and blocked the wind—most of it anyway. That was better than most in her position had.

Nell set a fat, red tomato on the cutting board and deftly sliced it into cubes. That's the way Miz Biggs liked her salad, with cubes of juicy tomatoes from her own garden. Of course, Nell did most of the garden work, while Miz Biggs sat on the porch drinking lemonade and fanning herself. Nell didn't have time for a garden of her own. It was all she could do to take care of the children and the Biggses. Miz Biggs wasn't bad. She was plump and happy, friendly, and rarely had a harsh word for anybody. Young Robert, who was seventeen, was stuck on himself, but never disrespectful. Boy just seemed to think he was better than most everybody else who crossed the Biggs's threshold. Then there was Mr. Wilton Biggs hisself, the big-shot owner of the gin in Greenville, and the man all the farmers had to do business with. You raised cotton in this county, you dealt with Biggs Ginning Company. Wilton Biggs set the price for ginning cotton to guarantee hisself a good margin so he could continue to live at a standard well above that enjoyed by his customers—and far, far beyond what any of the county's colored folk could even imagine.

Nell scrubbed the dirt from a handful of radishes and set to slicing them into thin circles. Nell had got used to Miz Biggs's cheerfulness, to Robert's arrogance, and even to Mr. Wilton Biggs's staring eyes and unrestrained hands. And if she occasionally had to suffer more than just a quick grope, if she sometimes had to suffer Mr. Biggs's advances—never when Miz Biggs or Robert were around, of course—then that's what she'd do. Because Nell Gaines had a job, a decent job that kept her two children fed and kept that old wolf from the door. It was a job she was lucky to have and if she didn't keep everybody happy— Miz Biggs, the boy, and Mr. Biggs—she'd end up right back in Milledgeville.

Nell was the best cook Velma Biggs had ever had, a conclusion Wilton Biggs would have reached even if Nell had burnt every pan of cornbread and every pot of black-eyed peas. But she didn't. Nope, just like she had told him at the prison farm, this gal could cook. Wilton figured she was directly responsible for the tightness of his trousers— both at his waist and below. Her fried chicken came out golden and crispy every time and her biscuits were big as cats' heads, fluffy and flaky. Hell, she even made vegetables taste good, adding liberal amounts of butter and drippings to flavor up even the bitterest turnip greens.

But that was really beside the point as far as Wilton was concerned. A big man—big in the community and big in his appetites—Wilton judged Nell about the finest looking nigra he'd ever seen. She could nearly pass for white, except for her coarse, dark hair, and despite those two little kids of hers, she had a body like Venus—but complete with arms. She had a fine smile that would have knocked a lesser man over and her eyes were more golden than brown. Yes indeed, she was a fine-looking woman. Wilton would have liked her even if all she ever did was cook and then clean up the kitchen.

Of course, that wasn't the limit to her duties around the Biggs house. Nope, there were certain other roles Nell was obliged to fill from time-to-time. And while he could tell that she'd rather be mixing batter or flouring chicken, Nell knew better than to complain or resist when it was time to satisfy her employer's other hungers. This she did with the same competence with which she prepared a macaroni pie or stuffed a turkey. Well, Wilton chuckled to himself, he was really the one doing the stuffing.

CHAPTER 2

Greenville

With school back in session, Robert Biggs had plans. These included some hands-on biology experiments. His assistant would be Susan Woods, the pretty daughter of the owner of the feed store. Susan was a grade behind him in school but was more mature than any of the girls in Robert's class. Well, more physically mature, anyway. Susan was happy, always giggling, reading movie magazines and talking about Hollywood stars. But she was the prettiest girl in school, a cheerleader, a good Methodist, and secretary of the junior class, and that made her the girl for Robert.

"Pop," Robert said as Nell cleared the dishes from the dinner table, "can I use the car tonight? I'm taking Susan to the pictures."

Wilton looked up from his chocolate pie. "It's your mother's circle night, son. She'll need the car to drive over to Miss Nancy's."

Dang. Robert glanced appealingly at his mother, who smiled at her handsome son, red-haired and freckled, just like his father. "What time is your show, dear?" she asked.

"Seven-fifteen. I told Susan I'd pick her up at ten till."

"Well, I don't see why you can't drop me off at Nancy's a little early and then swing by and pick up your date."

"Thanks, Mother!" Robert said, pushing back from the table. He put on his "grateful son" smile; as an only

13

child, he could usually get his mother to do anything he wanted.

"You be sure to treat Susan like a lady, you understand?"

"Yes ma'am."

"What are you going to see?" Wilton asked.

"The Call of the Wild."

"Sounds exciting."

"Yes sir. It's supposed to be very good," Robert replied. He did in fact plan for some excitement, but not at the picture show.

Nell was washing dishes by the time Robert eased the Buick out of the garage, backed down the driveway, and headed toward Miss Nancy's house. The women of Temple Baptist Church gathered for their circle meeting every Tuesday, except during the month of July, when those that could afford it—and the Biggses certainly could—took their annual vacations. Wilton watched as the car disappeared down Maple Street, then he turned his attentions toward the woman at the sink.

He came up behind Nell and placed his big freckled hands on her hips, leaning in close and nuzzling her neck, which was already damp from perspiration. "How 'bout it, Nell?"

Nell sighed, stared down at the soapy water and said, "Let me finish up here, Mr. Biggs." Wilton leaned into Nell so that she would better appreciate his sense of urgency.

"Hurry up, then."

Although Robert and Susan had known each other since childhood—Greenville wasn't a big town, after all— he had suddenly noticed her the previous spring. She had grown up, in all the right places. He had flirted with her at an ice cream social at the church, then they attended the prom as a couple and dated regularly all through the summer. Robert was more than a little frustrated by Susan's shy response to his physical advances, but he had finally gotten some cooperation when he began talking about love. It wasn't hard; all he had to do was paraphrase the lines of Clark Gable or Ronald Colman and use a few big words Susan didn't understand, and she practically swooned. In fact, he felt confident that the movies were going to enable him that very night to get what he wanted most from Susan.

Robert and Susan had already seen *The Call of the Wild*. They had paid attention to the story and could describe it in some detail. So, when Robert bought their tickets, fifteen cents apiece, and took Susan's hand, her heart beat a little faster. They sat on the right side of the theater, three rows back from the exit door leading to Tinker's Alley. Five minutes or so into the picture, during one of the night scenes which turned the theater dark, the two young lovers crept from their seats and quietly exited the theater into the alley.

Wilton had converted the attic over the garage into an unheated apartment in 1920 to house Velma's idiot brother. Unable to hold a job after coming back from the Great War, Stanley had worked for a while as the Biggs's gardener and general handyman. Wilton hadn't been willing to pay much, but then Stanley's work wasn't worth much. He had, however, been willing to provide room and board. So, he'd had a sink and a cold-water tap installed, and he and Stanley had carried an iron bedstead and mattress up the narrow exterior steps. An old chest of drawers, a floor lamp and a rocking chair had rounded out the furnishings. The gardener's tools—clippers, machete, sling blade—hung on nails along the wall next to the door.

Stanley had lasted less than two years before running off one night with the green grocer's wife, who had less brains than looks. Wilton and Velma hadn't heard from Stanley since. Good riddance. But the little apartment still had its uses.

Robert and Susan were tingling with excitement as they parked the car under the big oaks behind the church. Nothing was going on there on a Tuesday night and they would be back before anyone noticed it.

Robert led his date by the hand as they cut through the woods that separated the Wilton place from the rest of the town. "Listen out for wild pigs," he teased, goosing her at the same time. Susan shrieked and giggled. He helped her balance as she stepped on the stones bridging the small creek and then tugged as she struggled up the slippery bank on the other side. Reaching the edge of the woods, Robert pulled Susan behind a tree, her body hot against his. He peered out toward the house. The light was on in the living room. Pop was probably in there listening to the Philco.

Robert stepped from their hiding place and guided Susan toward the wooden stairs leading to the garage apartment. When they reached the bottom of the stairs, Robert put his finger to his lips and said, "Shhh."

Susan squeezed his hand with a smile.

Wilton and Nell lay side-by-side on the narrow bed, covered only with a thin sheet. Wilton was dozing, occasionally snoring, while Nell counted the minutes until she could be on her way home to her kids. *Like a big freckled hog.* She'd give him a little longer and then she'd shift or cough to wake him. Wilton was selfish in bed, but then he was selfish in life. He was there solely to tend to his own needs, and Nell understood that. She resented him for it, but that was the way life was.

And it could have been worse. She knew that from personal experience. Wilton Biggs, as repulsive as he was, had never hit her, had never been violent. It's not that she liked him, she didn't, but she understood the man. White or black, there was something elemental about all men. Call it love or call it lust or call it whatever you wanted to, they had to have sex. The more powerful they thought they were, the more they demanded it. And right now, Wilton Biggs was the most powerful man in her life. She said a quiet prayer for the day that would change.

That's when she heard the squeak on the stairs.

Robert turned the knob and pushed the door open slowly, entered the room and then pulled Susan in behind him. With his back to the room, he quietly pushed the door closed until it latched with a *click*. He turned now toward Susan with a broad smile on his face and leaned down to kiss her. That's when he saw movement from the corner of his eye.

Robert jerked back. Confused, he swept his arm out, shoving Susan behind him. He heard a loud snort from the corner of the room. *How could a boar have gotten up here?* Robert glanced to his right and grabbed the machete off its nail.

The boy heard a grunt and rustling sounds from the corner. His eyes adjusted to the dim interior in time to see a naked man—*Was that Pop?*—throw back a sheet and stand. But there was someone else there too, someone else laying on the bed.

"Oh, Sweet Jesus!" a voice moaned.

"What? What's happening?" His father was confused, disoriented. The other person—*a woman?*—was standing now, cowering behind him.

"What the hell is going on here?" Robert snapped.

"Son?"

Robert took a step forward. "What are you—" then he realized who the woman was. He completely forgot about the frightened girl behind him and brought the machete up as though it was a sword. "You black whore! What the hell are you doing in here?"

"Now, son..." Wilton began. Realizing he was naked, he turned to grab the sheet off the bed. As he did, Robert lunged forward, swinging the wide blade. It nicked Nell's arm. She yelped. The arc of the swinging blade threw Robert off balance. As he recovered, Wilton stepped forward.

"This ain't what you thi—"

Robert swung again blindly, catching his father just below his ribs, the force of the machete stopped only by its collision with Wilton's spine. The big man dropped to the floor like a sack of grain, blood pouring out of his severed bowels.

Susan screamed. Nell vomited. Robert froze. After a moment, he spun, grabbed Susan by her shoulders and hustled her through the doorway and down the stairs.

Nell stood motionless for a moment. She squatted next to Wilton and grabbed the handle of the machete. She tugged on it, but it was well and truly stuck. She looked at his chest to see if he was breathing. She looked at his eyes. Lifeless. She felt something warm on her toes and jerked her foot back from the spreading crimson puddle. Feeling bile rising again in her throat, Nell reached for her clothes on the bed and bolted toward the door.

Disappointment. That's the word, Robert thought as he guided the Buick through the dark west Georgia country-side, Susan sniffling at his side. He understood the weakness of the flesh. Heck, he'd been intending to partake in the joys of the flesh with Susan, but he wouldn't be breaking any marriage vows to do so. His father, on the other hand, had not only betrayed his mother, but to make matters worse, had been doing so with a colored woman. And not just any colored woman! Pop had been laying with one that served his family, that worked in his house.

Well, Robert had done what he had to do. It was unpleasant, but the righteous had to step in where others feared to tread. In hindsight, his only regret was that he hadn't finished the job by punishing that black wench too.

TUESDAY, MAY 12, 1936

CHAPTER 3

Los Angeles

"Let me get this straight," Billy Bryce said, staring across his cluttered desk at the Los Angeles *Standard's* Hollywood reporter, Joan Roswell. "You want to go all the way to Atlanta, Georgia to talk to some oddball writer who's never published anything, and you expect me to pay for it."

"That's correct, dear." Joan busied herself digging through her alligator skin purse, a gift from a New York businessman she'd met on her last trip east. She pulled out a Chesterfield and fitted it into the end of her long, ebony holder. "Do you have a light?" she asked, leaning forward.

Billy, a cigar smoker, tugged open the top drawer of his desk and removed a box of matches, flipping them across the desk. Joan caught them in two hands, struck one and lit her cigarette. "I'd think with my track record you would give me more credit for developing a story. I scooped everybody on the Shirley Temple case—"

"A story we couldn't run," Billy snapped.

"—and practically solved that murder-robbery case in Washington in February. Honestly, dear, that should have raised your opinion of my work and my instincts."

Billy leaned back in his swivel chair and eyed the pretty, blonde reporter. She had, in fact, broken several stories in the last few months, including a big scoop about the little actress, the publication of which the White House had prohibited. It had amounted to censorship of the press and Billy, unbeknownst to Joan, had protested vigorously to the paper's owner and publisher. But the publisher, a fat cat and ardent New Deal supporter, had acquiesced to a personal request from the President to quash the story. *How I hate politicians—and millionaires too!*

Joan had initially stumbled when Billy had sent her east over the winter to cover the appearance of film star Ginger Rogers at the President's annual polio fundraiser in Washington. She had been diverted by the handsome New Yorker and was otherwise engaged during the kidnapping of Rogers and the President's private secretary, Marguerite LeHand, after the ball. But Joan had gotten her second wind, had developed confidential sources inside the FBI, and had broken several headline-grabbing stories about the case. She had, to hear her tell it, even helped capture the Russian agent behind the whole plot to influence the upcoming presidential election.

Billy stared directly into Joan's green cat's eyes. "What makes this little nobody worth my money, not to mention your time?"

"This 'nobody,' as you call her, has just written the great American novel of the twentieth century, dear. If you had a literary bone in your body, you'd know about it."

"I'm a newspaper man. I don't have time to read."

"The book isn't even on sale yet, and already Warner, Zanuck, and Selznick are bidding for the screen rights," she said, naming the heads of the three largest studios in Hollywood.

"If it's not on sale, how does anybody even know about it?"

"MacMillan, the publisher, shared the galley proofs, dear. They sent them to friendly critics and the big studios' story editors in New York. That's how the studios find the stories for their next films." Joan shook her head and smiled. "And you live in the center of the motion picture universe. It's a good thing you have *me* covering Hollywood!"

"All right, I get it. But if the book's not even on sale yet and the studios haven't bought it yet, why do you think it's going to be such a big deal?"

"It's a Civil War novel. It's got heroes and villains, Yankees and Rebels, romance, action, comedy. The Book-of-the-Month Club has already snatched it up as its July selection. And the writer, well, they say she's quirky. She worked on the book for ten years and even her closest friends had no idea she was writing it."

Billy sat for a moment, staring silently at Joan. She had developed into a first-rate reporter, something Billy would not have imagined eight months earlier when he had been on the verge of firing the former actress. Joan had pleaded for a job where the work—and the income—would be steadier than what she had been able to scratch out as a bit player at the studios. And, Billy had to admit, she had worked hard. Maybe she was a little unconventional in her approach, but she covered Hollywood after all, and those movie people were pretty unconventional themselves.

"Budget?"

Joan smiled and removed a typewritten note from her alligator bag. "I've got it all itemized right here, dear. I can make the whole trip, transportation, room, board and expenses for a hundred twenty-five dollars."

"I'll give you fifty. Travel coach."

"But dear, I need to arrive refreshed and looking my best. That requires a compartment, not an uncomfortable chair with no leg room."

"You want to be a reporter? Learn to live like one."

"Oh, Billy!" Joan frowned. "You can't expect first-class work on a third-class budget. At least meet me halfway. Seventy-five, what do you say?"

"I say this isn't a bank. I don't have funds for you to go gallivanting all over the country like some celebrity."

"Well, dear, I can't cover the celebrities if you won't invest in my stories." Joan crossed her arms over her ample bosom and blew a stream of blue smoke toward the ceiling.

"All right. Seventy-five dollars," Billy growled, removing a voucher from his desk drawer. He grabbed one of his blue pencils and filled in the amount, the payee, and his initials. "Here," he handed the form to Joan, "take this down to Doris in bookkeeping. Tell her to call me if she has any questions."

"Thank you, dear," Joan said, standing. Her smile spread across her attractive face. She turned and walked toward Billy's closed office door. He couldn't help but appreciate the view.

"What's the name of this masterpiece, anyway?" he asked as she reached the door.

Joan glanced back over her shoulder and said, *"Gone with the Wind."*

THURSDAY, MAY 14, 1936

CHAPTER 4

Warm Springs

President Roosevelt was later than usual arriving for his semi-annual vacation at his Little White House in Warm Springs, the delay caused by the painful and lingering death in mid-April of his longest serving advisor, Louis McHenry Howe. The small, irascible man, whose clothes were always covered with ashes from his Sweet Caporal cigarillos, had been a constant presence in the lives of both FDR and his wife, Eleanor, since Roosevelt had served in the New York Assembly almost thirty years before. Louie had been a master strategist and a loyal friend to both Roosevelts, helping to keep FDR's political career alive after his legs were paralyzed by polio, and to build the confidence of Mrs. Roosevelt when she began her own schedule of public speaking. He had master-minded FDR's campaign for governor of New York in 1928 and built on it to help him win the presidency in 1932. Howe had finally died, the victim of his smoking habit, at the Naval Hospital in Washington on April 18, and had been given a White House funeral with full honors.

After the emotionally fraught months, President Roosevelt was particularly eager to get to Warm Springs, where he had undergone polio rehabilitation and established the Warm Springs Foundation in the 1920s, with the help of his long-time secretary, advisor, and confidante Marguerite "Missy" LeHand. The remote town in rural Georgia revived his spirits like no other place on earth, and he loved spending time with polio patients like himself. On the Foundation grounds, he did not have to feel the least bit self-conscious about his wasted legs or the fact that he could not walk without considerable assistance. Missy was equally fond of Warm Springs, where she had long served, with Eleanor's blessing, as Franklin Roosevelt's hostess. Missy had even had her own cottage built there, which she rented out to polio patients and their families who came to the Foundation for treatment.

An unusually versatile secretary, Missy also served as the First Lady's back-up hostess at the White House, and had recently found, much to her surprise, that she was a pretty good amateur detective. In recent months, she had helped solve two major crimes, a kidnapping and then a robbery-murder, while working with a resourceful FBI agent named Corey Wainwright. The cases had been very exciting, but Missy was happy to be in Warm Springs, where it was unlikely she would find herself embroiled in another crime.

The Little White House, completed in 1932, was a simple, one-story structure, with wide doorways to allow wheelchairs to glide through. Missy had her own bedroom and bath on the same side of the house as the kitchen, while the President's bedroom, bath, and a guest room were situated on the other side. A central entry hall and a combined living and dining room separated the two sides of the house.

Eleanor was not as taken with Warm Springs as her husband and his secretary and was usually glad to stay in Washington or make alternative travel plans when a trip to Georgia was scheduled. She was troubled by the abject poverty and the overt racism of the Jim Crow South, and had a hard time holding her tongue when she witnessed disturbing instances of injustice to black people. This time, however, she had relented, and now the three were companionably seated on the large back porch, which thrust like a ship's bow into the pines and hardwood trees.

It was a lovely late spring day, the trees filled with song birds, the sunlight filtering through the fresh green leaves. Gardenia bushes were heavy with white blossoms, and their sweet fragrance filled the air. Missy and Eleanor were both simply attired in cotton shirtwaist dresses—Missy's green-striped, Eleanor's light blue—and flat sports shoes. They had cardigan sweaters draped around their shoulders against the early morning chill. The President, as usual when he was not receiving guests in Warm Springs, wore a white shirt and tie, but no coat. Mrs. Roosevelt's knitting bag was parked beside her chair.

They had just finished a hearty breakfast of eggs, bacon, grits, and buttermilk biscuits, and began to sing the praises of the cook, Daisy Bonner, as she emerged from the house with a silver coffee pot to refresh their cups. Inveterate coffee drinkers all, they smilingly accepted Daisy's offer of a refill. The liquid was as thick and black as used motor oil, and none of them chose to dilute it with sugar or cream.

Mrs. Roosevelt returned her attention to the local newspaper, the *Meriwether Vindicator*, and the lurid account of a murder that had occurred the previous September. A prominent businessman from Greenville, the Meriwether County seat, had been sliced up with a machete, and his black cook had been tried and found guilty of the crime. She was being held at the Georgia State Prison in Milledgeville with her execution set for mid-June, and her final appeal had just been denied. The account said the cook, Nell Gaines, had a criminal record prior to going to work for the family of the man she killed.

"How dreadful," Mrs. Roosevelt murmured.

"What's that, Babs?" the President asked.

"I was just reading about this woman who is to be electrocuted next month for the murder of a Mr. Biggs over in Greenville." She glanced up at Daisy Bonner. "Her name is Nell Gaines. Do you know her, Daisy?" she asked.

Daisy pursed her lips. *Why do they always think we all know each other?* But, in fact, she did know the other black woman. "Yes'm," she told the First Lady. "She was married to one of my cousins, lived over to Coweta County. He was a no-good man and left her with two little kids to raise. She'd been working for Mr. and Miz Biggs for a couple of months."

Something in the tone of Daisy's voice made Eleanor look up and regard her sharply. Their eyes met; Daisy was well aware of Eleanor's concerns for the civil rights of all Americans, regardless of color, and unspoken words were exchanged. "Daisy," the First Lady said, "could I speak with you in the kitchen for a moment?"

"Yes'm," Daisy said, and followed Mrs. Roosevelt indoors.

"Uh oh," FDR said when the two were out of earshot.

"Uh oh what?" asked Missy, her wide blue eyes regarding her boss with amusement.

"I manage to get my wife out of Washington and away from her do-good causes for a few days, and I can tell she's already sniffed one out down here. Have you heard anything about this murder case?"

"No," Missy said, "but I can certainly ask around. I'm sure some of the folks at the Warm Springs Foundation can fill me in."

"Add that to your to-do list, Missy," the President said. "I know you have a lot on your plate, but I have the feeling my missus is about to stir up some trouble, and I need to be fully armed with facts."

"Well, if there is a wrong to be righted, there is no better person to have in your court than Mrs. Roosevelt," Missy said loyally.

"Right you are, Missy, as usual," the President agreed.

Twenty minutes later, Mrs. Roosevelt came striding back across the porch, a purposeful gleam in her eye. "Franklin," she said. "I should like to tour the state prison over in Milledgeville, and even though Governor Talmadge isn't one of your favorite people—and vice versa—I should hope he might allow it since so much of the cost of the new state prison under construction in Reidsville is being borne by the Works Progress Administration."

"I think that would be an excellent use of your time here," the President said. Turning to Missy, he said, "Do you think you can call the governor's office this morning and set that up?"

"Certainly!" Missy said. "I'll get on it right way." She grinned mischievously. "If he asks to speak to you, I'll just say you've gone swimming."

"Grand!" the President said. "I'll head down to the pools right away, so you can't be caught in a lie. And Babs, when you get to the prison, leave your pistol in the car, won't you?"

CHAPTER 5

Los Angeles

Joan Roswell stepped aboard the *Sunset Limited* at Los Angeles's Union Passenger Terminal, drawing admiring glances from the porters, the rather portly conductor, and most of the male passengers. She was wearing a form-fitting spring suit of lightweight beige wool and a bright red hat with a feather curling along the brim. Her shapely legs were clad in nylons, and she wore open-toed pumps of beige kid. Unable to convince Billy to fund her travels at the level of comfort she deserved, Joan was forced to stroll slowly along the center aisle of the coach car searching for her seat, a porter carrying her two suitcases trailing behind and rather enjoying his view and the orange-and-jasmine scent she exuded.

"Right there, miss," the porter said, nodding to a seat on the right-hand side of the car. He set down both bags and waited until Joan cleared the aisle and sat down. Grunting a bit, he lifted each piece of luggage onto the rack above her head. Once he had finished, he rubbed his hands together, smiled, and said, "Anything else I can get you?"

Joan flashed her brilliant smile, her green eyes twinkling with the excitement of her trip. "Where's the dining car, dear?"

"It's behind us, miss. Head back that way," he pointed to his right, "through two more coach cars, then the lounge, then two sleepers. Diner's just after that and if you want something a little simpler, there's a coffee shop just beyond the diner."

"Thank you, dear. You've been most helpful." She reached into her alligator purse and handed the man a quarter.

"Miss," the porter smiled and tipped his cap. Then he was off to assist other passengers. The train would be full for most of its two thousand-mile run to New Orleans, with passengers getting on and off at most stops, but particularly at the bigger cities of Tucson, El Paso, San Antonio, and Houston.

That was both good news and bad news for Joan. The bad news was that she had no control over who would end up sitting beside her for two nights and days. The good news was that the number of passengers traveling first class might allow her access to better accommodations. Joan removed a small gold-tone compact from her purse and checked her makeup. She applied pressed powder to her nose and touched up her reddish-orange lipstick, smiling at herself to make sure nothing was stuck in her teeth. *Time to go to work.*

By eight-thirty, the *Sunset* had already passed Alhambra and was on its way to Pomona, rolling toward the rapidly darkening eastern horizon. Joan turned to her seatmate and said, "I'm going to go get a bite to eat, if you'll excuse me." The plump—but not pleasingly—older woman, who had been perusing an article titled "I Love Life at 70" from the current *Reader's Digest*, offered a tight smile and torturously pulled herself up and out of her reclining seat. She stepped into the aisle to allow Joan to pass. "Thank you, dear," Joan said with a smile. Keeping her feet wide apart to offset the gentle swaying of the train, Joan walked to the end of the car, through its door and across the narrow catwalk connecting it to the next coach. She continued on through car after car until she reached the lounge.

Several overweight businessmen were straddling stools at the bar. Joan considered implementing her plan here, but it was early yet, and a quick reconnaissance revealed no appealing targets. She continued through the lounge, admiring the New Orleans French Quarter theme of the décor, and next came to the sleeper cars. *That cheap Billy! This is where I ought to be! And may be yet.*

The first two hours out of Los Angeles were always the busiest, given the 8 p.m. departure time, and many travelers looked forward to a fine meal in the *Sunset's* dining car as a fitting beginning to their trip. As she entered, Joan immediately began to scan the tables, all of which were currently filled. Groups of businessmen occupied several seats, men and women—*married couples?*—took up most of the rest. Three nuns were seated at a table on the right about two thirds of the way along the car.

"Just one, miss?" a white-jacketed attendant asked. "I can seat you with the sisters."

"Oh, no, dear, but thank you. I'm actually just passing through to the coffee shop." On Billy's miserly budget, Joan needed to stretch her funds as far as possible. There was no chance the holy sisters would buy her meal— and there were no men sitting alone.

"Certainly, miss. It's the very next car. Enjoy your evening."

Joan continued her trek through the dining car, her stomach growling as she looked down at the plates of chicken, fish, and beef on the tables. The nuns' table included a bottle of red wine. *I could use a glass or two.* Joan smiled and nodded as she walked past. The coffee shop was less crowded and much less formal. Stainless steel napkin holders flanked by salt and pepper shakers and sugar bowls stood against the side windows. It was darker and smokier in here and it took Joan's eyes a moment to adjust. Two soldiers wearing olive wool uniforms sat smoking and drinking coffee at one table. They turned and frankly inspected the pretty blonde at the doorway.

After another moment, Joan spied a young man sitting by himself at a table near the far end of the car. "Join us, sister?" one of the soldiers said, standing and smiling.

"Oh, thank you dear, but I've already got plans." *Soldiers don't have any money.* Joan walked toward the man at the table, her fingers dancing across the backs of the chairs as she passed. He looked up just as she reached him.

"Mind if I join you?" she asked. The man's startled expression gave way to a shy smile as he stood and pulled a chair out for Joan. "Please!" he said. "I was just thinking I'd love some company."

"My name is Joan, Joan Roswell." She offered her hand.

He took it and replied, "A pleasure. Sam Andrews."

"It's so nice to meet you, Sam Andrews," Joan said, smiling, her head in the red hat cocked to the side like an exotic bird. Sam appeared to be in his mid-twenties, nice-looking, with short, sandy colored hair, brown eyes and a lopsided grin. He was wearing an undistinguished but respectable gray suit. Best of all, he seemed to be alone. "Are you from Los Angeles?"

"Pasadena." He stared at the pretty woman, puzzled as to why she'd chosen his table. "How about you? Miss Roswell, right?"

"Right, dear. And please call me Joan. Actually, I live in Hollywood. I work for the LA *Standard*. I'm a reporter."

"A reporter? That sounds pretty exciting." Sam leaned across the small table and lowered his voice slightly. "Are you covering a story on the train?"

Joan tittered. "Oh no, dear. I'm heading east, to Atlanta. I'm going to be doing some interviews there."

"I'm heading to Atlanta too," Sam allowed with a smile.

"Isn't that wonderful?" Joan said. "We'll have lots of time to get to know each other!"

"Would you like something to drink?" Sam asked, waving one of the waiters over.

"What are you having, dear?"

"Just coffee for me."

"Why not make it two?" Joan smiled. Her plan seemed to be working out very nicely. "And I wonder if there is any pie left in the kitchen? To be honest, I'm famished!"

It turned out that Sam was a motion pictures fan. When he learned that Joan's beat was the major studios, he fired question after question at her as she hungrily devoured a grilled cheese sandwich and a piece of apple pie a la mode. "Have you ever met Gary Cooper? What's he like?"

"Coop? Why he's a darling! Just the nicest thing. Always on an even keel and always, always nice to everybody from his director to the gaffer."

"What about Ginger Rogers?" Sam asked. "Gosh, I wish I could dance like Fred Astaire. They make it so look so easy!"

"She's a peach," Joan said. "Just the sweetest, most down-to-earth person you could ever meet." She momentarily reflected on the interview Ginger had given her on a train waiting to pull out of Washington's Union Station in early February. Following a fund-raiser at the Shoreham Hotel, Ginger and Missy LeHand, the president's secretary, had been kidnapped while carrying the event's receipts to the bank. Joan had written a highly embellished version of the story for her newspaper, but Ginger hadn't complained. *Thank goodness Hollywood stars are used to having their words twisted*, Joan thought.

By the time the train pulled into Palm Springs, they'd been talking and laughing for over an hour. It was completely dark outside, and Joan was beginning to get tired—and impatient. She faked a yawn. "Oh!" she said, covering her mouth with her napkin, "Excuse me, Sam. I guess the long day is starting to catch up with me."

"Well, no wonder!" Sam exclaimed looking at his watch. "It's nearly ten-thirty." He set a fifty-cent piece on the table and said, "Can I walk you back to your compartment?"

"Ah, well, I'm actually up front in coach, dear." In response to Sam's frown Joan added, "But I do have a very comfortable reclining seat."

"I see." Sam's brow wrinkled thoughtfully, and he looked down at his hands. "Joan, if you're open to it, I'd like to make you a proposition."

"A proposition?" Joan arched her eyebrows.

He looked up. "Yes. I'm traveling on business and I have a very comfortable sleeper compartment. It's just in the next car."

"Why, Sam!" Joan smiled.

"C'mon, I'll show you." Sam stood and held out his hand to Joan. As Joan stood, the train lurched forward, causing her to lean into Sam. He smiled and cleared his throat. "This way," he said, pulling her by the hand as he headed toward the door of the car.

By the time they reached Sam's compartment, the porter had already pulled down the bed, turned down the covers and placed a mint on the pristine white pillow. Joan looked in from the doorway with Sam peering over her shoulder. "So comfortable," Joan purred. She stepped inside and this time it was Joan who tugged on Sam's hand. Immediately, he froze and blushed.

"Come on in, dear."

Sam smiled sheepishly. "I think maybe I've given you the wrong idea."

She dropped his hand. "Maybe you have, dear." Joan was perplexed. *Things had seemed to be going so well.*

"Well, you see, Joan, my proposition is simply that you take my compartment and I'll take your seat. That's all." Sam's face had turned cherry red.

"Oh?" Joan recovered from the surprise quickly. "How kind you are, dear! So gallant!"

He smiled shyly. "So, you accept?"

"Of course I do. Such a lovely gesture, really. I'm speechless." She gave him a huge smile, sucking in one cheek to create a dimple.

"Here." Sam reached into his pocket. "Here's my ticket. Give me yours and I'll be off to coach."

Joan dipped into her purse and pulled out the red ticket. "First car past the lounge, dear. I have two bags directly above the seat."

"I'll have a porter bring them to you." Sam nodded, clearly pleased with himself. "Well, good night then, Joan." He turned toward the end of the car, but Joan caught him by his sleeve.

She stood on tip-toe and kissed him on his cheek. "Good night, you sweet man."

Sam made his lonely way through the darkened train, found Joan's seat and had her bags delivered to his compartment. He interrupted the slumber of Joan's seatmate, who gave him a withering look before allowing him to climb into his seat. Sam settled in, loosened his tie and closed his eyes, but he couldn't sleep. And he couldn't stop smiling either.

FRIDAY, MAY 15, 1936

CHAPTER 6

Warm Springs

Early in the morning, Eleanor Roosevelt and her loyal secretary, Malvina "Tommy" Thompson, took off for Milledgeville. Even on vacation, Mrs. Roosevelt faithfully wrote her syndicated newspaper column, *My Day*, six days a week, which meant she would dictate it to Tommy who would then find a Western Union office to transmit it to the syndicate. Ahead of them they had a three-hour trip, much of it down two-lane and rutted dirt roads. Missy had made arrangements for them to spend the night at the Dempsey Hotel in Macon, so the First Lady could thoroughly inspect the prison without feeling pressed for time. Daisy Bonner had packed them a hamper of food for a picnic along the way.

Missy stood waving until the car had gone through the bump gate and past the Marine sentry, and then she walked through the living room-dining room of the Little White House and joined the President on the back porch. "What's on the agenda today, F.D.?" she asked, plopping down in a chair by the table.

He took a last swallow of his coffee and lit a Camel. "The usual," he said. "A swim, and I thought we might take a picnic up to Dowdell's Knob this afternoon. No reason Eleanor should have the monopoly on Daisy's fried chicken!" The knob, overlooking Pine Mountain Valley, had long been Franklin Roosevelt's favorite picnic spot. "We can include Grace and a few of the Foundation staff. Maybe Fred Botts can join us," he said, mentioning a young man who had arrived in the luggage car of a train as a patient in the mid-1920s and stayed on as registrar of patients. "Might be a good time to ask what they've heard about this Nell Gaines my wife is so interested in."

"Beat you to it," Missy said. "A few of us were talking about it yesterday down at the pool while you were swimming. Apparently, it's been very controversial. Mr. Biggs wasn't exactly popular in Meriwether County—his gin had a kind of monopoly among the small farmers and sharecroppers here, and he took full advantage with his pricing—and there were a lot of unanswered questions about the murder. His son, Robert, who is in high school, and his girlfriend have been missing since the night of the murder, and a lot of people think they saw something or even did something. Nell may have been the scapegoat in the whole affair. Unfortunately, it's hard for a colored person to be assured of justice here, especially when she's represented by an incompetent public defender, and faces an all-white, all-male jury."

The President puffed on his Camel and sat for a few moments, staring at the trees. "Penny for your thoughts, F.D." she said.

He turned to her with a wide grin. "I was just thinking, that if anyone asks me where Eleanor is, I can say, 'She's gone to prison,'" he said.

"What's she in for?" Missy interjected.

The President's face fell. "I guess I've used that joke a few times before," he said.

Missy grinned, showing slightly crooked teeth. "Only every time she tours a prison. But you can always come up with a new reason for why she's been sentenced. What's it going to be?"

FDR exhaled and made a broad gesture with his arms. "Refusing to succumb to the charms of Warm Springs," he said. "I never fail to understand it."

As the dark blue Ford Phaeton rolled along a dusty road west of Macon, Eleanor Roosevelt was trying to find something positive to say about rural Georgia for her *My Day* column. She wasn't having much luck. "I'm sorry, Tommy," she said, breaking off yet another sentence halfway through as she watched a farmer in faded overalls and a straw hat plowing behind a bony mule. "It's so difficult to look at the way so many of the people have to live here, so hard and poor and ugly. Of course, it's that way in other parts of the country too, and heaven knows the squalor in the slums of New York is just as dreadful. The things I saw when I was volunteering for the Junior League, prior to my marriage!"

Certainly, the poor Italian and Irish immigrants who lived in those slums at the turn of the century had been looked down upon by the wealthy of New York, but there was not this two-tier system, this complete segregation of the races, that one sees in the South, Eleanor thought. Not for the first time, she guiltily pondered her own ties to Georgia's past. Her paternal grandmother, who had died before Eleanor was born, was a Southern belle from Georgia whose family owned more than thirty slaves. *Including her own personal "shadow" slave who slept on a mat beside my grandmother's bed. Imagine!*

The reforms of Reconstruction hadn't lasted, and now Georgia had a Jim Crow system of laws and policies that forced its black residents into a second-class citizenship that mimicked slavery. *The casual cruelty is so sickening—and contagious*, she thought, remembering earlier in the week when she saw a young White House aide tossing a penny to a crowd of little ragged black children and howling with laughter as they tussled in the dust for it. She had to bite her tongue to keep from berating him, but she had spoken to Franklin about it. *Not that he would do anything about it.*

They passed an unpainted house, its porch sagging, a thin woman in a housedress sitting on the steps, chickens pecking around her bare feet. "Tommy, I guess it bothers me that so many of the people here seem simply...lazy," Eleanor said. "Their yards are full of trash, their children are dirty. They just don't seem to have much gumption."

"Maybe it's their diet," Tommy suggested gently. "They seem to live on the most dreadful foods, collards and grits and cornbread and syrup. That's hardly enough nutrition to fuel a day's hard work in the fields, never mind cleaning up the yard when you get home. And so few of these homes have indoor plumbing."

"You're right, of course," Eleanor said, sighing. "I just wish the white people weren't so hateful to the poor colored people. I guess everyone just needs someone to look down upon—and I'm as guilty of that as the next person for what I just said about the Georgians being lazy."

They passed a road sign advertising the Dempsey Hotel in Macon. Eleanor brightened. "We'll stop at the Dempsey and leave our bags there. Franklin said he spoke to the Rotary Club at the Dempsey once in the 20s, and the hotel had a Japanese tea room and even brought actresses in from New York to wear kimonos and act like geisha girls! I wonder if they still do that."

They didn't. The Dempsey, which had been the grandest hotel in middle Georgia when it opened in 1912, had lost much of its luster during the hard years of the Depression. Nine stories tall and built of brick, the embellishments on its façade desperately needed a cleaning, and the canvas awnings over its street-level windows were faded. The manager, a short, balding man whose name tag read "MR. NATIONS," greeted Mrs. Roosevelt effusively when she entered the lobby with Tommy and sent a bell boy to fetch their bags. His dark suit was shiny, and the collar of his shirt was frayed, but he wore a fresh rosebud in his buttonhole, and his smile was as genuine as his offer to do anything to make them comfortable.

"Perhaps you'd like an early luncheon before you head on to your, er, inspection tour?" he asked. "Our tea room is open, and I've reserved a table for you overlooking Cherry Street."

"Do you still have the geisha waitresses?" Eleanor asked, Daisy's picnic basket in the back of her mind.

A shadow passed over the genial manager's face. "Oh, those were the days, Mrs. Roosevelt," he said simply. "But I assure you we have very competent young women working in our tea room now, and we have a delicious menu." He patted his stomach. "I can attest to the quality of the cuisine! If I can recommend something, all the ladies in Macon rave about our chicken salad—though it probably doesn't measure up to what is served at the White House."

"You'd be surprised," Mrs. Roosevelt said, fully aware of the abysmal reputation of the White House kitchens overseen by her friend Henrietta Nesbitt. She quickly calculated that, since her husband would be on the ballot again in the fall, a visit to the dining room might be wiser than resorting to the picnic lunch. "Please, show us the way. I'd love a tall glass of iced tea, wouldn't you, Tommy?"

Mr. Nations proudly conducted them to a table which bore a hand-lettered sign, "Reserved for Mrs. Roosevelt & Party," and a vase of fresh red roses. "These came from my wife's garden," he said proudly. "I'll send them up to your room after lunch."

Once she and Tommy had ordered, Eleanor glanced out the window and saw that she had already attracted an audience. She waved and smiled at the friendly faces, glad her husband was still popular in Georgia. You never knew, with Eugene Talmadge doing his best to be a thorn in Franklin Roosevelt's side. Georgia's governor had dragged his feet in participating in every New Deal program, calling them "a combination of 'wet nursin,' frenzied finance, and plain damn foolishness." Because of a two-term limit for Georgia governors, he could not run for re-election this year, but there was talk that he would try to win the U. S. Senate seat held by Richard Russell. *And we thought we were through with these Southern populists when Huey Long was assassinated last year*, Eleanor thought. *Not that I am hoping someone shoots Governor Talmadge!*

FRIDAY, MAY 15, 1936

CHAPTER 7

On the *Sunset*

Joan slept soundly as the *Sunset Limited* streaked overnight through the arid desert of southern Arizona. When she finally awoke, the train was pulling into Tucson two minutes ahead of its eight-fifteen scheduled arrival. By the time she was dressed and groomed, the train, its population increased by newly boarded passengers, was again headed east toward Texas.

Sam was the first person she saw when she entered the dining car. He beckoned her over, still wearing his daffy, lop-sided grin. Joan, refreshed from her slumber, smiled, waved, and headed to the table.

"Good morning, dear. Aren't you the early riser!" Sam stood as Joan slipped into the opposite side of the booth.

"I was hoping I'd see you this morning," Sam said, resuming his seat opposite her. He had whiskers on his face, rumpled hair and although he had tightened his tie, his suit and shirt bore the wrinkles of an all-night ride in a coach seat.

Joan reached across the table and laid her hand on his forearm. "Thank you so much, dear, for giving me your stateroom. I just don't know how I could have coped with having to sit up all night. I must say, you look none the worse for wear. How do you do it?"

Sam blushed and grinned. "Oh, I was happy for you to have it. You look as though you slept very well—if you don't mind my saying."

"Oh, you flirt, you!" Joan tittered.

"May I have your order, miss?" a waiter asked from the side of the table.

Joan glanced at the menu card on the table. "I'll have the western omelet, wheat toast, and orange juice and black coffee, please."

"And for the gentleman?"

"Two over easy with bacon, potatoes, white toast, and milk, please."

The waiter withdrew, and Sam leaned forward. "You know, I had a hard time falling asleep last night."

"Oh, dear! And there I was enjoying the comfort of your compartment. You were so chivalrous to swap accommodations with me." Joan began to fear that her relationship with the comfortable bed might have been a one-night stand. "I will certainly understand if you want to move back in for our last night on the train."

"No, it's not like that." Sam glanced out the window at the monotonous brown landscape flashing past. "I had a hard time getting you off my mind." He looked back at Joan, grinning shyly again. "I've never met anyone like you, Joan. You're so intelligent and independent. And lovely," he added, looking down at the table cloth. A slow blush crept across his cheeks.

"I think I'm going to swoon," Joan said, smiling and giving his hand a quick squeeze. *If I play this right, I may be able to hang on to the stateroom for another night.* "I haven't met anyone like you either, Sam. So generous and so gallant that you would put the comforts of a total stranger ahead of your own. So many of the men I encounter in Hollywood see a young woman and they only have one thing on their minds." Sam's ears reddened. "But you! Well, you are different, Mr. Sam Andrews—and different in the best possible way." Their breakfast arrived. Joan took a sip of coffee and went from buttering up Sam to buttering her toast.

"Why do you have to go all the way to Atlanta?" Sam asked shoving a piece of bacon into his mouth with his fingers. He chewed a moment. "I thought all the movie people were in Hollywood."

"My editor thinks that way too," Joan replied. "But one must realize that most pictures begin somewhere else. They begin on stage in London or New York or, in this case, in the mind of a novelist in Atlanta. The word in Hollywood is that this will be the biggest picture ever. That's why I have to go all the way to Atlanta. What's your excuse?"

"A business meeting," Sam replied, concentrating on his eggs.

"Sam, would you like to come back to the compartment, you know, to change clothes and freshen up after breakfast?"

"That would be most welcome," he said, his face showing relief. "I must look rather a mess. I could sure use a shave and wash." The waiter returned with the bill, which Sam insisted on paying.

"Are you sure, dear?"

"Sure I'm sure," Sam replied, smiling. "I'm on a per diem."

"I've forgotten, dear. Tell me again the company you're with."

"It's not really a company. It's the Association of Golden State Baptists. I work in the accounting office."

"Oh."

CHAPTER 8

On the *Sunset*

No wonder he didn't invite me to share his bed, Joan thought as she headed back down the corridor of the swaying car away from the stateroom where Sam was freshening up. At her urging, he had said he might take a quick nap. *Too bad. He's really quite sweet.*

The door to the compartment next to Sam's opened and a young woman peeked out. She was wearing a perky navy hat on her wavy blond hair, with an attached veil pulled over her face. Joan caught just a glimpse as she pushed her door inward, then froze. *I know her!*

Before Joan could react, the woman had pulled her door closed and stepped behind Joan as though heading for the dining car. From the rear, the woman presented an attractive figure. She was wearing an expensively-cut navy skirt and matching jacket, the kind one would expect to see on the secretary of a corporate big shot. Joan straddled the doorway between the compartment and the corridor and watched the unsteady gait of the woman until she disappeared through the door at the end of the car.

Where have I seen that face?

It was the woman's large eyes that had caught her attention. They were familiar, wide-set, almost almond shaped and clear, challenging. *I've seen them on the big screen, that's for sure. It'll come to me, I just need to see her again. Well, I've got a couple of hours to kill. Why not?* She headed back to the dining car.

Joan stopped at the maître d's stand. The mystery woman was just being seated, her back to Joan.

"One, miss?"

"Yes—no, I'm meeting my friend there," Joan said, thinking quickly and pointing toward the woman in navy blue.

"Very good. Right this way, please." The maître d', dressed in a white jacket with gold trim, led Joan down the center aisle to the table. Joan sat on the bench facing the mystery woman who looked up with a puzzled expression.

"Mind if I join you, dear?" Joan asked settling in and accepting the menu from the maître d'.

"Not at all," the woman replied, turning to stare out the window.

"Good morning, ladies," a smiling waiter said, arriving at tableside. "Would you like some coffee or juice to get started?"

"Coffee and orange juice, please," the woman replied without looking up.

"Just coffee for me, dear," Joan replied, smiling at the white-jacketed server. "My name is Joan," she continued once the waiter had withdrawn.

"How do you do?" The woman continued to stare out the window at Arizona's brown rolling hills.

"Where are you heading?"

"East."

"Smart girl. If you have to go east, this is the best way to travel. Sit back, eat, drink, and let the Southern Pacific do the—" *Smart girl*! That was it! Joan smiled broadly, pleased that she'd solved the mystery of her companion's identity. Now, the riddle was why she was on the train to begin with. Where, exactly, was she going and why?

"It's certainly not every day that one has a chance to share coffee with Paramount's Ida Lupino, star of *Smart Girl*."

Ida Lupino shifted her gaze from the window and stared directly into Joan's green cat's eyes. "You recognized me in the corridor, didn't you?"

"Yes, but I couldn't place you at first. You know how it is when you meet someone out of their normal context. I thought your performance in *Smart Girl* was quite powerful, by the way."

"Thanks," the actress replied without enthusiasm. "Listen, Joan, is it? I'm traveling on personal business. I'd appreciate it if you'd respect my privacy."

"Mmmm. That will be difficult for me, dear. I'm a working reporter for the Los Angeles *Standard*." Lupino closed her eyes and sighed. "I seem to have stumbled upon a story. Why would one of Hollywood's up-and-coming actresses be traveling all the way across the country and all by herself?"

The waiter returned with two cups of coffee and an orange juice and set them on the table. "Would you care for some breakfast?"

"The assorted fruit for me, please," Ida said.

The waiter turned his attention to Joan. "I'll just stick with coffee for now. Do you mind if I smoke?" she asked looking back at Ida.

"Be my guest."

"So, what set of circumstances finds you streaking across the desert southwest on such a lovely morning?"

"It's a personal matter."

Joan fitted a Chesterfield into her ebony cigarette holder and spun the wheel on her lighter. "I've found, dear, that personal matters sometimes make the best stories. The public just loves to peek behind the curtains of its celebrities' homes. They love to see that their screen idols are real people. It makes you more relatable, if you will."

"I suppose that depends on what you find behind the curtain, doesn't it?"

Joan exhaled blue smoke. "I suppose it does. What's behind your curtain, Ida darling?"

"Give me one of your cigarettes."

The plate of fruit was empty and the ash tray half full. Joan's reporter's notebook lay open on the table, her pen beside it. Joan had been surprised, not only that she had been able to get Lupino to talk, but also by the story the starlet had told. In 1934, the popular young actress, under contract to Paramount Pictures, had been stricken by polio. She had been briefly unable to walk and feared her career might have come to an end at the ripe old age of sixteen. Fortunately, she had recovered quickly, though she had not regained complete use of her leg and hand.

"So I've been making trips to a little resort in Georgia," Ida confessed over a third cup of coffee. "They have natural mineral springs there and the waters are very restorative. They also have a top-notch medical staff."

"You mean Warm Springs, don't you?" Joan said, a grin playing at the corners of her mouth.

"You know it?"

"I guess everyone in America knows of it, with the Little White House being there. I was involved in one of the Birthday Balls this past winter. We raised quite a bit of money for the Warm Springs Foundation."

"Good for you, Joan." Ida finally began to relax. "I helped with one of the balls in L.A. So you know how devastating polio can be, not only to its victims but to their families as well. It is emotionally wrenching and very few families, especially in this Depression, have the wherewithal to afford the kind of care the disease calls for."

"And you're going back for treatment? It helps?"

"Yes, I am, and it does. I also go to help others, to give them some hope so they'll know that recovery is possible—at least for some of us. Have you actually visited Warm Springs, seen the good work being done

52

there? It would make a much better story than coercing sympathy for poor little Ida Lupino, the beautiful, rich, talented young movie star." Ida smiled tremulously across the table. "Let me ask you a favor, Joan, one that could benefit you and your newspaper and me as well."

"Go ahead, dear."

"If you tell the whole world that Ida Lupino is a polio victim, I'll lose my contract. The studio won't be able to insure any picture with me in it. Then I'll be just one more face selling apples on the corner."

"A very beautiful face, dear."

"But if you sit on my story, I'll give you an inside look at Warm Springs. I'll introduce you to some of the doctors and physical therapists—we call them physios— who are achieving terrific results in the treatment of polio patients and I'll even arrange for you to talk to some of the patients and their families. You can get a first-hand look at the difference the Foundation is making in people's lives, thanks in part to all the Hollywood stars who participate in the Birthday Balls. What do you say, Joan? It would be a much bigger story with much broader appeal."

Joan stared at the young woman thoughtfully, fixing Ida with her green cat's eyes. "I don't know, dear. I kind of like the idea of looking behind your curtain."

"A story about me would be self-defeating, Joan. A one-shot deal. I'd be a has-been by the time the afternoon editions hit the street. Who'd be interested after that? A broader story about polio and the things going on at Warm Springs, why that would give you fodder for dozens of articles! Who knows what kind of stories you'd turn up?"

CHAPTER 9

Milledgeville

The President's car with the First Lady at the wheel arrived in Milledgeville just after two o'clock. The little town had been Georgia's capital during the Civil War, and it still boasted some handsome antebellum homes, most in need of paint, and impressive public buildings. The former governor's mansion, a Greek Revival building with four tall, stately columns, was now the home of the president of the Georgia State College for Women. The prison was not of this grand ilk, however. They pulled in front of the grim, two-story brick structure, three miles outside of town, where a black woman in a broadly striped dress was mowing the sparse lawn while her guard snored under the only tree, his shotgun at his side.

Eleanor Roosevelt approached the woman, who abruptly stopped mowing and stared, her jaw dropping in disbelief. "Miz Roosevelt?" she asked.

"Yes, how kind of you to recognize me," Eleanor said, offering her hand.

The woman scrubbed her hand on the skirt of her uniform and gingerly offered the tips of her fingers to the distinguished guest while executing a clumsy curtsy. "How d'you do, ma'am," she said.

"Very well, thank you. Please tell me your name, and what you are here for," Eleanor said conversationally, as if she were greeting a guest at the White House.

"My name is Hettie Evans, and I'm here for murder," the woman said, looking at the ground. "I kilt my husband."

54

"I'm sure you had a good reason," Mrs. Roosevelt said reassuringly. "Can you tell me where we might find the warden's office?"

Hettie Evans pointed to the entrance of the building and said, "First door on the left. His secretary is Miz Betty Barnette. I 'spect they know you's coming."

Mrs. Roosevelt thanked her and advanced with Tommy in her wake. The guard under the tree never stirred. Hettie Evans resumed cutting the grass, shaking her head in wonder.

The inside of the building was just as grim as the outside. Dirty paint clung desperately to the plaster walls, and the place had a distinct odor of unwashed bodies and mildew and greasy food and something else. *Misery,* Eleanor thought. *It smells like human misery.* The warden's office door was open, so she walked in. A woman in her early thirties, her pale blonde hair coiled into a bun at the back of her neck, looked up from her typewriter and gave the White House guests a bright smile, showing crooked teeth outlined in red lipstick.

"Mrs. Roosevelt!" she said, jumping to her feet and smoothing the skirt of her blue cotton dress. "It's such an honor to have you here. I'm Betty Barnette, the warden's secretary." She walked around the desk, enthusiastically shaking the First Lady's hand. "I'll let Captain Carlson know you are here. He's been on the phone with Governor Talmadge."

Betty Barnette knocked on an inner door and then pushed it open. In a few seconds, Captain Carlson emerged. He was a rough-hewn man, hair cut in a short military bristle, and though he did not wear a uniform per se, it was clear he regarded his starched khaki shirt and trousers as one. *I bet his wife spends hours ironing his clothes,* Eleanor thought. *Or more likely, one of the prisoners!*

"Howdy do, Mrs. Roosevelt," he said in a slow drawl. Introductions were made, and he ushered his guests out to the central hall of the building. "Betty, get the kitchen to rustle up come coffee, and then meet us in the white men's dormitory," he ordered.

"Right away, sir," Betty said, and hurried down the hall. *She's like a blond Missy*, Eleanor thought. *Polite and efficient. I wonder if she has spunk too?*

"I can hardly survive an afternoon without my cup of Joe," Captain Carlson joked.

"Do you know why we call coffee a cup of Joe?" Mrs. Roosevelt asked, blue eyes twinkling.

"Why no, I never paid no mind to it," he said.

"It's named for Josephus Daniels, who was secretary of the navy during the Great War," she said. "My husband, President Roosevelt, was his assistant secretary. Mr. Daniels was very much opposed to sin in all forms, and he allowed nothing stronger than coffee to be served on navy bases and ships, even in the officer's mess. That's why it's called a 'cup of Joe.'"

"You don't say!" the warden responded. "I'll have to remember that. Well, let me show you one of the barracks first. The prisoners are all out in the fields right now, but you'll get an idea of how they live."

He led them upstairs into a long, high-ceilinged room, whose paint was in even worse shape than that in the entry hall. Two long rows of metal cots were lined up, carefully made up with dingy gray sheets and thread-bare blankets. Wooden posts supporting the ceiling served as rudimentary "closets," with clothing hanging from nails hammered into the posts. The stench of misery was even stronger in the room than in the hall, and Eleanor felt her eyes watering in sympathy for the people who lived there.

"We run a tight ship here," Captain Carlson said importantly. "The prisoners rise at five o'clock every morning, make their beds, dress, and head to the dining hall for breakfast. Then they are working by six."

"What sort of tasks do they undertake?" Mrs. Roosevelt asked.

"We put them to good use," the warden said. "The men make bricks and work in the carpentry shop, if they show any aptitude. The white women sew; they make all the uniforms in use here. Most of the colored inmates work in the fields."

"What is a typical day like for these field workers?" Mrs. Roosevelt asked.

"Well, as I said, they are at work by six. They get a fifteen-minute break at mid-day for lunch, then work until six at night—later in the summer, since there's more daylight and more to be done. Then they get their supper and it's lights out at eight."

"Where do they bathe?" Mrs. Roosevelt asked, noticing no lavatory facilities.

"We have a wash house outside, they can take one bath a week—whether they need it or not," he said, laughing at his own joke. "And for other, uh, needs, they have outhouses, it's what they've got at home, if they're lucky."

Betty joined them then, informing the warden that coffee and pound cake would be waiting in his office when they completed the tour. He thanked her curtly and ordered her to take notes.

"I am especially interested in your female prisoners," Mrs. Roosevelt said. "Do you offer any educational opportunities for them here?"

"What do you mean?" the warden asked suspiciously.

"Oh, training for better jobs, for example, or teaching them to read and write, if they don't know how," the First Lady replied. "The prison superintendent in West Virginia is doing marvelous things to rehabilitate the women there. Many of the prisoners come in with practically no education and no knowledge of how to live decently, and they are most appreciative of being able to return to their families better equipped to cope with the responsibilities of a home."

"The white women or the colored women?" the warden asked.

"Why, both," Mrs. Roosevelt said. "Why should they be treated any differently?"

"Well, it's kind of a waste to teach colored women anything other than how to be better field hands," Captain Carlson said dismissively. "Some of the smarter ones work in the kitchen, and we have a parole program where we place them in domestic jobs after they are let out."

"Such as Nell Gaines, for example?" Mrs. Roosevelt asked.

Captain Carlson's face turned red and he worked his mouth for a moment before replying. "Well, I can't be responsible for every parolee," he said. "Gaines was a model prisoner while she was here. I had no way of knowing she would go crazy and kill Mr. Biggs."

"No, of course not," Eleanor said soothingly. "Still, I should like to speak to her, if I may. I understand she is scheduled for execution in June. I want to offer any assistance the President and I might give her family."

"I'm sorry, that won't be possible," the warden said stiffly. "She's in solitary confinement on death row. State policy."

"Oh, that's a shame," Eleanor said blandly. "Shall we visit the farm now?"

CHAPTER 10

On the *Sunset*

"Well, it seems to me that you wouldn't want to ruin her career, would you? That wouldn't be a very Christian thing to do." Sam, up from his nap, freshly shaved and wearing clean clothes, was seated in the coffee shop with Joan, sipping from a bell-shaped glass of Coca-Cola. *A wonder what a few minutes with a sink and razor can do for a man*, Joan thought.

"I'm a newspaper reporter, Sam. My job is to tell the story and let the chips fall where they may. I wouldn't be doing it to hurt her career. I'd be doing it because it's a story the public has a right to know."

"Who decides it's a story the public has a right to know? Look," Sam pulled back one of the lace curtains covering the window. "See that big cactus out there?"

"Which one, dear? There are dozens of them."

"Pick one. It doesn't matter. The point is that every one of them has a story if you want to tell it. Just like everybody aboard this train. Heck, even I have a story. But not every story is worthy of the newspaper, Joan. What makes the fact that this poor woman had polio a news story?"

"But she's a movie star! She's battling this horrible disease. Fame and tragedy; I think the public would eat that up, don't you?"

"I understand that you need to find news that nobody else has discovered. But you're taking a very short-term view, if you ask me. Seems to me the smart play is to treat Miss Lupino's story as a confidence. Use it to open the door to other stories."

"Like all the goody-goody stuff they're doing at this Warm Springs resort?"

"Sure, but more than that. Look, she's an up-and-coming movie star, right? You said so yourself. A young one with a bright future, right? So, I'm guessing she's going to be around for a while. Gain her confidence. Treat her right. Don't look at her as a quick score; look at her as a long-term investment. She could feed you stories for years to come. Or do you already have a source inside Paramount?"

Joan sat quietly for a minute, staring into Sam's clear eyes. "How is it that you're so smart?" she asked, fighting to keep a grin at bay.

"Hey, I'm an accountant," he said with a shrug.

CHAPTER 11

Milledgeville

By the time Eleanor Roosevelt and Tommy had returned to the warden's office, she had seen as much as she could bear for one day. Dozens of women were working in the prison farm's fields, wearing filthy striped uniforms, supervised and threatened by guards bearing shotguns and pistols. They had no hats to protect their heads and eyes from the hot sun, though some had fashioned primitive turbans from rags to cover their hair. Throughout the tour, Captain Carlson had bragged about the production goals his prison farm had met as if he were doing the planting and hoeing and harvesting himself.

All of the women looked painfully thin, and the First Lady recognized the tell-tale signs of pellagra in the skin of some of the prisoners' hands and arms, a sure sign that they weren't being properly fed. Pellagra had killed tens of thousands of Southerners in recent years. The exact cause had not been determined, except that it had something to do with the corn-based diet so common among the poor. Eleanor thought of asking to see the kitchen—she had begun while Franklin was governor of New York to serve as his eyes and ears in institutions such as prisons, and he had instructed her to lift the lids on pots and see what was being cooked—but she was pretty certain she knew what she would find. Tired and demoralized, she accepted a cup of black coffee in the warden's office but found it hard to make pleasant conversation with him. She was relieved when Captain Carlson excused himself in

61

answer to a summons from a distant field where one of the guards had been bitten by a snake.

As the First Lady turned the Ford's ignition for the return trip to Macon, Betty Barnette appeared beside the car looking nervously over her shoulder.

"Mrs. Roosevelt," the secretary said breathlessly, "Captain Carlson goes home for lunch on the dot of one every day and comes back to the prison at two-thirty. Could you send someone else, someone you trust but who isn't so well-known as you are, to see Nell? I could sneak someone in while the warden was at lunch. She does have a story to tell, and I feel so sorry for her, with the baby on the way and all."

"The baby?" Eleanor said, taken aback.

"Yes, ma'am," Betty said, lowering her eyes. "She's due this month. That's why the execution has been set for mid-June. Governor Talmadge thought it was unjust to electrocute her before the baby was born. He said, it wasn't the baby's fault, after all."

"No, not fair at all," Mrs. Roosevelt said. "Thank you, Betty. I think I can get someone here on Monday."

CHAPTER 12

On the *Sunset*

The train was rolling through west Texas by the time the sun set. Ida Lupino had arrived early for her dinner with Joan Roswell. She wanted a few minutes to think over her position, weak as it was.

"The early bird gets the worm, or at least the best seat," Joan Roswell said, following a waiter to the table. Ida looked up to see Joan followed by an attractive young man. *He's not her type*, she thought immediately. *He's not flashy enough.* "Don't get up, dear," Joan said, sliding into the booth. The young man sat next to her. "Miss Lupino, I'd like you to meet Sam Andrews. Sam has been so hospitable to me on our trip so far."

"Miss Lupino," Sam said, shaking her hand. "I'm no doubt the envy of all the men here, dining with two lovely ladies." He had a crooked smile that Ida found appealing.

"Nice to meet you, Mr. Andrews."

"I'll feel a lot more comfortable if you'll just call me Sam."

"Isn't he just the sweetest thing?" Joan said, looking across the table as she pulled a cigarette from her purse.

A waiter arrived and took their drink orders: a martini for Joan, a Scotch neat for Ida, club soda for Sam. Once they were alone again, Ida looked at Joan and asked, "Have you thought about my proposal?"

Joan squinted as she blew a cloud of smoke toward the ceiling. "I have, dear." She paused. Ida tried not to fidget. "With advice from Sam here, I've decided to accept your offer—with conditions, of course."

"Such as?"

"I'll follow you to Warm Springs in a couple of days and you'll give me the behind-the-curtain tour. All access. No holds barred. I see whatever I want to see, soup to nuts."

"Agreed."

Sam was looking from Ida to Joan like a spectator at a tennis match.

"And once you get back to Hollywood, you feed me news from Paramount." Joan paused. "I don't mean studio press releases. I mean what's really going on behind the camera. What deals are being made, who's sleeping with whom" —Sam's ears reddened— "who's getting the next starring role. Anything and everything that's happening on the lot. I get it first. If I don't, well, I have a blockbuster story that I can use to fill the gap. Do you get my drift, dear?"

"I get it." Ida was working to contain her anger. She was at Joan's mercy. For now.

"So, what do you say? Do we have a deal?"

Ida fixed Joan with a resolute stare and said. "Yes." She extended her hand across the table and Joan shook it.

"Wonderful. And here are our drinks! Just in time to toast our new friendship!"

Is that what you call it? "Cheers," Ida said glumly, tapping her glass against Joan's and Sam's. She took a sip and began to relax. *I'll figure something out.* "What is it that you do, Sam?"

"I'm an accountant. Heading to Atlanta for a conference. I have to admit I never expected to find myself in such interesting company." He blushed.

"And what about you, Joan?" Ida asked. "Why are you going east?"

"I'm interviewing Margaret Mitchell about her new book."

"*Gone with the Wind*?" Ida sat up, the tension that her drink had helped release now returned and amplified. "Everybody in town's been talking about it. They say it's going to be the biggest picture ever. Joan, I'd be perfect for the part!"

"What part, dear?"

"Why Scarlett O'Hara, of course! I'm the right age, the right body type, the right personality. She has dark hair, but I do too, I'm just a bottle blonde because that's what Paramount wanted. You've got to put in a good word for me. It would be a career-making role, Joan." Ida was now leaning half-way across the table.

"She's the heroine, I take it?"

"Haven't you read the book?"

"It hasn't even been published yet, dear."

"But the galleys have been floating around town for weeks. I'm telling you Joan, *Gone with the Wind* is the most anticipated film of our generation, maybe ever. It'll make *Ben-Hur* look like a Mack Sennett comedy."

Sam cleared his throat. "If it's going to be that big a deal," he said, looking at Joan, "having Miss Lupino in the starring role would put you in a pretty enviable position. Biggest star, biggest picture, feeding you the inside dope."

Joan looked from the handsome young man to the eager starlet. "You might just have a point, Sam. You might just have a point."

By the time the dinner ended, Joan was feeling pretty good about her day. She had uncovered a Hollywood secret and better yet, with Sam's advice she had turned that secret to her long-term advantage. Now well fed, courtesy of Sam's per diem, she was heading back to his compartment in a relaxed and amorous mood.

"Well, I guess I'll say goodnight," Sam said as they reached the stateroom door. He offered his hand to Joan.

"Oh, no you don't, mister!" she said, pushing the door open and pulling him by the arm. Once they were both inside, Joan slammed the door closed and pressed against the startled Sam. "You need to be properly rewarded for your chivalry, generosity, and wisdom," she cooed, reaching up and kissing him.

Sam kissed back, but then shook his head and pushed away. "No, no, this is not proper. Forgive me."

"But, darling," Joan began.

"No buts. I apologize. What you must think of me!" Sam's face was red, a light sweat covering his forehead. He reached behind him and yanked open the door. "I'll meet you for breakfast, say eight o'clock?"

Joan was confused. "Breakfast?"

"Yes," Sam said, stepping into the corridor.

Joan blinked. This was not what she had planned. "Of course, dear. Eight o'clock."

"Well, good night then," Sam said, pulling the door closed.

"Good night," Joan said with a giggle.

SATURDAY, MAY 16, 1936

CHAPTER 13

Warm Springs

Eleanor Roosevelt was back at the Little White House well before noon on Saturday. After her visit to the prison farm, she had tossed and turned all night, and had hustled Tommy out of the Dempsey Hotel with no other breakfast than coffee, much to the disappointment of Mr. Nations, the manager. He had hoped to enhance his hotel's reputation by serving the First Lady a first-class Southern breakfast, to be captured in a photograph to hang in the lobby, of course.

She was in full voice when she strode into the Little White House, where she found her husband and Missy huddled over the day's dispatches from Washington. "Franklin," she said forcefully, "what is going on at the prison farm is outrageous! The poor women are being treated like slaves on a plantation!" She quickly outlined what she had seen, and then demanded, "You must do something about this, Franklin!"

FDR gave his wife a patient look. "Calm down, Babs," he said. "You know that state prisons are run by states, not the federal government. There's really nothing I or even the U.S. Congress can do about the conditions down there in Milledgeville. And as you also know, Governor Talmadge and I are barely on speaking terms these days. I doubt he'd appreciate any suggestions from me about how to run his prisons."

Eleanor stood staring at her husband for a full minute, fixing her eyes on his. "And you don't want to rile up all those Georgians and other Southern Democrats whose votes you need to get re-elected this fall, do you, Franklin?" she said acidly. When he didn't reply, she stormed out onto the back porch. FDR sighed, lit a Camel, and said to Missy, "See if you can find out what's eating her so, would you?"

"Of course, F.D." Missy rose from her chair, smoothing her silvery black hair, and joined the First Lady on the back porch. "Would you like a cup of coffee or a little something to eat, Mrs. R?" she asked. "Daisy is here, and I know she'd be glad to prepare you something."

"No, Missy, I'm not hungry," Eleanor said, sighing. "Just frustrated. I heard the most awful news yesterday when I was in Milledgeville. That poor Nell Gaines is pregnant, and that is the only thing that is holding up her execution. As soon as her baby is born, she'll go to the electric chair."

"Gosh," Missy said softly, tears springing to her blue eyes. "No wonder you are upset. Is there anything I can do?"

"Well, since you asked," Eleanor said, turning to face the younger woman. "There is. I failed to get a meeting with Nell. The warden there is a Neanderthal; he simply refused to let me see her. But he has a very nice secretary—she reminds me of you, in fact—and she told me she could slip someone in to see Nell one day while the warden is at lunch. I thought of you."

"Of course I would do it," Missy said immediately. "As long as F.D. approves."

"I will see that he does," Eleanor said with determination.

Missy laughed. "I know you will." She paused for a moment. "You know, Mrs. R, there are so many things we can't change in this world. Even the power of the presidency has its limitations. I don't think we can make Georgia reform its prison system, for example, or treat its colored inmates any better. But maybe we can make a difference for Nell Gaines and her baby. I'm willing to try."

Eleanor hugged her. "Thank you, Missy," she said simply. "Now, let's go tell Franklin our plans."

CHAPTER 14

On the *Sunset*

A bleary-eyed Sam was seated in the dining car alongside Ida by the time Joan sauntered in for breakfast at half past eight. The train was slowing as it approached Houston's Grand Central Station and many passengers were lined up at the ends of each car ready to disembark.

"Good morning, dears!" Joan said with a smile as she sat across from Sam. "Don't we look chipper this morning!"

"Good morning, Joan," Ida said with a nod. "We ordered coffee for you." She nodded to a small stainless-steel pot sitting on the table next to an unused china cup and saucer.

"How thoughtful! Thank you, dear." Joan smiled as she reached for the pot.

"Thank Sam," Ida said. "It was his idea."

"Ha! I'm not surprised. He is such a gentleman." Joan beamed at her benefactor as she recalled his clumsy exit from the previous evening. "And how did you pass the night, Sam?"

"With some difficulty, I have to admit. I was doing all right until a Mexican lady got on with a little boy about ten o'clock. He was having a hard time settling in and I offered to hold him for a few minutes. Well, that did it. His momma fell asleep and then he fell asleep and I didn't think it would be right to wake her up and give him back, so I just had to hold him. I didn't sleep much and now my eyelids feel like sandpaper."

"Oh, dear." Joan giggled and put her hand over her mouth. "You really are a prince, Sam Andrews! After breakfast, you go straight to my compartment and take a nap, do you understand?"

"Thank you, Joan," Sam said with a tired grin, so relieved at the gesture that he forgot that it was actually *his* compartment she was offering. Sam waved over one of the waiters and the trio placed their orders.

Once the waiter had retreated to the kitchen, Ida began to talk. "Since our conversation last night," she said, looking Joan in the eye, "I've had some additional thoughts about our little agreement."

"Really dear?" Joan said, trying to sound nonchalant.

"As I agreed yesterday, Joan, I'll show you around Warm Springs, help acquaint you with the treatments being offered there and introduce you to some of the staff and patients. I'm sure you and your readers will find it uplifting. It will give you a chance to see how all the money you helped raise makes a real difference in the lives of real people."

"You raised money for polio?" Sam asked with a note of admiration.

"I was part of the team at the Washington ball back in February," Joan replied. *A very tiny part.*

"There's one more thing which I think can work to everyone's advantage," Ida said. "You're going to Atlanta to interview Margaret Mitchell, right?"

"Correct, dear."

"You agree to suggest me for the part of Scarlett O'Hara and we have a deal."

Joan hesitated for a moment, a smile on her lips, her eyes shifting from Ida's to Sam's and back to Ida's. "Shake on it," Joan said, extending her hand across the table.

"Well done, both of you," Sam said with a relieved smile.

"Ladies, gentleman, your breakfast," the waiter said, setting plates of hot food on the table.

At the Little White House, FDR immediately agreed to the plan Eleanor and Missy presented to him, and the First Lady, much cheered, retired to the guest room to dictate her *My Day* column to Tommy. As soon as she was out of earshot, the President sat Missy down for a little talk.

"One thing I've always appreciated about you, Missy, is that you have a good, sound head on your shoulders," he said. "You're idealistic, but practical too, unlike my missus. Whatever you find out tomorrow, I'm going to seriously consider your recommendation."

"Thank you, F.D.," Missy said simply. "Your confidence means the world to me."

The President took a long drag on his Camel, which he was smoking through an ivory holder. "I'm betting, though, that this is going to warrant some investigating, something beyond even your considerable capabilities. So, I want you to place a call to the Department of Justice this morning, straight to J. Edgar Hoover himself. Tell him to send your friend Corey Wainwright down here on the double. Hoover will figure out some federal angle to justify an agent on the scene. You two work well together, and I don't think you'll mind having his company, am I right?"

Missy blushed and smiled broadly at the prospect of working with the handsome FBI agent again. "Right as usual, sir," she said. "Thanks!"

"I'm sure neither of you is very hungry right now," Sam said once they had finished breakfast on the *Sunset*, "but I'd like to invite you both to dinner this evening—if you don't have other plans."

The two women exchanged looks. "What did you have in mind, Sam?" Ida asked.

"Well, we arrive in New Orleans about four o'clock and the *Crescent Limited* to Atlanta doesn't leave until eleven. That gives us either a lot of time to explore the New Orleans train station or plenty of time to have dinner in town. I did some reading before we left Los Angeles and New Orleans is noted for its fine French cuisine."

"Among other things," Joan added.

"What do you say? Would you both join me? My treat?"

"I'd love to, Sam. That's very thoughtful," Ida said, smiling and placing her hand on his forearm.

"And you're sure your per diem can handle both of us, dear?" Joan asked, cocking her head.

"It'll come close enough," he answered with a laugh. "How about it?"

"Count me in, dear," Joan purred.

CHAPTER 15

New Orleans

The *Sunset Limited* arrived at New Orleans Union Station at 4:04 pm, having lost only four minutes over its 2,069-mile route. By five-thirty, Joan, Ida, and Sam had checked their bags at the station and were sharing a cab heading east on Loyola Avenue toward the city's famous French Quarter.

"I know just the place," Joan announced.

"You've been here before?" Ida asked.

"No, but a friend of mine owns a place here. It's supposed to be quite good. Driver, take us to Pat O'Brien's."

"Very good, miss."

The flow of air through the open windows of the taxi masked the evening's humidity. When Sam paid the cabbie and the trio climbed out of the car at the corner of Royal and St. Peter Streets, they were engulfed by the warm, thick air and their ears were overwhelmed with the bustle of the evening crowd and the sounds of jazz music floating out onto the dirty streets from a dozen open doorways.

"Here we go!" Joan said, grabbing Sam by the hand and pulling him inside Pat O'Brien's. "Table for three, please," Joan shouted to a black-jacketed waiter carrying a tray of violently colored drinks.

"Hold on, sis," the man said. "Be with you in a sec."

Beyond the bar, two pianists sat facing each other across their respective instruments as they banged out a lively duet. Sam looked around with wide eyes at the colorful array of snappily-dressed customers mingling with a few who looked like they had spent the last few nights sleeping on the curb.

"Quite a joint, isn't it?" Joan said loudly, straining to be heard over the buzz of the restaurant.

"Three, you said?" the waiter asked them, his tray now tucked under one arm. "I've got a table over here." He wound his way among the early diners with Joan following. Sam trailed along behind Ida until they reached a round wrought iron table with three matching chairs set against a photo-covered wall. "Here you go, folks," the waiter said, pulling out chairs for the two women. "Get settled in and someone will be right over to take your drink order."

"Here," Ida said, pulling her chair against the wall. "Scoot around so that you have a good view of the pianos." Sam did as she suggested. Ida was behind the table, Joan and Sam flanking her.

"What can I get you folks to drink?" It was a different waiter, same black jacket and black bow-tie, but a little older and heavier, his brow covered in perspiration.

"Gin and tonic for me," Ida said with a smile.

"I'll have a scotch and soda," Joan said, her eyes dancing from table to table and back to the waiter.

"And for you, sir?"

"Just bring me a, um, Coke, please."

"All right, that's a gin and tonic, a scotch and soda, a rum and Coke," the waiter repeated.

"Waiter," Joan said, "I'm a friend of Pat's. Please make sure I get the discount."

"A friend of Pat's?" the waiter asked with a smile. "You got it, sweetheart!" With that he bustled away across the noisy, crowded dining room toward the bar.

Ida leaned toward Joan and shouted, "Are you really a friend of Pat's?"

"More of an acquaintance, actually," Joan said, pulling a cigarette from her purse and plugging it into her ebony holder. "We worked on a picture together a couple of years ago."

"Really?" Sam asked, impressed. "Which one?"

"*Here Comes the Navy*. Pat and Jimmy Cagney were the leads. I was an extra in the dance scene and in the wedding scene at the end. I was the girl dancing just beyond Gloria Stuart's shoulder."

"Wow! What are they like? O'Brien and Cagney?"

"Wonderful performers. Always very professional. And great pals. They've known each other for years. You know, the film community is really quite small, isn't that right, Ida, dear? Everybody knows everybody."

"It sounds like a lot of fun," Sam said, turning toward Ida. "Do you know Pat too?"

"I've never worked with him. He's over at Warner's, isn't he, Joan?"

"That's right," Joan said, blowing a cloud of blue smoke into the fog hanging below the ceiling.

"Most of my pictures so far have been at Paramount," Ida said. "Maybe I'll get lucky and work with him some day." Across the room, the pianos broke into a Dixieland rag.

"Here we are," the waiter reappeared, lifting drinks from his tray to the table. "Something to eat to go with these?"

"What would you recommend, dear?" Joan asked.

He wiped his sleeve across his damp forehead and smiled. "Well, for friends of Pat's, I always recommend the fresh oysters. We feature them raw, broiled in butter, fried, just about any way you'd like 'em."

"I'll have fried oysters," Joan said, smiling.

"Shrimp loaf for me," Ida said.

"I think I'd like to try the oysters," Sam said. "What's the best way to eat them?"

"Oh, the best way is just as the Good Lord made 'em, raw. Of course, a dash of Tabasco makes 'em that much better."

"Fine. I'll have the raw oysters with the taba…"

"Tabasco. Very good, sir."

"Well," Sam said, looking to his companions, "here's to a night on the town with two attractive ladies. Cheers!" He took a large sip of his drink and frowned. "This Coke tastes funny. Kind of flat."

"Oh, it's just the water down here," Joan allowed. "You know how it is on the coast."

"Hmm." Sam took another sip.

By the time he finished his oysters and his second drink, Sam was looking a little pale. "My head feels all fuzzy."

Joan winked at Ida. "Not enough sleep last night, darling. You were too busy spelling that poor mother. It's catching up with you." Joan signaled to the waiter, held up her finger and then waved it in a circle. "How'd you like the oysters?"

"Really different. I don't know if I could make a steady diet of them."

"A nice break from train food, though, right?" Ida said.

"For sure." Sam smiled as the waiter set another round of drinks on the table.

Before long, Sam had loosened his tie and was attempting to sing along with the dueling pianos. "Sam, dear," Joan said, reaching across the small table and taking hold of his hand. "I think it's time we settled up and headed back to the station." She caught their waiter's eye and motioned for the check.

"I'm just starting to relax, you know," Sam said, smiling at Ida and Joan. "I didn't realize how nice it was to get off that train. Whew! Two nights sitting up in a chair!"

"One more to go, dear," Joan said.

"Here you go, folks." The waiter set the check in front of Sam. "Hope you enjoyed your evening and hope to see you back again soon."

As Sam dug in his pocket for cash, Joan picked up the bill and studied it. "Just a moment, waiter. I distinctly told you that I'm a friend of Pat's."

"Yes, ma'am. Here in New Orleans, everybody's a friend of Pat's! Have a nice evening."

"Well! The gall of that man!"

"Joan, Joan, Joan! Don't get so upset! We're having a good time, aren't we? Besides, it's worth ever' penny. Ever' penny. And he gets a tip to boot. I've never had a better time. Have you, Ida? Have you, Joan?"

"I don't know that I have," Ida agreed, laughing. "Come on, big boy. Let's get you back to the train."

CHAPTER 16

On the *Crescent*

The *Crescent Limited's* Virginia green locomotive was trimmed with gold and silver and belching black smoke by the time Joan and Ida maneuvered Sam aboard at ten-forty-five. They'd taken a cab back from the French Quarter and Sam had fallen asleep nestled between them in the back seat.

"Some guys have all the luck," the driver had muttered, shaking his head, when he dropped them at the Loyola Avenue entrance to the station.

"I'm in the next car. Good night, Sam. Thanks for dinner," Ida said, kissing Sam on his clammy cheek and heading along the corridor.

"G'night," Sam replied, placing a hand on the wall to steady himself. Outside on the platform a whistle blew and the conductor shouted, "All aboard!"

"Come on, dear," Joan said. "I'll help you get settled."

"No, no, no. You take the stateroom, Joan. I'll just go find that little boy and his mom and sit with them."

"That was the other train, dear, last night. Besides, if you think I'm going to let all those oysters go to waste you've got another think coming." Joan pushed the door open and shouldered the unsteady Sam into the small compartment. "Look, dear, they've already turned down the sheets for us," she purred.

"For us," Sam mumbled, leaning heavily on Joan's shoulder. She pushed the door closed with her foot and held Sam by his lapels.

"Let's get you out of these uncomfortable clothes." Joan eased his coat over his shoulders and down his arms. "That's better, isn't it?" She reached down for his belt buckle and began to unfasten it. "If you think dinner was fun..." Joan laughed. "Sit down." Sam did as he was instructed.

Joan untied his shoes and slipped them off, tossing them into a corner. "Won't need those until breakfast. Now, we don't need these trousers any more, do we?" Joan knelt and began to tug Sam's pants off by the cuffs.

"Joan?"

"Yes, dear?"

"Joan, I think I love you."

"Now's your chance to prove it." Joan giggled.

"Joan?"

"Yes, dear?"

"I don't feel so hot." Then he threw up all over her.

SUNDAY, MAY 17, 1936

CHAPTER 17

On the *Crescent*

"Well?" Ida asked when Joan walked into the dining car the next morning. Joan's eyes were red and she appeared tired. "How was your night?"

"Four times."

"My God! Four times? Are you serious?"

Joan fixed her companion with a withering look. "He threw up four times. I didn't get to sleep until four o'clock and that was only after I was sure that everything was out of his system. He's still out, poor guy. I don't think he's ever had a night like that before."

"Poor boy," Ida said, chuckling. "He really is a sweetheart, you know. Last night notwithstanding, you really are a lucky girl."

"Me? Oh, he's not interested in me. He's a Baptist, for God's sake."

"Even Baptists can be romantic, Joan."

"He's not really my type, dear."

Ida laughed.

The cat's eyes sunglasses looked out of place perched on top of Sam's nose. He walked unsteadily to the table and sat next to Ida. He landed hard, almost slipping off his seat.

"Nice glasses, Sam," Ida said, trying not to laugh.

"Shhh!" He held a finger up to his lips. "Not so loud. There's a drummer pounding away inside my head. The glasses are Joan's. She loaned them to me. Otherwise it's so bright it's like a hundred needles sticking me in the eyes."

"And such handsome eyes, too," Ida said, stealing a look across the table at Joan. Ida reached up and pulled the glasses down slightly. "Oh my! What a lovely shade of red. How about some coffee?" She poured some from the pot on the table into Sam's cup.

Sam cleared his throat. "I don't ever want to spend the night on another train."

"The porter doesn't want you to either, dear," Joan said. "I thought the poor man was going to be sick himself after the third go 'round."

"Hmmm." Sam placed a hand on either side of his place mat to steady himself. "The train is really rocking this morning." Ida and Joan exchanged quick looks.

"Something to eat, sir?" the waiter asked.

"No, please!"

Joan smiled up at the waiter. "Perhaps you could bring our friend some dry toast?" she asked with raised eyebrows.

"Yes, ma'am. Coming right up."

"Oh, don't say that, dear."

"Ida, it was certainly a pleasure to meet you. I can't wait to go see your movies now," Sam said. The three traveling companions were standing on the platform at Atlanta's main depot early Sunday afternoon as travelers flowed around them like water around the rocks in a stream.

"Thank you, Sam. I enjoyed getting to know you as well. Thanks for your good advice about Joan. I'm sure she and I will be able to help each other out." Ida shook Sam's hand and then gave him a quick hug and peck on the cheek. "Take care. I've still got one more train to catch."

As if on cue, a muffled voice came over the public address system announcing the departure of another train from Track Two. "See you in a day or two," Ida said, shaking hands with Joan. "Remember, Train Forty-Five. It stops right at Warm Springs. Call from the station and I'll send a car for you. And remember to put in a good word for me with Miss Mitchell."

"Will do, dear. Goodbye for now." Joan watched as Ida moved off looking for her next train.

"I'm really sorry I made such a mess of last night," Sam was saying when she turned back toward him. His ears had turned red and he was staring down at the toes of his brown shoes.

"You have nothing to apologize for, dear. Why, this whole journey you've always put my best interests first. I truly appreciate that. You were never anything but a gentleman."

"Gentlemen don't get drunk and puke on their companions. I'm really quite ashamed of myself. I should have known better than to drink all those drinks. I've certainly learned my lesson. Demon Rum."

"Sam Andrews," Joan said in a scolding voice, "don't ever think that you aren't a fine, fine man. Why, any girl would be proud to call you her beau."

"Any girl?"

"Any girl!" Joan stood on her tiptoes and kissed Sam full on the mouth, right in front of God and everybody else in the Atlanta depot.

MONDAY, MAY 18, 1936

CHAPTER 18

Warm Springs

Even though it would leave him without both his first- and second-string secretaries for the day, FDR had insisted Missy take Grace Tully along on her journey to the prison farm. Grace, who had worked for FDR as Missy's assistant since he ran for governor of New York in 1928, was a good-humored, dimpled woman in her mid-30s, an Irish-Catholic like Missy. The two were the closest of friends, often vacationing together when their boss was off on one of his fishing cruises. They had spent a week in California the previous fall, where Grace had been on hand for the Shirley Temple kidnapping caper.

Missy had arranged to borrow a maroon Hudson convertible coupe from one of the doctors at the Warm Springs Foundation rather than taking the President's personal car, which might raise suspicion. She had also borrowed something else from the Foundation but decided to wait until they were closer to Milledgeville before she sprang it on Grace. Their boss rolled his wheelchair onto the front porch of the Little White House to bid them good-bye, and, eyes twinkling, recited a ditty that Louis Howe had written about Missy years before:

"Our darling Missy does I fear
Desire to copy Paul Revere.
But timid ones at home should bide
When she invites them for a ride."

"You can't scare me, Boss," Grace proclaimed. "I've taken many a ride with Missy and she's a perfectly competent driver."

As it was a lovely clear day, the top had been rolled down, and the two women had tied broad scarves over their hair to keep it from flying in the wind. Missy wore her darkened glasses as she usually did when outdoors. They had decided to return that evening rather than staying overnight in Macon, as they would not be spending more than an hour in Milledgeville. Daisy Bonner had packed a hamper with fried chicken, biscuits, and jars of cold sweet tea to sustain them on their trip.

"Are you nervous?" Grace asked as they rolled down the road.

"A little," Missy admitted. "Though I spoke by phone Friday with the warden's secretary, Betty Barnette, and she was very nice. She gave me specific instructions about where to enter and where to park. If anyone asks us, we're to say we are with the state health department and are just checking on Nell Gaines's pregnancy and narrowing down her due date."

"The better to schedule her execution, my dear?" Grace asked.

"Something like that," Missy said. "Oh, I feel so sorry for that woman. Mrs. Roosevelt wants us to find out who the father of the baby is—she's betting it's Mr. Biggs—and anything she can tell us about what happened that night that didn't come out at the trial. Apparently, the lawyer the court appointed to defend her didn't do much defending."

To distract themselves from their grim mission, the two women chattered about work, the news from old friends at the Warm Springs Foundation and the latest Shirley Temple movie, *Captain January*, which Grace had seen at The President movie theater in nearby Manchester on Saturday afternoon. During their California vacation, the tiny star had been kidnapped from the train on which they were riding. Over a frantic weekend in San Francisco, Missy and Grace had worked with Corey Wainwright, then the FBI agent-in-charge there, to find her. News coverage of the crime had been quashed by FDR himself, much to the displeasure—for different reasons—of the reporter on the scene, Joan Roswell, and J. Edgar Hoover.

"To think she started filming that movie the day after she got home from her ordeal!" Grace said. "And she's marvelous. Wait until you see her dancing with Buddy Ebsen in their musical number 'At the Codfish Ball.' By the way, what do you hear from Corey lately? I'd think with him based in Washington now you'd be seeing him all the time."

Missy blushed. "Funny you should ask. Mr. Hoover has kept him pretty busy," she said. "After we wrapped up that mess from the Birthday Ball, he had to settle things in San Francisco before he could move, and then as soon as he got to Washington, Hoover sent him out of town on a case that took almost a month." Corey had again been instrumental in solving a crime when Missy and the actress Ginger Rogers had been waylaid on the way to the bank with a large deposit from the President's Birthday Ball fund-raising event at the Shoreham Hotel in late January. "But it just so happens that the Boss instructed me to call Mr. Hoover Saturday and get Corey sent down here to help investigate this case, if it turns out there's anything to investigate. If not, he'll get to enjoy a nice holiday in the Georgia sunshine."

"That's grand!" Grace said. "Now all we need is Joan Roswell and we'll have the old gang back together again. I wonder what she's up to these days."

"I don't care," Missy said. "As long as she's far, far away from here!"

CHAPTER 19

Atlanta

The elegant Georgian Terrace Hotel on Peachtree Street in midtown Atlanta was one of the city's finer hotels. *Wish I could afford to stay here*, Joan thought as she followed a waiter to a table in the hotel's gracious, high-ceilinged dining room. Instead, she was staying three blocks down the street at a flop house called the Heart of Dixie Inn. Joan was sure her "roommates" were as pleased to see her leave the room as she was to escape it. *Roaches like their privacy.*

With the money she had saved from her travel allowance by cozying up to Sam on the train, Joan felt she could afford to splurge on a luncheon meeting with the author, Miss Mitchell. Her interview had been arranged by a publicist at MacMillan, the publishing house which had purchased Mitchell's novel.

"Have you met Miss Mitchell before?" the publicist had asked.

"No, dear."

"Be prepared. She's a little different."

"Different than what, dear?"

"You'll see."

Now Joan was seated, facing the dining room's entrance and waiting to see just how "different"— and how punctual—the author would be. Joan removed her notebook and pen from her alligator purse and set them beside her place setting on top of the linen covered table. The silverware was embossed with the hotel's "GT" logo. A crystal water glass stood at each place.

At five minutes after noon, a diminutive, thirty-ish woman with dark, wavy hair, wearing a prim navy dress with a white lace collar, a wide-brimmed straw hat, and ankle strap heels, walked through the lobby and into the dining room. She paused and spoke to the maître d' who led her to Joan's table.

Joan stood and extended her hand, looking down at the little woman. "I'm Joan Roswell," she said, offering her friendliest smile. "You must be Margaret Mitchell. It's so nice of you to meet with me."

"Peggy Marsh," the author said, clasping Joan's hand in her navy-gloved one and regarding the reporter with quizzical blue eyes. "I seem to be better known these days by my pen name." Her accent reminded Joan of honey dripping from a spoon: *Ah seem to be bettuh known these days bah mah pen name.* "Socially, I am Mrs. John Marsh."

"Oh?" Joan asked.

"It's sort of a funny story. John was the best man at my first wedding," Miss Mitchell said as she took her seat. "That marriage was a disaster, so I'd appreciate it if you don't mention it in your story. But John is a wonderful man. He's been so supportive of my writing, even bought me my typewriter." *Even bawt me mah tahpwrahtuh.*

"Well," Joan began tentatively, "you are certainly the talk of Hollywood."

"You're from one of the papers in Los Angeles, is that right?"

"That's right, dear, the *Standard.* I'm the Hollywood reporter. I cover the motion picture business. Everything and everybody from Shirley Temple to Ginger Rogers and now Margaret Mitchell. They say your book is going to become the biggest film of all time."

"Really? Who's 'they'?" Miss Mitchell asked as she removed her gloves and slid them into her purse.

Joan smiled and cocked her head. "Oh, people in the know around the studios."

"What do you think?" the author asked.

"There's a certain unity of opinion on the topic. I hear you have several suitors, that's always a good sign. MGM, RKO, Warner's, Fox. Those are heavy hitters. They all make quality pictures."

"Well, I don't know about any of that," Miss Mitchell said. "It just about killed me correcting the final galleys, and I gladly turned over the movie negotiations to my publisher and editor."

"What kind of money are they hoping to get?" Joan asked.

Miss Mitchell's dark eyebrows rose against her pale skin. "Goodness. What a question. I can't imagine."

She's not giving me much for my story, Joan thought. She tried another gambit. "I understand the story is about the Civil War," she said.

"You haven't read it?" Miss Mitchell asked incredulously. "You mean you've come all the way across the country to interview me and you haven't even read my book?"

Uh oh. Joan gritted her teeth but kept her smile in place. "It's not available yet, is it, dear? At least not to working girls like me."

Then, to Joan's surprise, Miss Mitchell threw her head back, her dark hair bouncing, and laughed. "You know, I have to tell you something. I'm impressed that you can talk your editor into spending the money to send you all the way to Atlanta, Georgia without reading the book. You must be quite persuasive."

Joan grinned. "Let's just say that I've had a good run of scoops lately and that my editor wants to see that run continued."

"I started out as a newspaper reporter myself, you know," Miss Mitchell confided. "I wrote for the *Atlanta Journal* for four years, wrote everything from features to obituaries. I know a thing or two about pitching stories to crusty old male editors." She reached into her purse and pulled out a package of cigarettes, offering one to Joan. *This is going better*, Joan thought. *At least she didn't get up and storm out of the place when I admitted I hadn't read her masterpiece!*

The waiter arrived and took their orders: Cobb salad for Joan and baked ham and sides for Miss Mitchell. He quickly returned with glasses of iced tea garnished with lemon slices and a basket of hot buttered rolls.

"So," Joan resumed, "what was your inspiration for the book?"

Miss Mitchell took a sip of her sweet tea. "I was born and raised here in Atlanta. Except for a year at Smith College in Massachusetts, I've lived here my whole life, so I grew up being dragged hither and yon on Sunday afternoons, visiting relatives. When I was a child, we were seen and not heard, so I spent hours and hours listening to old folks—my grandmother and my aunts and uncles mostly—telling their stories from the years during and after the war. Some of the men had been in the cavalry, and it was awful to sit on their knees, because they'd start bouncing around like they were still riding their horses in the war."

"Do Southerners truly call it the Civil War? I've heard otherwise."

"Well, some people down here still call it the War of Northern Aggression, but yes, the Civil War," Miss Mitchell said with a grin. "I was ten years old before I found out the Confederates had lost, and I just couldn't believe it. That Robert E. Lee, who was such a Southern gentleman, was defeated by the likes of Ulysses S. Grant was just an abomination! I also did a tremendous amount of historical research, old newspapers, diaries, letters, and the like. I wanted my novel to be historically accurate, even if it was fiction."

"Any surprises along the way?" Joan asked, enjoying her interview subject more than she had expected.

"I was surprised to find how important Atlanta was to the war effort; you know, at the time it wasn't even the capital of Georgia. But it was an important railroad town, and all the supplies from the Deep South to Virginia, where so much of the fighting was taking place, were sent through Atlanta. In fact, its name before it became Atlanta was Terminus. Milledgeville was the capital back then. Milledgeville lost the capitol, but it kept the state lunatic asylum." She grinned mischievously. "You know how to tell the capitol from the asylum?"

"How, dear?"

"The capitol has a dome," Miss Mitchell said innocently.

Joan laughed again. *This lady is a gas. I wonder if her book is funny?* "The war ended more than seventy years ago," Joan pointed out. "Do you think people still care about it?"

"Why, certainly!" Miss Mitchell said. "Here in the South, there are still signs of the destruction of Sherman's March to the Sea. When I was a little girl, my grandmother took me on a buggy ride near her old home place outside of Jonesboro. We rode through mile after mile of what she called 'Sherman's sentinels.'"

"What are those?"

"The brick and stone chimneys that were all that was left of hundreds of homes after Sherman burned them. People haven't forgotten here. I doubt they've forgotten in Gettysburg and places like that in the North, either. But my book isn't all moonlight-on-magnolias, and my characters are very flawed people."

"Tell me about your main characters," Joan said, rapidly taking notes. "Your heroine is named Scarlett, right?"

"Originally, her name was Pansy, but I changed it to Scarlett last year," Miss Mitchell said. "She's a young woman when the book opens. Very headstrong, very spoiled, her father's favorite child. The book is really her story, following her from just before the war when she has her eyes set on marrying a young man from a neighboring plantation, all the way through Reconstruction. The old world has disappeared, 'gone with the wind,' as the title says. By then, with sheer gumption, she's made a small fortune and partially regained a place in the society of the new South, but at a terrible cost to herself and everyone around her. She's become a hardened adventuress."

"Who should play her in the picture?"

"Miriam Hopkins would be a perfect Scarlett O'Hara," Miss Mitchell said enthusiastically. "She was born in Savannah, so she has the right accent. She played the title role in *Jezebel* on Broadway a couple of years ago, didn't she? I don't know why they cast Bette Davis for that part in the movie."

"Miriam's a wonderful actress, but she's a little mature for the part, isn't she?" Joan said. "You said this Scarlett is a young woman?"

"Yes, she's just sixteen at the start of the book. You're probably right. Miriam Hopkins is probably about my age, mid-thirties."

"How about Ida Lupino?" Joan asked quickly. "She's just the right age. She's done some very good work. She has excellent emotional range."

"Sounds Italian," Miss Mitchell said, wrinkling her nose.

"She was born in England, but you'd never know it from her movie work," Joan said. "She doesn't have a British accent."

"Never heard of her. I don't know if anyone from England could handle the Southern dialect," Miss Mitchell said. "But casting won't be up to me, I don't suppose."

The waiter arrived with their luncheon dishes, and they spent a few minutes digging into their food. Joan found her Cobb salad a fair copy of the one originated at the Brown Derby in Hollywood and was happy to be eating at a table that wasn't rocking along a railroad track. "Okay," she said, after a few bites, "Tell me a little bit about the main male character. His name is Rhett Butler?"

"Yes, Rhett Butler, a rogue from Charleston, where he's been exiled from polite society," Miss Mitchell said, daintily wiping her lips with a linen napkin.

"Sounds like my kind of man!" Joan laughed.

Miss Mitchell confided, "He and Scarlett are two of a kind, but she doesn't know it. Her mammy says he's a mule in horse's harness."

"The buzz all over Hollywood is that Clark Gable would be the perfect Rhett Butler," Joan said. "What do you think?"

The author frowned. "Oh, I don't think so. It's too bad Charles Boyer can't lose that French accent, he would be perfect. I saw Jack Holt in *The Littlest Rebel* with Shirley Temple last Christmas. He was playing a Union captain, but I think he would make a good Rhett Butler. But, once again, it will be up to the studio, I suppose."

"Have you ever been out to Hollywood?" Joan asked.

"No, but Hollywood has come here," Miss Mitchell said. "I interviewed Rudolph Valentino right here at the Georgian Terrace. He was mesmerizing. He picked me up in his arms and carried me into the hotel, just like in *The Sheikh*!"

As they ate their lunch, Miss Mitchell regaled Joan with stories about how she had begun writing her novel while recovering from a badly broken ankle and had stuffed the chapters into dozens of manila envelopes hidden all over her apartment. "I never thought anything would come of it, to be honest," she said, "and then Harold Latham, from MacMillan, came here looking for new writers and he talked me into handing it over. Harold had to buy a new suitcase to hold all my envelopes, so he could take the book on the train. I even found two envelopes under a bed that had a broken caster. I was using the envelopes to make all the legs even!"

"I have a long train ride back to California," Joan said. "Do you have a copy you can loan me?"

"Well, as you noted, it won't be published until July." Mitchell picked up her fork and stared into Joan's green eyes. "But, if you're really interested, I'll see if I can scrounge up an advance copy before you head back."

"That would be lovely, dear. Train trips are so long and lonely, and I never find anything to occupy my time." Joan took a small bite of Cobb salad and watched as Miss Mitchell cut into her ham. "This doesn't have anything to do with the book, dear," Joan said, pointing with her fork toward Mitchell's plate, "but what exactly is that side dish?"

Mitchell looked down and laughed. "Those are hominy grits."

"And what, may I ask, are grits?"

"You've never had grits?"

"I'm from California, dear. We don't have any grits trees out west."

CHAPTER 20

Milledgeville

Missy and Grace stopped for gas in Gray, and both women planned to use the ladies' room while the attendant filled up the Hudson's gas tank. That's when Missy shared her surprise with Grace.

"When I was at the Foundation arranging for the car, Grace," she said. "I had a thought about some disguises for us."

"Disguises?" Grace asked.

"Yes," Missy said. "I thought if we were supposed to be from the health department, one of us should have a nurse's uniform, and I was able to borrow one at the Foundation. I think it would fit you."

"Me?" Grace said. "Why not you? At least you've had experience pretending to be a nurse, when you and the Boss were setting things up at Warm Springs and he christened himself ol' Doc Roosevelt and you Nurse LeHand."

"I know, I know," Missy said. "But I'm, uh, a good bit slimmer than the nurse who loaned me the uniform, and I'm afraid I would just swim in it. It might be closer to your size."

Grace sighed in resignation. "The diet starts as soon as we get back to Washington. Did you bring me white shoes and white stockings too, I suppose?"

"Yup. And a blood pressure cuff and stethoscope." Missy smiled and handed her a small suitcase. "I know you'll look like *Sue Barton, Student Nurse* when you're all dressed."

"And what's your disguise going to be?" Grace asked, taking the suitcase.

Missy lifted a clipboard from the backseat. "This. I'm a social worker."

Twenty minutes later, Grace was appropriately suited up, though she insisted Missy raise the top of the convertible to keep her white nurse's cap from blowing off her head. Missy removed her sporty hairband, smoothed her hair, and settled an appropriately serious hat on her own head.

When they arrived at the prison farm a few minutes past one, they presented themselves to Betty Barnette, who quickly ushered them down a long hallway. "You won't be disturbed here," she said. "Nell is the only prisoner on death row right now." She chose a brass key from a large ring in her hand and opened a heavy wooden door with a small viewing window set at eye level.

"Nell?" she said. "You have some ladies from the health department who want to examine you." She pulled a chain to turn on a naked light bulb hanging from the ceiling on a wire. Turning to Missy she said, "I'll be back in forty-five minutes. That should give you plenty of time, won't it?"

"I think so," Missy said, but both she and Grace were almost dumbstruck by the sight before them.

Nell Gaines lay on a narrow cot in the small cell, which reeked from the contents of a slop bucket in the corner. Her belly bulged with the baby she was carrying, but her arms and legs were like sticks. Her face was swollen, her hair matted. She listlessly raised herself to a sitting position, never making eye contact with her visitors. *I've never seen a more miserable human being,* Missy thought.

"Good afternoon, Mrs. Gaines," she said formally. "I'm Miss LeHand, and this is Miss Tully. We want to check on your, er, condition, and ask you a few questions."

Nell Gaines simply nodded.

"First, I think we should check your blood pressure," Missy said, nodding at Grace. Her assistant snapped open the small suitcase that contained the blood pressure cuff and stethoscope and made a good pretense of competence as she wrapped the cuff around Nell's arm. The two secretaries had watched the President's doctor take his blood pressure dozens of times and were familiar with the mechanics, if not how to interpret a reading.

"Very good," Grace said. She then produced a wooden tongue depressor from the suitcase. "Please say 'ah,'" she said, and when Nell complied, she looked down her throat, though in the dimly lit room she couldn't tell anything except Nell had recently consumed coffee.

"How have you been feeling?" Grace asked. "Is the baby, uh, moving?"

Nell nodded. "I ain't getting much sleep," she said. "Not that anyone would expect me to."

An awkward pause followed, and Missy decided it was time to lay their cards on the table.

"Mrs. Gaines," she said. "We've got a confession to make. We're not from the state health department at all." She fumbled in her purse, pulling out her wallet, and extracted her White House identification card to show to Nell. "The First Lady, Mrs. Eleanor Roosevelt, sent us to see you. She wants to find out what really happened with Mr. Biggs, and if you feel you got a fair trial."

Nell Gaines stared at the two women, and then she began to wail.

CHAPTER 21

Atlanta

Joan and Miss Mitchell parted with a handshake on the hotel's circular driveway. "I'll send my secretary to your hotel with an advance copy of the book. Where did you say you are staying?"

"Right here, of course," Joan lied, thinking, *I'm sure I can make some arrangement with the desk clerk to hold the book for me.* "Thank you, dear. I look forward to reading it. And thank you for your time. It's been a real pleasure. Are you coming out to Hollywood to watch the filming?"

"We'll see," Miss Mitchell said. "That still seems a long way off to me."

"If you do, be sure to let me know. I'll treat you to dinner—courtesy of the *Standard,* of course."

Joan watched as Miss Mitchell crossed Peachtree Street, cars honking as she dodged through the midday traffic, then she turned and walked back inside the Georgian Terrace. Joan found a comfortable upholstered chair in a corner of the lobby, sat down, and began to write.

MITCHELL LOOKING AHEAD TO PICTURE

By Joan Roswell, Special to the AP—Atlanta, Georgia—*Gone with the Wind* author Margaret Mitchell is looking forward to the motion picture version of her soon-to-be-released novel. The book, which has impressed early reviewers and attracted the fervent attention of Hollywood's biggest producers, is a Civil War-era tale following the exploits of wealthy, beautiful, young Scarlett O'Hara.

In an exclusive wide-ranging interview with this reporter, the twice-married Miss Mitchell predicted that the film version of her novel would be "an outstanding picture." Apparently, the motion picture industry agrees, for this reporter has learned that the major studios are engaged in a bidding war to land the screen rights to *Gone with the Wind* and bring this classic story of America's most turbulent period to theaters across the country and around the world.

Joan's article, when she finally finished the first draft, ran to more than two thousand words and covered Mitchell's inspiration for the story, her views on the old and new South, and her hopes to visit the film set and meet the cast that would bring her characters to life. *Not too bad*, Joan thought, after she reread the draft for the third time. *Hope it's still readable after Billy finishes with it!*

The reporter checked her watch. It was after five o'clock now and the traffic on Peachtree Street had gotten much heavier as workers left downtown and headed to their midtown and uptown neighborhoods and supper.

She had missed the afternoon train to Warm Springs, but another departed in the morning at eight. *Looks like another night with my six-legged friends*, she thought as she headed toward the Heart of Dixie.

CHAPTER 22

Milledgeville

By the time Nell Gaines had finished telling her story, Grace and Missy were seated on either side of her on the cot, their arms around the sobbing young woman. They didn't notice the stench in the room, or the fleas hopping around on the cot's thin mattress. They had forgotten everything except the horrifying story Nell had told them about her indentured servitude to the Biggs family, Wilton Biggs's sexual abuse, the events on the night of the murder and the gross miscarriage of justice that had landed her on death row.

They sat in silence, rubbing Nell's back. Suddenly, they heard pattering footsteps in the hall.

It was Betty Barnette.

"The warden is back early!" she hissed. "You've got to get out of here!"

Missy and Grace leapt to their feet, gathering up their belongings as Betty impatiently stood by the door. "Hurry, hurry," she said. "I'll lose my job if he finds out, and God knows what he'll do to Nell!"

Missy pressed Nell's hand before she left the cell. "I promise to help you," she said simply, then she scurried out the door.

"This way," Betty said, herding the secretaries down the central hall. "I'll hide you in the laundry room. The prisoners are hanging out the wash today, so there shouldn't be anyone in there."

In the laundry, Betty located two huge wheeled canvas carts heaped with dirty sheets. "Here," she said, helping Grace into the first. "I hate to do it, but I've got to cover you up, just to be safe." She did the same for Missy. "Now, stay quiet," she said. "I'm going to lock the doors in case anyone should try to come in, but I'm not the only one with a key."

The suspension of Missy's senses that had begun under the onslaught of Nell's story returned with a vengeance as she huddled under the dirty sheets. Within minutes, she felt like her skin was on fire as tiny insects bit her. *Am I going to have to cut off my hair to get rid of them?* she wondered. The smell of unwashed bodies was almost intolerable, and she felt bile rise up in her throat.

After what seemed like hours but was probably only thirty minutes, she heard the rattle of the key in the door again. Missy held her breath as footsteps came straight to her cart. "It's me," Betty said. "The warden's gone. He had an appointment in Macon and just stopped by to pick up something he'd forgotten."

Missy and Grace sprang from their hiding places. Missy had to laugh at Grace, whose nurse's hat was wildly askew. Both women began to scratch furiously as they followed Betty out of the room and down the hall.

Once back in the car, they were silent for several miles, digesting all that had happened, then Missy said, "I think we've earned a night at the Dempsey Hotel. I can't bear driving home with all these critters crawling in my hair."

"I agree!" Grace said. "I was thinking, 'Well, at least I have some other clothes to change into."

"Lucky you," Missy said. "I'm going to send you out shopping for me in Macon while I take a long, hot shower."

"At least the top is down and can blow some of the stink off us," Grace said.

They were silent again, then Missy said, "At least we're not Nell Gaines. Grace, we've got to save that wretched woman."

CHAPTER 23

Atlanta

"Well, look what the cat dragged in," Elliott Norton said with a laugh when Corey Wainwright walked into the Federal Bureau of Investigation's Atlanta office on Monday evening. "What brings you to the beating heart of the South?"

Special Agent Wainwright dropped his suitcase on the floor in front of Norton's desk and flexed his shoulders. "I'm surprised to find you still at work. Hoover says you boys down here have assumed the work habits of the natives: in by nine and gone by four." Corey laughed and dodged as Norton flung a wadded-up ball of paper at his head. The two men had joined the FBI at about the same time in 1933 and had crossed paths while they trained at different regional offices and later in Washington conferences of special-agents-in-charge.

Norton walked around his cluttered desk and stuck out his hand. "Welcome to Dixie. Had too much of the square heads up at headquarters? You here on business or pleasure?"

"You think I'd be in your office if I wasn't here on official business?"

"Well, you sure look like you've been working," Norton appraised his visitor. Corey was tall and athletically built, with a square jaw, cleft chin and deep blue eyes. Like all FBI agents, Corey had begun the day impeccably dressed, with a fedora on his head, starched white shirt, subdued tie and highly polished shoes. But a long day on the train and a walk through the humid Atlanta streets had left him looking a bit wilted. "By the way, it's May in Atlanta, a little late in the spring for wool."

"Thanks for the tip. My train just arrived from D.C. Mr. Hoover's ordered me to Warm Springs, wherever that is."

"Warm Springs? The Little White House? I heard you'd been cozying up to the big shots, Corey. I guess this is proof positive. You want a cup of coffee?" Norton asked turning toward a hot plate holding a pot of God-only-knows-how-old coffee.

"To tell you the truth, I'd like something a little more substantial. Sitting on a train all night and day doesn't give you a very restful start to an assignment. What time you closing this place down?"

"Hey, you're from headquarters. Say the word and we're out of here."

"'The word.' Let's go get something to eat and you can fill me in on the lay of the land down here."

"But Talmadge is a Democrat, right?" Corey asked Norton over a dinner of fried chicken and mashed potatoes at Aunt Sue's Home Cooked Meals on Forsyth Street.

"Sure. All of 'em down here are Democrats. There hasn't been a Republican elected since Reconstruction. But that doesn't mean he likes the President. Roosevelt's too cozy with labor and too friendly with the Negroes, at least by Talmadge's standard. Of course, that's a pretty low bar. It's a different world down here than what you were used to out in San Francisco, Corey. I should say 'two different worlds.'"

"How so?"

"Well, like I said, there's only one political party. You win the Democratic nomination and you're in. But the biggest difference is that there's a white world and a colored world and the two cross paths only within a very strict social code."

"Elaborate."

"Blacks can work for whites, in their homes and in their businesses, but only in menial positions. Whites never work for blacks. They don't eat together, they don't socialize together, and they don't go to church together. Different neighborhoods, different business districts."

"I've seen some of that in Washington," Corey said with a nod. "I think that may have something to do with why I'm down here."

"You're going to tackle race relations?" Norton sat back and whistled. "Good luck, friend. Say, before you head out tomorrow, how about putting in a good word for me. Maybe I can get your job when you get eaten up by Jim Crow." Norton laughed, but Corey didn't think it was funny. "So, what's your assignment, really?"

"I'm not sure. Something about a black woman accused of killing a white man, the man she worked for as a domestic. The President's secretary is supposed to fill me in on the details."

"Well, cheers," Norton said, lifting his tea glass. "Politics, crime, and race. What could possibly go wrong?"

TUESDAY, MAY 19, 1936

CHAPTER 24

Atlanta

Corey had enjoyed catching up with his old friend, had enjoyed the meal and a long restful night in a comfortable bed. He had checked out of the Imperial Hotel at 7 a.m. and taken a taxi the few blocks to Terminal Station, the large twin-towered train depot on Spring Street. He paid seventy-five cents for a coach ticket on the eight o'clock train to Columbus, bought a newspaper and then ordered coffee and a biscuit at the station's café.

An uneventful news day. Former President Herbert Hoover had denied he had any interest in running as a candidate for president that fall. *That's a relief for the GOP*, Corey thought. The governor of New Jersey had punched a reporter he disliked at a formal dinner at Rockefeller Center's Rainbow Room. *I can think of a reporter I'd like to punch, but I'd never hit a lady.* The Yankees had not played the night before, which was a shame, because Corey was following with interest the new big hitter on the team, a kid named DiMaggio.

A muffled voice sounded over the public address system, spewing forth a long string of destinations being served by a soon-to-depart train on Track Six. Corey couldn't keep up with the list of unfamiliar place names, spoken in a slow-as-molasses drawl. Listening to the speaker was like trying to understand the radio playing next door by pressing your ear against the wall. He glanced at his watch, checked his ticket, and then headed toward Track Four, suitcase in hand. Norton had been right about his attire; his poplin suit was much better suited to Atlanta's spring weather.

Once the train had entered the station and the passengers had disembarked, Corey climbed aboard. He turned to the car on his right, holding his suitcase in front of him until he found a pair of vacant seats. He hefted his bag into the overhead rack, removed his hat and set it on top of the suitcase, and settled into the seat by the window. *At least I'll have a good view. And maybe I'll get lucky and nobody will sit beside me.*

After a few minutes, Corey felt a slight lurch. He looked out the window to see travelers, porters, and baggage slowly gliding past the window. He checked his watch again: eight o'clock. *You have to hand it to the Southern Railway, right on time.*

The train was winding its way out of downtown Atlanta, still moving slowly. Corey watched buildings and neighborhoods slipping by and then felt someone settle into the seat beside him. He turned toward his seatmate and received a rude shock.

"Good morning, dear," Joan Roswell said with a wide smile.

"Let me guess," Joan said looking into Corey Wainwright's blue eyes. "You're hot on the trail of a Russian spy—no, a bank robber, or better yet a whole gang of bank robbers—who have been terrorizing the hard-working depositors of the deep South." She tittered.

Corey smiled, wishing he'd picked a different train. "Nothing so dramatic. How is it that of all the trains in the entire country, you happen to be on mine?"

"Just good fortune, I guess." Joan leaned over, pressing her shoulder against the burly agent's. "A reward for good behavior, maybe?" She batted her eyes.

"Where are you headed?" Corey asked. *Please, please don't say 'Warm Springs'!*

111

"Warm Springs, to the polio asylum down there. A friend of mine is going to show me around the place. I might do a series of stories on the treatments and the patients."

"Well, that makes sense. Sort of a follow-up to all the stories you wrote about that Birthday Ball affair in Washington over the winter."

"Stories I couldn't have uncovered without your help, dear. Now tell me," she said, placing her hand on Corey's forearm, "where are you going and why?"

Corey attempted a laugh, but the situation was more annoying than humorous. "Like you, I am headed to Warm Springs. That's the 'where.' As to the 'why,' I really don't know. Mr. Hoover said to get on the first train south and report to the President at the Little White House, so here I sit."

"Ooh, a mystery. I like mysteries. I already smell a good story. How is dear Mr. Hoover, by the way? He's been such a darling since I got back to Los Angeles. Why, hardly a week passes that I don't get a sweet note from him. Oh, but pretend I didn't say that, dear, or at least that you didn't hear it. I really must learn to be more discreet." Joan tittered again. Corey gritted his teeth.

"He's fine, up to his neck in fighting crime, of course, but he just wrapped up a big case with the arrest of Alvin Karpis in New Orleans. Karpis was the brains behind the Barker Gang."

"I read about that in the newspaper. And Mr. Hoover took part in the arrest himself. My, my. That must be very inspiring for you, working for a man who's not afraid to take the same risks his agents take."

"Oh, sure. Inspiring." Corey knew that the Karpis arrest had been about as risky as a kid climbing on a merry-go-round, but Hoover had been embarrassed at a congressional hearing when he had admitted he had never made an arrest in his life. His participation in the Karpis bust had been a set-up to help him save face.

"At any rate, if Mr. Hoover has dispatched you to Warm Springs, then I'm sure he has a very good reason," Joan paused, patted Corey on the arm and added, "and a very good story behind it."

Corey glanced at his watch. Two and a half more hours and twenty more stops. *I should have walked.*

CHAPTER 25

Warm Springs

Train No. 45 from Atlanta arrived on schedule at 10:52 am. The morning was warm and humid with clouds already forming that promised afternoon showers. Ever the gentleman, Corey offered his hand to Joan as she stepped down from the carriage's metal steps and onto the track level apron of the small depot.

"So this is Warm Springs," Joan said, looking around. "Not much to it, is there?"

"Doesn't seem to be," Corey answered. Behind him, the station master blew a shrill whistle and waved a red flag toward the engineer. The locomotive belched black smoke and gave a short blast of its steam whistle and the train began to move slowly southwestward in the direction of its next stop four miles away at Nebula.

"Do you have someone meeting you, dear?" Joan asked as the racket from the train receded down the tracks.

"I expect a car from the Little White House to pick me up. They know I'm on this train. What about you? Do you have a ride from here?"

"Oh, don't worry about me, dear. I'll call for a car. I have a little business to take care of first. Wonderful to see you again, Corey Wainwright." Joan batted her eyes. "Hopefully our paths will cross again before you head back to Washington."

"I'll look forward to it," Corey replied with a polite smile. *With loathing.*

Joan walked inside and scanned the dim interior for the Western Union counter. Even in small, rural stations, one could usually find a telegraph office. The railroads still used telegraphy extensively to keep track of the arrivals and departures of their traffic.

She headed toward a counter at the back of the narrow waiting room. There was a young man wearing faded overalls and a sun-bleached white shirt leaning there, his elbows on the counter. On the business side of the counter was a short, chubby older man wearing thick round glasses that made his eyes look too large for his face. He had on a dark green apron from the pockets of which stuck several short, yellow pencils. Joan formed a line behind the young man.

"Well, congratulations, Thomas! A boy, huh? That's just wonderful. And May Ruth is doing all right?"

"She's tired. Took near all night to punch that little fellow out. They's both asleep when I left to come over here. Sara's with 'em 'til I get back."

The short man smiled, reached down below his counter and set a white form in front of his customer. "I guess you're wanting to share the joyful news, then."

"Yes sir. Want to send a telegram to May Ruth's folks over in Carolina."

"What's her daddy's name?"

"Horace Fleming. Lives in Gaffney, South Carolina."

"All right. Got it. What you want the message to say?"

"'Thomas Morgan Vickery, Junior was born this morning at 5:58 a.m. He weighed eight pounds. May Ruth and Tommy are both fine.' Got that?"

The short man moved his pencil back along the form, touching each word in turn. He looked up with a frown on his face. "That's going to be a pretty expensive message, Thomas. You know we charge by the word, right?"

"You do? I never sent a telegram. How much is all that worth?"

"Well, it's sixty cents per ten words." The clerk turned the form around, so his customer could read it. "See these numbers here?" He pointed to the time of birth. "Each number counts as one word. All told, you've got over twenty words here so that runs your total up to a dollar eighty cents."

"Oh, I can't spend that kinda money!" Thomas protested.

"Well, of course not. Here," the helpful clerk said, "let's save a little money." He quickly moved his pencil back across the message form, scratching out several words. Once he was finished, he read the revised message to himself and, satisfied, read it aloud to Thomas. "How's this: 'Junior born 6 a.m. Eight pounds. Mom and baby fine.'? That puts us at ten words and your bill at sixty cents."

"Wonderful!" Thomas said, digging into the pockets of his overalls. He produced two quarters and a dime and placed them on the counter. "Money well spent."

"Congratulations again, Thomas," the clerk said, reaching across the counter to shake the young man's hand. "I'll look forward to meeting your new little man. And I'll send this out full priority. They should have it by this afternoon."

The proud young father departed and Joan took his place at the counter. "How can I help you, miss?" the clerk asked, peering at the pretty and stylishly dressed young woman standing before him.

"I'd like to send a telegram to Los Angeles, please."

The clerk chuckled. "Didn't think you were from around here. You visitin' the polio Foundation or the Little White House?"

"The Foundation." Joan smiled and cocked her head, again sucking in one cheek to form a dimple. *It worked on Sam.* "How did you guess?"

"Don't mind me saying so, miss, but you're not dressed like one of our local ladies, so I figured you to be from somewheres else. And there ain't but two reasons why someone would come to Warm Springs, unless they got family here."

The door to the tracks opened letting in a bright shaft of late morning light. Joan turned toward a plump woman striding toward the counter.

"Good morning, Bob!"

"Good morning, Miss Tully," the clerk answered.

"Oh!" Grace stopped short, her hand going to her mouth. "My goodness! Joan Roswell, what in the world are you doing in Warm Springs?"

"She's come to visit the Foundation," Bob replied helpfully.

Joan looked from Bob to Grace, smiled and held out her hand. "That's right, dear. It's so nice to see you again. I'm working on some human-interest stories, sort of a follow-up to our little adventure over the winter."

"Who are you working with, Dr. Irwin? He's the medical director."

"Well, I certainly hope to meet him. I'll also be meeting with some of the staff, taking a look at the treatments being administered to the patients, and learning how the Birthday Ball funds are being used. That sort of thing."

"That sounds wonderful, Joan. Good publicity will help tell the story of the fine work that's being done by the Foundation. Can't wait to read your stories." Grace let go of Joan's hand and turned back to Bob. "Miss LeHand and I were in Milledgeville yesterday, and I thought I'd stop by and see if there were any messages for us."

"A few, I think," Bob said, turning from the counter toward a wall of mail boxes mounted on the wall. From one on the bottom row he pulled several yellow envelopes. "Here you go, Miss Tully. That's all for now."

"Thanks, Bob. Nice to see you again, Joan." Grace whirled and headed back toward the door. Joan watched through the window as Grace climbed into the back seat of a large black Lincoln phaeton. At least two other people were in the back seat. One of them was Corey Wainwright. The other was Missy LeHand.

"You're a reporter, then, Miss Roswell?" Bob asked, jerking Joan's attention back inside.

"Yes," Joan smiled. "That's right. And I want to send a message to my editor in Los Angeles." Bob pulled another white form from beneath the counter.

She dictated a concise message and paid her sixty cents. "I'll get this right out for you, miss."

"Thank you, Bob." She snapped her purse closed, then paused. "Say, Bob, what's in Milledgeville, anyway?"

Bob chuckled again. "Oh, there's lots in Milledgeville. Used to be the state capital. Bet you didn't know that."

"Is that a fact?"

"Yep, wasn't 'til after the Civil War that the capital moved to Atlanta. There's a big insane asylum in Milledgeville and the state prison farm. And two colleges too. So, there's still a good bit goes on there."

"Hmm. So colorful. I'm finding Georgia to be quite an interesting place. Well, thank you, dear. I'll be staying out at the Foundation for a couple of days if any messages come for me." Joan patted Bob's forearm and gave him another faux-dimpled smile. "You've been so helpful, Bob. I always say if you want to find out something about a town, check in first with the Western Union man. Thank you."

"Oh, happy to help. Hope to see you again."

118

"I hope so too, dear. I hope so too."

Warm Springs, Georgia? Billy Bryce thought as he reread the telegram. *She's going to drive me to an early grave, spending money in Warm Springs, Georgia.* PURSUING STORY SERIES STOP FUNDS SUFFICIENT FOR NOW. *Well, that's a good thing, because there won't be any more. Hope you're going to have enough to get back.* Billy reconsidered that last thought.

CHAPTER 26

Warm Springs

"How was your trip?" Ida asked as Joan settled into a maroon Hudson convertible coupe.

"Fine, dear. I happened to see an old friend on the train and so I had a nice visit on the ride down."

"What a coincidence," Ida said, pulling the car out onto state highway 85 and heading south.

Joan stared out the window at the forest of pine trees. "Oh, I don't think so dear. I think our White House friends are up to something."

"Like what?"

"I don't know, but I plan to find out." Joan turned back to her driver. "And how are you getting along?"

"Very well," Ida replied with a smile. "I have rented a cute little cottage on the Foundation grounds, and there's room for you to stay with me, so don't worry about paying for a hotel room."

"How thoughtful, dear," Joan said. *That means I'll get to eat on the way home.*

"It's so relaxing here," Ida continued. "No producers, no studio bosses, no agents or publicity people. It's quiet, too. By nine o'clock, everybody goes to bed and all you can hear are the crickets and the tree frogs. I can understand why the President likes to come here."

"Sounds dreadful," Joan said with a pretty grimace, fishing a cigarette from her purse. "What's in store for me today?"

"I'm going to give you a quick tour of the place, then we'll have some lunch in the dining hall, and after

120

that, if the weather holds up, I thought you might like to take a dip in the warm springs."

"Tell me about the pools," Joan said. "What makes these pools different from the ones all over Beverly Hills, dear?"

"Temperature for one thing. As the name suggests, the water is warm, just under ninety degrees. That's sort of like a warm bath at home. Plus, the water has a lot of magnesium in it, so it's buoyant. People who ordinarily couldn't stand without assistance can often do so in the pools."

"And the patients like that, do they?"

"Yes, they seem to."

"Does the water actually heal anybody or is this all just a placebo that fools the patients into thinking they're better?"

"That's a good question for you to ask Dr. Irwin, the medical director. President Roosevelt first visited the place back in 1924 because he heard about a young boy who regained the use of his legs after swimming in the pool here."

"Mmmm. So maybe there is some therapeutic value?"

"I don't know. I feel better after taking a swim. But they have an excellent staff of physical therapists who work with us, and they do pioneering orthopedic surgery too. They also have a custom brace shop, so each patient has braces made that fit their own needs to a T."

"How bad is your case?"

"I couldn't even walk at first. That was two years ago. Fortunately, I've recovered most of my muscular control but I'm still not back to normal with my left leg and hand."

Joan looked over at Ida. "Well, you're doing a fine job of driving, dear." She smiled. Ida smiled back.

A few minutes later, Ida pulled the Hudson into a parking space in front of a large building with white columns. "Here we are. This is Georgia Hall, the main building. The dining hall is inside. Let me buy you lunch."

Joan followed Ida along the sidewalk and inside to a wide windowed portico that ran horizontally across the front of the building. Several pedestal fans stood inside the open windows, pulling air from the front windows and out the back. "It's a lot cooler in here."

"Yes. They're expecting thunderstorms late this afternoon, so we should hit the pool right after lunch, if you're up for that. Did you bring a bathing suit?"

"No. I didn't expect to be swimming. I came east for another purpose, as you know."

"Of course! And how was your interview with Miss Mitchell?" Ida asked eagerly as they entered the dining room and looked for an empty table.

"Quite fascinating. She's certainly a colorful character in her own right."

"And did you keep your end of our bargain? Did you suggest me for the part?"

Joan smiled. "Of course I did, dear! Miss Mitchell was quite enthusiastic about it. She said you were on her short list that she expects to submit to the studio, although she still isn't sure which one is going to win the bidding war."

"Oooo!" Ida squealed, grabbing Joan's arm. "That would be so marvelous! Every young actress in Hollywood wants that part." The news added a spring to the young woman's step. They found two seats at an unoccupied table for four and pulled out the cane-backed chairs.

"Goodness, this is very up-scale," Joan said, looking approvingly at the starched white linen tablecloth, pretty china and silver-plated dinnerware. "I had no idea."

"Yes, it's part of what Mr. Roosevelt calls 'the Warm Springs Spirit,'" Ida explained.

"The Warm Springs Spirit?"

"Everything about Warm Springs encourages hope, optimism and, well, fun," Ida said. "So many of these patients have been shut away in dark bedrooms, feeling useless, a burden on their families. When they come to Warm Springs, they learn to use what muscles they have, and with the treatments and better braces, many of them find they can work again, even if they can't all walk again. Why, Mr. Roosevelt hired a patient from here, Toi Bachelder, to serve on the secretarial staff at the White House!"

Joan looked around the room. Staff and patients were chattering together and laughing. The only thing that differentiated them were the wheelchairs, crutches, and braces of the patients.

A tall black man in a spotless white jacket, a snappy black bowtie at his neck, approached with menus and urged them to take their time deciding on their meal. "I'll keep an eye out for you," he said. "Meanwhile, how 'bout some tall glasses of iced tea?" Joan was glad she had gotten her ears warmed up on Margaret Mitchell's Southern accent. It sounded like the man was offering that Italian sparkling wine, "asti."

"That would be lovely, James," Ida said. "Thank you." When the waiter headed for the beverage station, she warned Joan, "They like it really sweet here. It's a good thing the ice melts fast!"

A heavy, middle-aged woman with gray streaks in her brown hair and deep wrinkles around her sunken eyes walked by. Ida looked up and smiled. "Hello, aren't you Velma? We met yesterday afternoon at the pool. Would you like to join us?"

Velma looked down with a blank stare, then she recognized Ida and offered a thin smile. "Hello, Miz Lupino. Who's your friend?"

"This is one of my Hollywood friends. Velma Biggs, meet Joan Roswell."

"Nice to meet you, Miz Roswell. Are you an actress too?"

"No, I'm a reporter. I cover the motion picture industry and that means I sometimes get to spend time with delightful people like Ida." Joan smiled, hoping she was coming across as sincere.

Velma's face clouded. "A reporter? What paper do you work for?"

"It's OK, Velma," Ida said, reaching over and giving the woman's hand a quick squeeze. "Joan's here to do some stories on Warm Springs. She helped raise a bunch of money for the Foundation last winter. She worked with Ginger Rogers and the people from the White House on several of the big Birthday Balls honoring President Roosevelt." Ida glanced toward Joan, who was staring at the older woman. "Isn't that right, Joan?" she asked with an edge in her voice.

"Oh, yes, yes, dear. So true. I just had to visit Warm Springs personally to see the good use to which that money is being put."

Velma's face relaxed. She offered another thin smile. "Well, I'm sure you'll be pleased. Not everybody leaves cured, Miz Roswell, but everybody leaves better. Thanks for the invitation, Miz Lupino, but I was just looking for Miz Cumbee. I'm supposed to help her with the registration for the square dance that's being held tonight."

"Sounds like a lot of fun," Ida said with a smile. "See you later, Velma. And please, call me Ida. Every time I hear someone say Miz Lupino I look for my mother!"

"What a Dora Doom," Joan said just loud enough for Ida to hear. "What's her problem?"

Ida spoke under her breath. "Last summer her Negro cook murdered her husband, with whom, incidentally, she was having an affair. That's bad enough, of course, even though the cook was tried, convicted, and sentenced to death. But what really broke her heart was the disappearance of her son. Apparently, it all happened at the same time. The boy and his girlfriend up and vanished. She's been volunteering here to help take her mind off things. Poor woman's left with an empty house, a missing son, and a dead husband who was cheating on her."

Joan stared after Velma as she left the dining room. "Yes, and now she has to eat her own cooking."

CHAPTER 27

Ida and Joan took an early afternoon dip in the outdoor pool, Joan wearing a borrowed, shapeless, navy-colored one-piece swimsuit and a dingy white rubber bathing cap that she wouldn't have been caught dead in at any California pool. But after her cross-country train trip, two nights in a roach hotel, plus the ride down from Atlanta, she had to admit the warm waters felt good.

"This is actually quite relaxing," Joan said, resting her arms on the corner of the pool. "How often do the cripples swim—once a day, twice a day? At their whim or with the guidance of a doctor?"

"Patients, Joan, or polios. Don't ever call these people—my people—cripples. The whole idea of this place is to heal them. That includes both physically and mentally. Why, President Roosevelt said it was here in the springs that he regained the confidence to get back into politics. Save up your questions. I'll introduce you to one of the physical therapists here. You can ask her."

"Thank you, dear. I'm glad this little side trip worked out...for both of us." Joan paddled over to the pool's ladder and climbed out. She pulled off the bathing cap, loosening her lovely mane of blond hair, and toweled off, then headed for a bench against the dressing room wall and spent a few enjoyable moments sitting in the sunshine. *All I need to make this a perfect afternoon is a White Russian—the drink or the man.*

"Joan, I'd like you to meet Janice Howe." Joan shaded her eyes against the afternoon sun and looked up to find Ida standing in front of her with an attractive and lissome young woman in a form-fitting bathing suit.

"Janice is one of the physical therapists who work with the patients here. She's been working with me, in fact."

"A pleasure to meet you, dear," Joan said, sitting up straight and offering her hand. "Do you have time to join us? Ida said you would be able to answer some of my questions about the treatments you provide your patients."

"I'll do my best," Janice said as she and Ida joined Joan on the bench. "Ida tells me you're from Los Angeles and that you used to be in pictures."

"That's right, dear. More recently I've worked with the people at the White House to raise money for the Foundation. Ida invited me to come down and see how that money is being put to use." Joan reached down by her side for her purse, which looked out of place beside the pool, but which held her pen and note pad. "Do you mind if I take some notes?"

"Not if it will help our patients," Janice replied.

"How admirable. Tell me, dear, what are your qualifications to work with polio patients?"

"Well, I earned a bachelor's degree with a certificate in physical therapy from Peabody College in Nashville."

"I see. And what are some of the treatments you provide your patients?"

"Well, Ida tells me that you've already sampled our warm pools. The pools are sort of the basis for our work because without them, I doubt the Foundation would exist. That's what first attracted President Roosevelt to Warm Springs. Of course, he wasn't president then. He bought the place and turned it into a private foundation about ten years ago. As you can see," Janice continued, looking over her shoulder at the therapists and patients in the pool, "we like to combine massage and moderate exercise with the soothing waters from the springs."

"What good does moderate exercise actually do? You can't cure polio, can you?"

Janice shook her head. "No, not yet anyway, but maybe someday. Better yet, we'd love to be able to prevent polio. Meanwhile, the exercise helps preserve what muscle function they have, and some muscles can be developed further to compensate for the weak ones. Look at that young man over there," she said, nodding to a dark-haired boy in the pool. "Notice how big his shoulders are? That helps him get in and out of cars, manage his crutches and the like. In a way, his arms become his legs. No matter what ails you, most doctors will prescribe some physical activity."

"Like the square dance I heard about?"

Janice laughed. "Yes, like the square dance."

"Forgive me, dear, but when I look around at all the crutches and canes and wheelchairs here, why, it seems almost cruel to hold a dance."

"Oh, no ma'am, not at all!" Janice said, smiling at Joan. "Just the opposite. It's wonderful. The patients forget their limitations when they get out on that dance floor. And that's just the point, you see. They begin to realize that there are still more things they *can* do than they *can't* do. The impact of a simple square dance, well, that may be the most powerful therapy we offer. Come to the dance tonight and see for yourself."

"I believe I will, dear."

CHAPTER 28

Coweta County

Susan Woods mopped her brow with a yellow bandana and set the sweat-stained straw hat back on her head. She had been working for hours and she was dripping wet. And here it was only May! As if the sun wasn't hot enough, it was so humid you had to part the air to move along the rows of corn. Susan hated corn. She hated the weeds that sprouted overnight like Jack's famous beanstalk. She hated the hoe that had rubbed angry red blisters on the palms of both hands. Most of all, she hated her banishment to Aunt Cleo's farm just east of Moreland in rural Coweta County.

That's what happens when a girl tries to have a little fun: everything just turns to poop. For Susan, it had all started the night that Robert had picked her up to go to the picture show. Of course, the picture show was the last thing on their minds. He was so cute. She'd had dreams about him from the first time he smiled at her in the school lunchroom the previous spring, when he finally realized she'd grown up, and that she was just the girl for him, the star quarterback of the football team. When he had suggested it was time to "consummate their love"—he was always using mature phrases like that, but then again, Robert was an Eagle Scout—she was only too willing. There wasn't another boy like him in the high school. He was smart, a terrific athlete, so handsome he was almost pretty, and—best of all—his daddy was rich, so he always had money to take her to the movies. When Robert had proposed that they "consummate their love"—whatever that meant—Susan had enthusiastically kissed him with her mouth open.

So now here I stand, holding on to this hoe and hoping there ain't no more snakes along this row. She'd killed one the day before and Aunt Cleo had got all over her.

"Girl! Don't you know better'n to kill a black snake?"

"No'm. I reckon I don't. I don't want to get kilt by a snake."

"Black snake won't kill you. Won't even bother you if you don't bother it." Aunt Cleo had picked up the headless snake by its tail and held it a foot from Susan who had leaned back on her heels in revulsion. "Don't kill any more snakes like this, Susan. Just kill the copperheads and rattlesnakes."

"How am I supposed to know the difference?"

Aunt Cleo had flung the snake into the trees at the end of the row, wiped her hand on her apron and wandered away muttering something about a "dumb city girl."

She'd been a city girl all right, if her stint living in Phenix City, Alabama counted. It had started when she and Robert had crept their way up the steps to the garage apartment where Robert's no-count uncle had used to live. Then everything had gone haywire. Something had happened in that darkened room above the garage. Before Susan even knew what was going on, Robert had spun her around and hustled her down the stairs. They'd run inside Robert's house for a minute, then they'd hightailed it back through the woods and to the car.

They didn't stop until they crossed the state line and reached Phenix City. Robert had left Susan and the car behind a rundown motor court and gone to the little office out front to pay for a room. He'd unlocked the room, turned off all the lights and then come and gotten her and led her inside. He'd locked the door and they'd finally been alone, several hours later and one state west of where they had planned. The first round of love-making had been quick and it had hurt a little—*so that's what consummation means!* —but the second was more satisfying and when Robert had fallen asleep, Susan had curled up beside him, comforted by the warmth of his body and the slow, even sound of his breathing.

"Get to work! You supposed to be hoeing, not standing there daydreamin' about God only knows what!" Aunt Cleo hollered from two rows over.

Witch! She ain't had a man since before Prohibition because they had to be drunk to want to be with her. Susan turned back toward the weeds and brought the hoe down with a *thunk*.

Phenix City had been fun for a while. Eye-opening to say the least. Susan had never seen some of the ways people made a living in that town. Every two weeks, the soldiers from the big Army base across the river flooded into town for the gambling, the drink, and the women, all of which could be purchased at market prices. She had read about some of those professions in the Holy Bible. It wasn't nothing like Greenville.

For a few days, Susan had avoided detection at the motel, but then one day, the little manager man had caught her and Robert leaving the room together. He'd looked at them, smiled and said, "Good evening," like he didn't even care that they were living in a sinful condition. Nope, nothing at all like Greenville.

At first, they were eating out at least once a day, but pretty soon they were buying loaf bread and boloney at the supermarket and making sandwiches in the room. Gotta save money, Robert had said, until he could find a job. He had encouraged Susan to look for a job too, but the only jobs she seemed qualified for were hard. Of course, in hindsight they weren't any harder than standing here in the sweltering heat of the cornfield. Susan had a mind to throw down her hoe, walk back to the house, pack her things, and walk to Newnan. *Bet I could find a job there. I could work in a café or a restaurant, make some good tip money.*

It would probably work. They wouldn't know about her in a town as big as Newnan, wouldn't know that she'd been "ruint," as her father had screamed when she had finally ridden the Greyhound bus home. To be honest, she'd gotten homesick. Sure, the sex was fun at first, but after a while, that's all there was. When Robert wasn't working the job he'd gotten at the mill, he'd had his head stuck in that old Bible of his or was listening to that preacher-lady on the radio. By then they had moved out of the motor court into a shabby one-room apartment, and he expected her to keep it clean and prepare him a hot meal every night.

The radio, bought at a pawn shop for two dollars, had been a mixed blessing. On the one hand, Susan would have gone plumb crazy had it not been for the radio. She listened to it all day. Her favorite program was *Backstage Wife*. Susan loved everything to do with show business and she empathized with the ups and downs the show's heroine suffered through five days a week. How exciting it would be to be married to a matinee idol!

But in the evening, Robert would tune in after supper and listen to one of the radio preachers. He had followed Deacon Knox from Chicago until his ministry had collapsed in a political scandal over the winter. Lately, he'd become enthralled with Aimee Semple McPherson out in California. Susan had been interested for a while, especially after Robert explained that Sister Aimee preached at the Angelus Temple in Los Angeles, and that movie stars like Charlie Chaplin often attended her services.

After listening to Sister Aimee, Robert would start a long monologue on sin, and Susan would sometimes ask,

"Well, what about us? Aren't we living in sin?" She always whispered when she said "in sin."

Robert would sigh and explain, "We're all sinners. That's what the Apostle Paul writes about in Romans. We all give in to the flesh, we all submit to sin. That's why Jesus Christ died on the cross. He died for our souls so that we could be cleansed and leave our corrupt bodies behind and be taken up to the glory of the Lord God almighty."

"Why don't we go out to California?" Susan said one night. "You could go work for that preacher-lady and I could go be an actress at MGM or Warner Brothers or Paramount."

"I have a lot more to learn before I can preach the gospel like Sister Aimee or Deacon Knox," Robert said. "And we've got to save up a lot more money if we're going to drive all the way to California."

As if they could save any money. He wasn't making enough money to do more than pay for their room and food. She was wearing the same clothes day in and day out, and it had gotten so cold during the winter that she had to stay in the room almost all the time because she didn't have a coat. That radio, and the occasional movie magazines she bought with nickels filched from Robert's pockets, were just about her only connections to the outside world—except for church on Sunday. And honestly, rather than go to church in the same old worn dress week-after-week and listen to the same old white-headed preacher pound on the same old pulpit and warn against the wages of sin, Susan would much rather read her magazines and keep up with her favorite film stars like Ginger Rogers and Ida Lupino.

"Robert, let's go home," she had whined one cold March night as they huddled under the thin blanket on their lumpy mattress. He had rolled over to face her.

"I don't want to go back, baby," Robert had said. "In the past few months, I've realized I have a much higher calling than anything I could do in Greenville. That's why I spend so much time reading my Bible and listening to Sister Aimee on the radio. When I get enough money saved, we'll go out to Los Angeles together."

"How much do you have saved?" Susan had asked.

"Not a lot. Look, I'm not saying it's going to happen tomorrow, or next week or next month. But look at all the obstacles the apostles overcame to serve their Lord."

Susan had started to cry. "I don't care about those ol' apostles," she said. "I just miss my mama, and my friends. I love you, Robert, but I'm tired of living this way."

He agreed then to buy her a bus ticket and let her go home, on the condition that she didn't breathe a word to anyone about where he was. He'd promised to send for her once he got settled in Los Angeles.

They made love that night for the last time. The next day, Robert drove her across the river to Columbus and put her on the two o'clock bus for Greenville. She'd given him a long goodbye kiss that had been the envy of every other man in the grimy terminal. She hadn't been able to say "goodbye" because of the lump in her throat, but she'd waved and blown him kisses as the bus pulled out onto the road. He had not responded with as much enthusiasm, but he was a boy, after all.

It had been late afternoon by the time she walked from the filling station where the bus stopped out to her house. She had knocked on the front door, which, mercifully, had been opened by her mother.

She'd thought that her mother was going to squeeze all the air from her lungs. Mother was crying and smiling and squealing. But her daddy had only frowned, called her a harlot, and sent her upstairs to her bedroom without anything to eat. Susan had dutifully complied, sitting tired and hungry on the edge of her bed as her father thundered at her mother so loudly that she was sure every neighbor on the street could hear the ruckus.

The next morning, her mother had awakened her before dawn, thrown some old clothes in a suitcase and hustled her into the back of the car before any of the neighbors were out and about. Mother had crawled into the front seat. "Stay down on the floor," she had ordered.

A few minutes later, the driver's door had opened, and her father had climbed in. He started the car and pulled out onto the street.

"Where we going?" Susan had asked.

"Keep quiet," her father had barked.

"I'm hungry and I want to be at home."

"You need to do some growing up—and not the kind you been doing," Father had said. "You need to learn responsibility and discipline and the value of work." Neither he nor Mother had spoken again until forty-five minutes later when they turned off onto a dirt road and pulled into the yard at Aunt Cleo's. Susan's stocky aunt, her father's twin sister, was standing on the front porch holding a broom in one hand and looking like the matron of a women's prison.

Susan blinked. Sweat rolled down her forehead and burned her eyes. She reached the end of the corn row, straightened her back and walked around to the next row. There was always a next row. She wiped her sleeve across her forehead. *You know, Phenix City wasn't that bad after all.*

CHAPTER 29

Warm Springs

The dance was held in the dining room after supper, with the tables and chairs pushed against the walls to make a dance floor. A portable public address system consisting of a floor microphone and speakers had been set up, and a tall, rangy man wearing faded overalls, a red-checked long-sleeved shirt, and a string tie served as the caller. His weather-beaten face was enlivened by twinkling blue eyes. Next to him, on a small table, sat a Victrola and a stack of records.

Joan and Ida stood against a wall, watching as wheelchair-bound patients rolled out on to the dance floor. Next to the double entrance doors, Velma Biggs sat behind a folding wooden table greeting the patients and their families and checking off their names as they came in.

Ida leaned over toward Joan and pointed to the man at the microphone. "That's Buddy," she said. "He's terrific. He comes out every Tuesday evening to call the dances. He'll have them dancing like pros in no time."

Joan nodded, but she was skeptical that these cripples could do anything resembling a dance.

Buddy stepped up to the mic and tapped on it with his index finger, causing a loud thumping sound to carry through the speakers. "I have to start every dance that way," he said with a broad smile revealing uneven, tobacco-stained teeth. *He has an even broader accent than Margaret Mitchell*, Joan thought, hearing his words as *Ah hafta staht ever daynce thataway.*

"Are y'all ready for a good time?" A muffled response proved unsatisfactory to Buddy. "Oh my. I see I have some work to do with this bunch. I said, 'Are y'all ready for a good time?'" Shouts, laughter, and smiles were returned, enough to convince Buddy to proceed.

"How many of y'all have square danced before?" One hand went up among the fourteen patients on the floor. "Good, good! That means we won't have to unlearn bad habits!" Buddy smiled to let everyone know he was joshin'. "Now here's how we gone git started. Pair off. That means in twos, just like on Noah's ark—preferably a she-person and a he-person in each couple." Some of the family members along the wall chuckled. "That's it. Now, we've got fourteen folks out there, but as this is square dancing, we need squares of eight people each—that's four couples per square. Got it?"

Buddy turned to the spectators. "Who'll volunteer to fill out these squares? I just need one more couple over here," he pointed to his right. "How about you two?" he asked a middle-aged couple. "Ain't nothin' to it. I'll tell you exactly what to do." Glad not to have been called out to the floor, several of the other spectators along the wall began to clap and encourage the new couple. As they made their way to the dance floor, Buddy asked the woman, "Is he good at following directions?"

She laughed and nodded. "Yessir. We've been married for fifteen years!"

Buddy threw back his head and laughed. "All right. Now I want you to form a square with the other couples in your group. The couple with their backs to me, raise your hands. That's it. You're couple number one, got it? This ain't so hard, is it?" Everyone laughed. "Now couple number one, to your right is couple number two. All the number twos, raise your hands." Hands went up. "Very good. I can tell this is a smarter group than we had last week! Now straight across from couple number one—

137

everybody put your hands down for a minute. Straight across from couple number one and to the right of couple number two is couple number three. That means that the remaining couple is…?"

"Couple number four!" everybody replied.

"You got it! Now couples number one and number three are what we call the 'heads.' That makes couples two and four the 'not heads!'" Everybody laughed. "No, not really. Couples two and four are what we call the 'corners.' All right then, couples hold hands. Boys on the left, girls on the right. Now, there's just one more thing you need to know before we start dancing. Where you're standing—or sitting—right now, facing the other couples of your square, that's what we call 'home.' So when I say 'go home,' that's right where you want to end up. Any questions?"

Buddy's eyes scanned the two squares in front of him. He leaned over and picked a record off the stack and slipped it out of its paper sleeve. "Here's a nice piece to get us started off. It's called 'Arkansas Traveler'. You might know it. Been around for a long time. This recording is by the Loblolly Boys." The bluegrass music began, and Buddy called out, "Now bow to your partner. Say high to the corners." His voice assumed a sing-song rhythm. "Now join hands and circle to the left."

Joan watched as the wheelchair dancers followed Buddy's directions, grinning and laughing and having fun. Her eyes strayed to the table by the door where Velma Biggs sat, her head keeping time with the fiddle music playing through the speakers.

"Excuse me, dear," Joan whispered to Ida. Joan walked over to the table and sat down beside Velma, who continued to follow the dancing.

"I was so sorry to hear about your recent troubles, dear," Joan said leaning toward the older woman's ear.

Velma stopped keeping the beat and half turned toward Joan.

"I come here to forget about it. I guess some people can't let me have any peace." She didn't appear to be angry, just sad.

"In my experience, dear, peace often comes by facing an issue. By talking about it."

"Now circle to the right," Buddy called out. "No, darling, your other right! That's it! Good."

Velma had forgotten about the dancing now, her attention focused on the reporter, who said, "Sometimes it helps for you to tell your side of the story, to set the record straight."

"You really think so?"

"I know so. You have a lot of friends around here, from what I've been told."

"It doesn't... it hasn't felt that way. Not since it all happened. People, my friends, well, it's like they've forgotten about me or maybe they're ashamed of me."

Joan laid her hand on Velma's. "Now, dear, they haven't forgotten. They just need to know the story from your perspective, so they can understand the kind of help you need."

Velma looked away, back to the dancers wheeling around the floor, tears pooling in her eyes. "I'd like to tell my story. Just to get it off my chest. I reckon Mr. Biggs got what he deserved and Nell, well she's gonna get her just desserts too, but what I really want, what I really need, is to get my boy back. I don't know where he's gone or if he's all right. Maybe if I share my story it'll find its way to him and he'll come home."

Joan patted Velma's hand. "It might help. And Velma," Joan said, staring into the woman's troubled gray eyes, "I'm a very good listener."

An hour later, the square dance ended, and the patients and their families made their ways down the wide corridors of Georgia Hall and out into the cooling evening air. Joan stood near one of the pedestal-mounted fans that kept air flowing beneath the building's high ceiling, watching and listening. She was struck by the good humor, the laughter, and happy banter of the people leaving the dance. It was, as Ida had said, as though these poor cripples had forgotten their wretched condition, if only temporarily.

"It'd make a good scene in a picture, wouldn't it?" Ida said from behind her. "How hope is resilient, and life goes on even in the face of tragedy and disappointment."

"I have to admit, I'm quite impressed," Joan replied.

As the boisterous group exited the building and made its way toward the dormitory and cottages, Velma Biggs came and stood beside Joan.

"I'd like to tell you my story," she said shyly.

CHAPTER 30

Warm Springs

Eleanor Roosevelt had spent Tuesday at the Pine Mountain Valley Resettlement Project, a "sister" to the Arthurdale Resettlement Project she so loved in West Virginia. In both places, impoverished rural and city families were provided with small, neat frame houses and put to work in agricultural and food processing pursuits, with an emphasis on modern techniques and conservation of natural resources. There was a dairy, poultry farm, and hog farm, as well as a canning plant. For most of the people, it was the nicest place they had ever lived. Children from the elementary school had turned out to sing for the First Lady, all waving tiny American flags, and she had visited with mothers in several of the homes. So it wasn't until that evening that she was able to hear the story Missy and Grace had to share about their meeting with Nell.

Mrs. Roosevelt, the President, the two secretaries and Corey Wainwright gathered in the living area of the Little White House after dinner. Daisy had prepared Brunswick stew, one of the President's favorite Southern dishes, and they were still sipping their after-dinner coffee. Although Mrs. Roosevelt was knitting, as usual, her ears were keenly tuned to the story Missy told.

"I don't think I've ever seen a more miserable person," Missy began, lighting a Lucky Strike and tossing the match into the stone fireplace. It was a little warm for a fire, but the President was a bit cold-natured and liked the friendly feeling a fire gave to a room. "Have you, Grace?"

"No," Grace said. "She's just pitiful. It's like the baby is sapping everything out of her body. Plus, the conditions in that cell were just...unspeakable."

Missy nodded and surreptitiously scratched a flea bite on her ankle. She and Grace had shared their misadventure with the President, who had let loose a bellowing laugh about their pestilent hideaway in the laundry and cheerfully reimbursed Missy for their night's stay at the Dempsey Hotel.

"F.D. is right," Missy admitted, "that we can't do anything about the conditions of the Georgia prison farm; it's a state issue, not a federal one. But if what Nell told us is true, and we can prove it, we may be able to find the real culprit in the murder and save her from the electric chair."

Corey, his steely blue eyes fastened on Missy's pale and lovely face, asked, "So the story she told doesn't exactly jibe with the one presented in court?" Corey had practiced law in his native Kansas for several years before joining the FBI and had spent the afternoon at the courthouse in Greenville reading the trial transcript.

"Well, in some respects," Missy said. "She did have a criminal record, that's why she was at the prison farm in the first place. She had used a knife on her estranged husband, who came to her house one night drunk, beat her, and threatened the children. Here in Georgia, there is a policy of paroling women prisoners into domestic work. The families that hire them must make reports to the warden each month. But according to Nell, the warden has instituted his own practice of allowing prospective employers to personally choose their parolee. For a price."

Eleanor Roosevelt looked up. "You mean Captain Carlson takes bribes?" she asked sharply.

"Yes, Mrs. R," Missy said. "I confirmed that with his secretary, Betty Barnette. I don't know that Betty would say that openly—she's terribly afraid of losing her job—but she thinks his practice is just despicable, and I take it he hasn't done anything much to earn her loyalty." She smiled. "We can't all work for Franklin Roosevelt, can we, Grace?"

Grace smiled. Eleanor sniffed and jabbed a needle into the moss-green sweater she was knitting. "So, I suppose he lined up all his candidates for Mr. Biggs and he looked them up and down like they were prize cattle and picked Nell."

"Pretty much," Missy said. "She had an idea what she might be in for, but she was desperate to get out of the prison and see her children, and Mr. Biggs was offering a fair wage. However, it didn't take long after she went to work there that he started making unwanted advances on her."

FDR took a long drag on his Camel. "Not much she could do about it, was there?" he said. "She couldn't refuse him, or he'd send her right back to prison. And the warden would probably have to pay back his bribe money to Biggs, so he'd treat her especially harshly."

"That's right," said Missy. "So, she complied. And that was what she was doing the night of his murder."

CHAPTER 31

Warm Springs

"It was a Tuesday, just like this one, and on Tuesdays me and some of the other ladies from our church have our circle meeting." Velma Biggs and Joan Roswell were seated in a wooden swing on the lawn outside Georgia Hall. With the help of bright moonlight, Joan could just see to make notes in her pad. "We always hear a report on home missions and another on foreign missions and then we pray for missionaries. You know it takes quite a strong calling to pick up and go around the world to China or someplace like that and spread the gospel. I do so admire those men and their wives that do that."

"What happened that night?" Joan asked, steering the conversation back to the murder.

"Well, Robert asked Mr. Biggs if he could use the car and Mr. Biggs said it was my circle night." Joan tapped her pen on the pad. "But I said, 'well why don't you just drop me off at Miss Nancy's'—it was Nancy's week to host. We rotate among the group so that everyone has a turn twice a year, except we don't meet at all for the month of July on account of lots of our members are farm ladies and they just have too much work to do."

"What happened next?" Joan asked, trying to move the conversation along before the Second Coming.

"Robert dropped me off at Nancy's—Nancy Mason, lives over on Oakmont near the church. And then he went over to pick up his date, Susan Woods. Now Susan was a year behind Robert in school, but just the prettiest girl and real grown up. Her daddy owns the feed store. He's got everything in that store, my word. Mr. Biggs says that if Leo Woods don't have it, you don't need it."

"After Robert dropped you off, did you see him again?"

Velma's eyes clouded over like the sky before a storm. "No." She pulled a handkerchief from her pocket and dabbed at the corners of her eyes. She cleared her throat and continued. "Another lady had driven to the meeting. I knew Robert and Susan would still be at the picture show, so I asked her to carry me home." Velma paused again, staring down. She cleared her throat. "She dropped me off and I walked up the sidewalk and opened the front door. Everything was quiet. I don't know how or why, but I knew right then that something was wrong. Mr. Biggs wasn't in his chair. He usually sits in his reclining chair and either listens to the radio or reads the afternoon paper until he falls asleep. He wasn't there, so I went back to the bedroom, but he wasn't there either. So, I put down my things and took off my jewelry and changed into some more comfortable clothes. I mean I don't wear my Sunday clothes to circle meetings, but I still want to look nice, you know?"

"Of course you do, dear. Did you go look for Mr. Biggs?"

"Yes. I went back to the kitchen, but of course Nell wasn't there. She was always bad to run off as soon as she could after I would leave the house. I'd come home sometimes and find dishes that weren't washed or food that hadn't been put away. She was so lazy that I'm not sure why we kept her around. It's not like we couldn't find another cook, you understand."

"What did you do next?"

"Well, I looked through the kitchen, but like I said, nobody was there. I poured myself a glass of buttermilk from the icebox and walked outside. I thought maybe Mr. Biggs had gone out there to check on the dogs or something. He always kept three of four good bird dogs to hunt with and sometimes he'd piddle with them in the evening."

"Was he with the dogs?"

"I never made it to the kennel, but no, he wasn't with the dogs."

"Why didn't you make it to the kennel?"

"I came out the back door and started toward the kennel which is below the garage, just on the edge of the woods there. That's when I saw the footprints on the steps."

"The footprints?"

"Somebody—of course we found out later just who that somebody was—had tracked blood down the steps from the little apartment above the garage. That's when my heart just flipped over and started hammering so fast."

"How did you feel at that point?" Joan asked, scribbling in her notepad.

"I was scared. Scared to death. I started to go up those stairs, but I lost my nerve, I guess. That's when I went back in the house and called Sheriff Young. He told me there was probably nothing to worry about but that I'd done the right thing, to not touch anything and to stay inside the house until he got there."

"How fast did he get there?"

"Ten minutes or so. A real long ten minutes." Velma shuddered and licked her lips.

"Would you like something to drink, dear?" Joan asked. "I could go get you a cup of water."

Velma looked up at Joan with a shy smile. "I'd like something stronger."

CHAPTER 32

Warm Springs

"But did Nell Gaines kill this fellow Biggs?" FDR asked Missy, lighting another Camel.

"No," Missy said firmly. "She says it was his son, Robert, who did it, and I believe her."

"His son!" exclaimed Mrs. Roosevelt, putting down her knitting. "Why on earth?"

"I don't think it was premeditated or even intentional," Missy said. "Nell and Mr. Biggs had started using an apartment over the garage behind the house for their, er, assignations."

"No one used the apartment on a regular basis?" Corey asked.

"Nell said that at one time, someone had lived there who kind of kept up the yard, and the gardening tools were hanging on the wall," Missy said. "Nell said on Tuesday nights, when Mrs. Biggs had her church social meeting, Mr. Biggs would take her up there. Well, they were lying in the bed, Mr. Biggs asleep, when Nell heard someone coming up the stairs. The door opened, and it was Robert with his girlfriend."

"Susan Woods," Eleanor said. "Daisy said she had disappeared along with Robert the night of the murder."

"That's right," Missy nodded. "Apparently it was a like-father-like-son situation. Robert had gotten the bright idea of bringing Susan up there for some privacy. When he realized what was going on and who his father was in the bed with, he grabbed a machete off the wall and attacked Nell with it. With all the fumbling around for cover and such, Mr. Biggs got in the way. Nell doesn't think he meant to kill his father, but he cut him wide open. When he realized what he had done, he and the girl ran for it."

Grace took up the tale. "So, here's poor Nell, covered in blood. She tried to pull the machete out, thinking she might could save Mr. Biggs's life, but all she did was get her fingerprints all over the handle. She threw on her dress and grabbed her shoes, and she tracked bloody footprints all the way down the stairs."

"Well, that's one point for scientific policing any way," Corey commented, using one of J. Edgar Hoover's favorite terms. "Poor soul."

CHAPTER 33

Greenville

Velma drove Joan to her house, explaining that she'd had to use part of Mr. Biggs's life insurance proceeds to buy the used Chevrolet. Their Buick, she said, had disappeared along with Robert and the girl. Inside the house, Velma had gone to the pantry and pulled out a bottle of red wine.

"We don't really drink socially, but Dr. Raper up at the Foundation said a little red wine every day was good for the heart, so me and Mr. Biggs would have a glass most nights before bedtime." Velma struggled with the cork screw for what seemed to Joan an hour, finally pulling it free from the bottle. "Oh dear. I may have gotten a little bit of the cork in there. Mr. Biggs usually handled this." She poured the wine into two small jelly glasses, handing one to Joan and joining her at the kitchen table.

"Don't worry, dear," Joan said with a smile, "I'll drink around it." *In your dreams. Ugh! Smells like kerosene.* "Tell me what happened after the sheriff got here."

Velma's eyes took on a faraway look. "He came inside to check on me and asked where I'd been, what time I'd got home, when I'd seen Mr. Biggs last, and things of that nature. I walked him back outside and showed him the footprints on the steps. It was pretty dark by then, but he had this big flashlight. He looked at the steps real careful. Then he drew his pistol. That's when I liked to have fainted.

"Well, Sheriff Young starts up those creaky steps and I start up right behind him. 'Now hold on, Velma,' he says to me. 'We don't know what's up there. You best to wait right here. And don't touch nothing either.' So that's what I did. He went on up the stairs and went inside the apartment up there. After a few minutes Sheriff Young comes back down the steps, walking real careful so he doesn't step on the footprints that's already there.

"'Me and you need to go inside and talk,' he says, and I knew right away that the talk wasn't going to be pleasant. When we got back in here, his face was grim and pale. He sat right there where you're sitting, and he told me Mr. Biggs was dead." Velma paused, the tide of her memory washing over her. She raised her glass to her lips with a shaky hand and took a sip.

She cleared her throat. "He wouldn't let me go up there. I was in shock. My mind was spinning around, and I was fearful of how I was going to tell Robert. Sheriff Young got on the phone and called for his detective to come over and then he called the coroner.

"'Where's your boy?' he asked. I told him he was at the picture show. He called the theater and asked the manager to find Robert and send him home. The manager called back about ten minutes later and said Robert wasn't there." Velma reached behind her and picked up a small picture frame from the kitchen counter. "This is Robert," she said, staring at the photograph. "This is when he got his Eagle Scout badge."

"And the girl?" Joan asked.

"Let me see." Velma heaved herself out of the chair and walked into the den, picking up a heavy book from a side table. "Here's last year's school annual." She sat back down at the table and flipped through the pages, stopping at a row of portraits. She stabbed at one of them with her chubby finger. "That's Susan."

Joan leaned forward. "She's a pretty girl." The bright face staring back was smiling broadly, her eyes clear, her hair arranged in a style popular with Hollywood starlets. "And neither of them was still at the theater?"

Velma shook her head. "No. Well, before too long, we had sheriff's cars and a county van parked in the drive and they'd set up some flood lights to help them look for clues. I kept waiting for Robert to get home. I wanted him here so bad, but at the same time I couldn't bear to have to tell him about his daddy."

Joan looked up from her pad as Velma wiped her eyes with her lace-edged handkerchief. "When did the sheriff tell you what had happened?"

"It was pretty late. He came into the kitchen again and pulled the curtains closed. Said they were removing the body."

"Did you see your husband?"

"No, they wouldn't let me watch. I didn't see Mr. Biggs until a couple of days later at the funeral home."

"That must have been very painful for you, dear."

"It was. But, of course, what came next was even worse."

CHAPTER 34

Warm Springs

"Nell didn't do herself any favors with the way she reacted to Robert's handiwork," Missy said. "She was terrified for herself, and for her children. She ran home—she lives in a little house about a mile from the Biggs's home—packed a few things, told her mother what had happened, and hid in the woods. But the sheriff got out the bloodhounds, and they quickly tracked her down. She was arrested and charged with the murder and put in the county jail."

"Did she have a competent defense attorney?" Mrs. Roosevelt asked.

Corey broke in vehemently. "Calling that guy a defense attorney is an insult to defense attorneys everywhere," he said. "I spent the afternoon reading the trial transcript. Every line trumpets his incompetence. He called no defense witnesses and wouldn't even put Nell on the stand. The trial, if you can call it that, lasted four hours, and the jury, which was all-white and all-male, returned its verdict in ten minutes. Her attorney filed an appeal, as a matter of form, and then dropped the case."

"Ah, the 'justice system' in Georgia," the President said.

They all sat silently for a few minutes. Daisy Bonner came in to refill their coffee cups. Finally, Eleanor Roosevelt spoke up. "What about the baby, Missy?" she asked. "I don't suppose it was evident that she was expecting at the time of the trial, but soon after…? Would Nell tell you who the father of the child is?"

Missy nodded, turning her wide blue eyes to Eleanor's. "She said it has to be Mr. Biggs's child. She hasn't had relations with anyone else, and she didn't have any idea until she was sent to the prison farm that she was pregnant. Once it became obvious, Governor Talmadge got involved and decided that if she was denied clemency by the parole board, he would delay the execution until after the baby comes. And that's exactly what has happened."

"The poor baby," Eleanor said. Missy looked at her with quick sympathy, knowing she still mourned the first Franklin Delano Roosevelt, Jr., who had died as an infant. Mrs. Roosevelt always said he was the biggest and most beautiful of her six children.

The President broke the silence. "Well, we've got to decide where we go from here," he said. "Corey, you could ask to see the presiding judge, but I doubt you would find much sympathy there."

Corey grimaced. "No sir, Mr. President. His nickname is 'Two Pistols' Johnson because of the pair of loaded weapons he displays prominently when he's on the bench. But I think a call on the defense attorney is warranted, to see if he made any effort to track down Robert Biggs, and then I'll visit Robert's mother and Susan's parents and see if I can get them to tell me where she is."

"Excellent, Corey!" the President said. "I'll put one of my Secret Service agents, Jim Rawlings, and a car at your disposal. It never hurts to have back up." He took another deep drag on his Camel. "For my part, I am going to reach out to my good friend Cason Calloway over in Hamilton," he said, referring to the textile mill owner who had led efforts to raise the money to build Georgia Hall at the Foundation. "Surely he knows of a competent attorney who would be willing to represent Mrs. Gaines, once we've got some new evidence to present. Oh, and that reminds me, when you see that sorry excuse for an attorney, make sure he is no longer representing Mrs. Gaines. We want him out of the way, so we can bring in competent counsel."

"Yessir," Corey said. "It will be a pleasure."

"There's something else going on that concerns me, F.D.," Missy said quietly.

"I'm not sure I can take any more bad news!" the President joked. "What is it?"

Missy glanced at Corey, who nodded his head. "Well, when Corey was on the train coming from Atlanta, he met an old friend of ours, that reporter from the Los Angeles *Standard*, Joan Roswell. She claimed she was coming here to do a series of stories on the Foundation's work, which strikes me as a little odd, since her beat is supposed to be Hollywood. Would you mind if I take some time tomorrow to find out what she's up to?"

"Certainly," the President said. "She's a sneaky one. You never know where she'll turn up." He then turned to Grace. "My dear, I'm afraid I will have to ask you to step into Missy's shoes for a few hours. I hope you don't mind."

Grace put on a great show of reluctance, and then grinned widely, showing her dimples. "Always a pleasure, Boss." She said.

Eleanor excused herself. "I need to speak to Daisy for a moment," she said.

CHAPTER 35

Greenville

"So, the sheriff thinks Nell lured your husband into a sordid affair and then tried to extort money from him," Joan said.

"Blackmail. That's what he called it. Mr. Biggs wouldn't give it to her, so she nearly cut him in two. They took her fingerprints off the murder weapon, an old machete. Bloody fingerprints. They also matched up the bloody footprints on the stairs with her foot. Wasn't the first time she'd cut a man either. She was serving time for cutting the father of her children. All that came out at her trial."

"Why would the authorities—even in a place like this—allow a woman with a past like that to work in a decent home like yours?" Joan asked.

"Oh, they claim it helps rehabilitate them, but I'm not much of a believer. Not now. So they convicted her of the murder, but of course they never could tie her into Robert's disappearance. Nor the girl's either."

"What do you think happened?" Joan asked. "You must have a theory."

"Sure," Velma said, dropping her eyes to the handkerchief in her hand. "Nell didn't get what she wanted from my husband. Well, she did, and she didn't. But he refused to pay her. Mr. Biggs was a man, with all a man's faults, but he was decent too. When he realized what he'd done, he knew he had to come clean before the Lord. He wouldn't pay so she killed him. Then she went down and stole some money from our bedroom. Mr. Biggs always kept a hundred dollars for emergencies. That was gone."

"What about your son?"

"My guess, my belief, is that Nell got hold of some of her kin. You know they're all related: cousins and aunts and uncles. And they all watch out for each other. Lie for each other like as not. Well, she called her kin and they came running. I think they got Robert and Susan. I think they kidnapped them, stole the car and they're going to use them to bargain Nell out of prison. That's what I think."

Joan thought for a moment, tapping the end of her pen against her lips. "Seems like they would have made their move by now. Kidnappers usually like to move pretty quickly. Keeps the police on their heels."

Velma arched her eyebrows and pursed her lips. "You think?"

"Well, I have done some consulting for the FBI."

"Maybe you can help find Robert." Velma laid a hand on Joan's shoulder. "I'd appreciate any help you could give. He's all I have left now."

"I don't want to promise what I can't deliver," Joan said, looking into Velma's pleading gray eyes, "but I'll make inquiries with my FBI contacts."

WEDNESDAY, MAY 20, 1936

CHAPTER 36

Greenville

Melvin Jugg had never really wanted to be an attorney, but after he flunked out of the University of Georgia and wasn't much help around his father's medical practice—he just couldn't get the hang of filing patient charts alphabetically—his Uncle Clarence agreed to let him read law at his office over in LaGrange. The boy did like to read, which didn't require much exertion, and after five years of reading, running errands, and tagging along with his uncle to court, he was finally admitted to the bar. *It sure helped that Uncle Clarence was good buddies with the president of the bar association!* Melvin had proudly hung his shingle out in Greenville and waited for the clients to come. And waited. And waited.

That had been three years ago, and Melvin was still living at home with his parents and eking out a bare living by taking any case the presiding judge threw his way. The worst had been defending that colored woman, Nell Gaines, who had cut her employer to ribbons with a machete last fall. No one had expected him to get her off, which was a good thing, because he hadn't even tried. He could barely stand to look at her during their brief conferences at the jail, and he hadn't believed anything she told him. *Tried to pin it on Robert Biggs, a fine Christian boy like that! For shame!*

Now that he didn't have to read law any more, Melvin spent most of his time in the scruffy one-room office he rented behind the courthouse reading *True Detective Mysteries* magazine and the novels of Erle

Stanley Gardner, featuring the brilliant defense lawyer Perry Mason. He dreamed of working out of a fancy suite of offices in Los Angeles with the delectable Della Street as his private secretary, ready to come into work at any hour of the day or night, and an able gumshoe like Paul Drake to do his bidding.

Jugg was deeply engrossed in *The Case of the Sleepwalker's Niece* when he heard a sharp rap at his office door. Reluctantly laying down the book, he opened his door to find two tall, broad-shouldered, conservatively-dressed men in fedora hats standing there. One of the men reached into his jacket pocket and flipped open a leather case holding a badge. "Mr. Jugg? I'm Corey Wainwright with the FBI. This is Agent Rawlings with President Roosevelt's Secret Service detail. We'd like to ask you some questions."

The hair on Melvin Jugg's neck stood on end and his eyes bulged out of his head. "S-s-sure!" he stuttered. "Please have a seat!"

CHAPTER 37

Greenville

When Joan had gotten back to Ida's rented cottage at the Warm Springs Foundation Tuesday night, she had filled in the young starlet on the story Velma Biggs had told, rousing her curiosity. "Something about Velma's story doesn't add up," Joan had said. "Think about all the gang kidnappings in this country before Hoover and his boys got things under control. Kidnappers like the Barker Gang were usually pretty well organized and financed. They had guns, for one thing, and fast cars. To think that a poor, black family living in the Georgia sticks could pull off a spur-of-the moment kidnapping is beyond something even a Hollywood screenwriter could imagine."

"You're right," Ida said slowly. "I think Velma is just grabbing at straws."

On Wednesday morning, following her early-morning therapy session, Ida drove Joan to Greenville to track down Susan Woods's family. Once again, she had been able to borrow Dr. Raper's maroon Hudson, which she had used to pick up Joan at the train station.

There's more to this story than Velma is sharing; maybe even more than she knows, Joan thought as she and Ida traveled north on Highway 41. With the Hudson's top down, the warm, moist air blew over their faces and rushed through their hair.

On the way out of town, Joan had visited her friend Bob at the Western Union counter. Sam Andrew's generosity on the train trip had saved Joan most of her travel advance. Bunking with Ida in the cottage on the grounds of the Warm Springs Foundation had likewise proven economical, but Joan knew that without some journalistic output, Billy Bryce would soon lose his patience and she intended to stay on her editor's good side. With that motivation, Joan sent a short telegram to her boss in Los Angeles.

ANTICIPATE FEATURE POLIO FOUNDATION STOP PLEASE AUTHORIZE COLLECT TELEGRAM STOP

She also got Bob to track down the Woods's address in Greenville, which was thirteen miles north of Warm Springs. She had timed their arrival for mid-morning when she calculated Mr. Woods would not be at home. Joan believed a woman-to-woman approach was usually the most productive. Ida slowed down as they reached the city limits and then found the courthouse square. They drove three-quarters of the way around it, just as Bob had said, and a few minutes later, they reached the Woods's house on the LaGrange Highway.

It was a sturdy-looking, white frame dwelling with four square columns across the front supporting a two-story porch. The Woods appeared to be weathering the Depression in a manner more comfortable than most rural Georgians. The house itself was in good repair, the front yard was recently mowed, and the bushes around the porch were trimmed and neat. To the side of the house next to the driveway, a small rose garden added vibrant color to the surroundings.

"Pull up in front," Joan directed.

"I could just park in the driveway."

"In my line of work," Joan said, staring at the large house and the fields beyond it, "one sometimes has to make a quick getaway. By the mailbox is fine."

Ida pulled the car off the road, set the parking brake, and killed the engine. She reached for the door handle, but

Joan laid her hand on her arm. "Sometimes one-on-one is best, dear. I hope you don't mind waiting here."

"Oh, sure," Ida said. "I'll just wait over there in the shade." She pointed to a swing hanging from the heavy branch of a big oak tree dominating the front yard.

"Thank you, dear," Joan said, opening her own door and sliding out of the car. She smoothed her tight, cream-colored skirt, picked up her alligator purse and headed up the pea gravel walk. *I don't understand how these people stand the constant heat and humidity.*

The coolness of the shaded front porch was a welcome relief. The front door was open and Joan could see through the screen door all the way to the back of the house. She took a deep breath and knocked on the black wooden frame of the screen door. Within a few moments, she heard the sound of footsteps approaching. A stocky black woman appeared on the other side of the screen, holding a striped dish towel in her hand.

"Yes'm?"

"I'm here to see Mrs. Woods. Is she in?"

"Yes'm. I'll fetch her." The woman turned and disappeared into the darker interior. Soon a middle-aged woman in a print house dress and apron took the maid's place at the door and said, "I'm Mrs. Woods."

"How do you do? I'm Joan Roswell, a reporter for the Los Angeles *Standard*. I'd like to ask you a few questions about the Biggs murder and the disappearance of your daughter."

"A reporter?" Mrs. Woods's hand went up to her hair, held in place by a net, and unconsciously patted it into place. "Why, surely all of that's old news by now. Why would a Los Angeles paper have any interest in my daughter?"

"I've spoken with Velma Biggs," Joan continued, ignoring the question. "She believes Susan was kidnapped along with her son."

Mrs. Woods crossed her arms, still on the other side of the screen. "Velma is free to believe whatever she wants," she said belligerently.

"Do you believe they were kidnapped?"

"We certainly never received a ransom note. I don't expect we will."

"Why is that, dear?"

"That murder was what—eight months ago? If those children had been kidnapped, don't you think we'd have heard from the kidnappers by now?"

"Perhaps, unless the same thing happened to your daughter that happened to the Lindbergh baby."

Mrs. Woods gasped. "What a horrible thing to say! I don't know who you really are, miss, but I trust you can find your own way off our property."

"Of course I wasn't speculating about Susan, Mrs. Woods, only trying to understand what —"

"Get out of here before I call the law!"

"Mrs. Woods, please, I just want to help—" Mrs. Woods wheeled about and disappeared down the hallway.

That really didn't go as well as I had hoped. Joan stood for another moment trying to figure out a way forward. From inside the house, she heard Mrs. Woods speaking. "Mary, it's Sharon Woods. Would you connect me with the sheriff's office? No, everything's all right. I just have a nosy reporter bothering me." There was a moment or two of silence, then Joan heard, "Is that right? Well, it serves her right for taking up with a drunk. You'd a thought she'd learned her lesson by now."

Joan turned and stepped off the porch. She motioned to Ida, who got out of the swing and headed toward the car.

"How did it go?" Ida asked when they reached the car.

"Not too well. Mrs. Woods didn't seem too concerned that her only child has been missing for eight months." Joan opened the car door as Ida made her way around to the driver's side. "There's something about this whole thing that just doesn't fit together." Joan looked back at the house and shook her head.

Ida started the car. "You coming?"

Joan looked at Ida and held up one finger. Then she strode over to the mailbox, which had its red flag up, and looked inside. A single letter awaited the mail carrier. Joan pulled it out and read the address.

Miss Sally Wilson
c/o Miss Cleo Woods
R. F. D. 6
Moreland, Georgia

Joan smiled broadly, replaced the letter, returned to the car and slid onto the front seat. "How far is it to Moreland?"

CHAPTER 38

Greenville

"I read the transcript from the trial," Corey said. He and Agent Rawlings were seated in two wobbly straight-backed chairs facing Melvin Jugg, who was perched at the edge of a squeaky rolling chair behind his desk. "I couldn't quite figure out your defense strategy. You gave an opening statement, and asked a few questions of the sheriff, but you didn't put up any witnesses or even put the defendant on the stand."

"Well, Mr. Wainwright," Jugg said, feeling the sweat break out on his face and wishing his mother had remembered to give him a fresh handkerchief that morning, "It was pretty cut and dried. Miz Gaines's fingerprints were all over the weapon, her bloody footprints had been found on the stairs. There wasn't anyone else on the premises who might have done such a thing."

Corey gave Jugg a steely-eyed look and hardened his square jaw. "From my own investigations," he said, "I've learned that there very likely was a witness. Wasn't Mr. Biggs's son Robert on the scene? With his girlfriend Susan Woods?"

"Well, that was just a rumor," Jugg said. "I couldn't confirm it in any way, so it didn't seem material."

"Didn't Mrs. Gaines tell you Robert was there?" Corey persisted.

"That's privileged information between me and my client," Jugg said primly.

Corey was silent for a moment and continued to stare at Jugg with his sternest expression. Jugg broke into a fresh sweat. "I happen to know she shared that information with you," Corey said. "Further, I happen to know that Mrs. Gaines was wounded with the machete when Robert attacked her, and that she claimed he was the one who killed Mr. Biggs. Why didn't this come out in court?"

"Now, listen here," Jugg said, wondering briefly and desperately how Perry Mason would have answered these questions, "this is all water under the bridge now. The case was turned down on appeal—"

"Thanks to you," Corey interjected. "You provided no grounds for the appeal."

"—and Miz Gaines has gotten her sentence, to be carried out in a few weeks. I have already notified Judge Johnson that I've resigned from the case."

"Did you make any effort at all to find Robert Biggs?" Corey asked. "Or his girlfriend Susan Woods?

"Of course not!" Jugg sputtered. "I never looked for him. You have to understand, Mr. Wainwright...Uh, you're not from around here, are you?"

"No," Corey said. "I'm from Kansas. I practiced law there for five years before joining the Bureau in 1933."

"Well, if you were from around here, you'd understand why I did what I did with that trial. I'm just trying to make an honest living here," Jugg said. "You can't go after the son of the most prominent family in town on the word of a colored woman, whose only motivation for telling such a lie is to save her own skin—not and hope to keep practicing law or even live here after the trial. It's just not done."

As Corey continued to stare at him, Jugg summoned up his inner Perry Mason. "Look here," he demanded. "What business is this of the FBI? This is a local case, not a federal one."

Corey stood up and put on his hat. "Thank you, Mr. Jugg," he said. "I think I've got all the information I need.

Now, would you kindly direct me to the homes of Mrs. Velma Biggs and Mr. Leo Woods?"

CHAPTER 39

Greenville

Returning to the central square in Greenville, Joan directed Ida to stop at a Texaco station near the courthouse. She flirted with the mechanic, claiming to be lost and asking directions to Moreland. The man pulled a road map from a wire rack and opened it across his cluttered desk.

"Hold that end down there, sweetheart," the man said as an oscillating fan swept across the room. "We're right here, see," he said, pointing with his fat, grease-stained finger to the map, "and what you want is to take Highway 41 straight north. Moreland is only about eighteen miles, but you have to be very careful," he said, looking from the map to Joan's green eyes.

"Careful?"

"Yep, if you aren't careful you can drive right through it without knowing it." He laughed.

Joan joined in, leaning against his shoulder. "You're such a help, dear. A knight in shining armor."

"Well, happy to help two pretty ladies on a mission of mercy. I hope you find your aunt's house and that everything's all right. You know how telephones are. Sometimes they work and sometimes they don't. Don't let the fact that she's not answering concern you. She's probably out working in the yard or something."

"I'm sure you're right, dear. It's just that she's sixty and since Uncle Bird died, she's been out there all alone. I thought since I was visiting down at Warm Springs I'd drive up and surprise her."

"Well, good luck to you, then. Here, let me," he said, reaching across the desk and picking up the map. "I know how difficult it is for you ladies to fold a map." He made it look easy and then handed it to Joan. "Here. Compliments of me and Texaco."

"Oh, you are a dear," Joan said, smiling and forcing herself to ignore the mingled scents of sweat, oil, grease, and gasoline that surrounded the mechanic like after-shave. She blew him a kiss and returned to the car where Ida sat waiting.

"Tell me again why we're going to Moreland?" Ida said.

"There was an outbound letter in the Woods's mailbox," Joan said. "It was addressed to Sally Wilson, in care of a Miss Cleo Woods in Moreland."

"So?"

"So, I'm playing a hunch, Ida."

"I don't get it."

"Sally Wilson's initials are SW, same as Susan Woods's. And Sally, whoever she is, is obviously staying with this Cleo, who I figure is a relative of Leo and Sharon Woods. With me so far?"

"Yes," Ida said without conviction.

"If you had a daughter to hide, where would you hide her? You'd put her out in the sticks where nobody would know to look, and you'd put her with somebody you could trust, somebody like a family member."

Ida thought for a minute, her eyes staring at the gray ribbon of highway stretching out ahead. "Yeah, I guess so."

"Well, my hunch is that Cleo is an aunt or a cousin or something and Sally is really Susan. If we find Susan, I'll bet you a nickel she can lead us to Robert. We find Robert and maybe we can bring a little relief and comfort to poor Velma Biggs."

Joan and Ida stopped at the post office in Moreland and asked directions to Cleo Woods's house. "Want me to call ahead and let her know you're coming?" the jovial post master asked.

Joan smiled and said, "Oh, no, dear. It's a surprise. I haven't seen her in years. Nobody from the Texas branch of the family has visited since before Coolidge became president. I can't wait to see her!"

They climbed back into the Hudson and drove back south two miles to a one-lane country road and turned left. Before long, just as the post master had said, the road turned to gravel, then to a rutted dirt track.

"That must be it," Ida said, slowing down as they rounded a bend in the road. She nodded toward a simple, one-story farm house standing between two old oak trees. A young woman in a faded yellow frock was sweeping the dirt front yard with a straw broom as chickens strutted about pecking at the ground. Ida turned the car back in the direction from which they'd come and stopped in the shade of a tall pine tree. "I'll wait," she said.

Joan climbed out of the car, leaving the passenger door open to create a breeze for Ida. She walked toward the young woman, who looked up at her approach. *No question: this is Susan Woods. Her eyes are the same even if her face looks older and more tanned than the school portrait.* The young woman stopped sweeping.

"Hello, Susan," Joan said, continuing to walk toward her. "My name is Joan and I'd like to talk to you about Robert Biggs."

"How'd you know I was here?" Susan asked the pretty woman in front of her.

"I'm a reporter, dear. We have ways of finding people."

"A reporter? What are you doing here? Nothing ever happens around here that anybody'd be interested in—

unless they like watching corn grow—which ain't very fascinating, if you ask me."

"I wanted to talk to you, dear. I wanted to find out about the night you and Robert Biggs left town."

Susan hesitated. "I'm not supposed to talk about that."

"About what, dear?"

"About the killing. That's what you want to know, ain't it?"

"Yes. I want to know what happened and where Robert is. Is he safe? Are you?"

"Why you want to know about it? You're not from around here, I can tell."

"I'm a friend of Robert's mother. She is quite worried about him. I'm sure your parents are worried about you too, dear." Joan suspected that wasn't really the case.

"Well, if they are, they know right where to find me," Susan said, frowning and looking around. She stared toward the house behind her. "I'll tell you what I know if you'll get me outta here."

"Aren't you free to leave?"

"Heck no! If Aunt Cleo catches us talking, she's liable to shoot you and whip me with a strop. I am hot and tired and bored, but free—nope." Somewhere at the back of the house, a screen door slammed, and Susan looked over her shoulder. "She's coming. What do you say, reporter lady? I got a pretty good story to tell. You wanna hear it?"

"Get in the car," Joan said.

The girl dropped the broom and ran toward the car, scattering two chickens. Joan turned to follow and heard the screech of the screen door on the front of the house.

"Where do you think you're going?" a stocky, tanned woman asked, an open shotgun cradled in her arms. Her hair was pulled back in a tight bun giving her face a pinched, severe look. Her boots looked incongruous beneath the hem of her blue-checked dress.

"C'mon!" Susan shouted, sliding into the front seat. Ida cranked the engine to life.

Joan turned to face the woman but continued to walk slowly backwards toward the car. "Miss Woods? Joan Roswell from the Los Angeles *Standard*. You have a lovely place here." Cleo Woods stepped down one cinder block step into the yard, snapping the shotgun shut as she did so.

"Get out of that car, Susan!" Cleo hollered.

Joan spun and bolted for the car as fast as her tight skirt would allow. She reached the open door and dove inside as Ida popped the clutch and the car jerked forward. Ida wrestled the wheel around to the left and the car fishtailed as its rear wheels fought for traction in the dirt. In the rearview mirror, Ida watched as in slow motion as the gun came up to Cleo's shoulder.

"Duck!" she shouted, as her foot slammed down on the accelerator. The car hesitated and then shot forward, its engine screaming, blue smoke billowing from the tail pipe. Ida saw a flash from the muzzle of the gun and heard the pinging sound as tiny lead pellets rattled off the car. Before Cleo could fire again, the three women and their car were safely around the bend in the road.

"Oh, my word!" A red-faced Joan exclaimed, her hand to her throat, her heart pounding. "That's the first time I've ever been shot at off a movie set!"

"Oh, relax," Susan said, laughing. "It's only bird shot." Then her eyes grew wide as she recognized the driver. "Hey, aren't you…Ida Lupino?"

CHAPTER 40

Warm Springs

Right after breakfast Wednesday morning, Missy walked over to the Foundation office, passing by the little wood-frame white cottage she owned. She'd had it built in 1927 at FDR's urging. "It will be good rental income for you, Missy," he had assured her. "The staff here will handle it, all you have to do is put the checks in the bank."

It hadn't quite turned out that way. Renters were rather few and far between, though occasionally polio patients' families liked to come in for a week or two at a time and stay on the grounds. Missy usually got a handful of checks a year. She was cheered to see that the house appeared to be occupied this week. *I'll have to remember to ask who is renting it. I'd like to go by and say hello.*

At the Foundation office, she tracked down Fred Botts, the former patient who had joined the staff ten years before. Fred was a favorite of the President's, both for his good humor and his beautiful singing voice. They often invited him to come over for dinner and impromptu concerts. "Hi, Fred," Missy said. "I wonder if you can help me? I'm trying to find a woman named Joan Roswell who is visiting the Foundation this week."

"A patient?" Fred asked, frowning. "I don't remember that name from my registration records."

"No, actually she's a newspaper reporter, from Los Angeles," Missy said. "Grace Tully saw her at the train station yesterday. She said she was here doing some stories about the Foundation's work."

"What does she look like?" Fred said. "I might have seen her around."

"Blonde, about my height, sort of a flashy dresser," Missy said. She put on a Southern accent. "Buttah wudden meyelt in huh mow-yuth."

"Huh?" Fred asked.

"I said, 'butter wouldn't melt in her mouth,'" Missy said. "You know the type. Calls everyone 'dear,' just when she's stabbing them in the back with a poison pen."

"Oh! I know who you're talking about," Fred said. "She's staying with Ida Lupino."

"Ida Lupino, the Hollywood actress?" Missy said, surprised. "Why is she here?"

"She had polio a couple of years ago and she's been coming for therapy in between making movies," Fred said. "Very hush-hush, you understand. If word got out in Hollywood that she'd had polio, it could ruin her career. But, yes, she's here. In fact, she rented your cottage."

For once, Missy was completely at a loss for words. "Thanks, Fred," she finally said. "Have you seen them today?"

"Yes," Fred said, "early this morning they were at breakfast, and then I saw them drive off in Dr. Raper's car."

CHAPTER 41

Greenville

Corey and Agent Rawlings drove first to the Biggs's house, but the maid who answered the door said Mrs. Biggs was not well that day and could not be disturbed. Corey left his card and asked her to call him when she felt better. When the two men reached the Woods home shortly before noon, there was a ruckus going on inside that they could clearly hear as they stood on the porch outside the screen door.

"Why didn't you call me?" a man's voice demanded. "I'd have come right home!"

"Well, she would have been gone by then," a woman replied. "How was I to know she'd find out Susan is at your sister's? I sure didn't tell her anything. I got right on the phone to call the sheriff!"

"Well, why didn't he come?" the man asked.

"I, uh, well, I guess I got to talking with Mary—she always knows the gossip—and I just forgot," the woman said defensively. "Like I said, that woman was gone by then, I figured she'd just headed home to Los Angeles."

Corey turned to Jim Rawlings and raised his eyebrows. "Looks like our little chicken has flown the coop," he said as he rapped on the door.

Missy used Fred's phone to call the Hotel Warm Springs and the Little White House. She left an urgent message at the hotel for Corey, asking him to meet her at her cottage. In her call to the Little White House, she shared the latest developments with Grace.

"Can you believe that?" Missy said. "They've rented my house! Fortunately, I have my own key, so I'm going over there to wait for them. Beard the lion in its den, so to speak."

"Or lioness in this case," Grace said. "Watch out for her claws!"

Missy stopped by the cafeteria and asked the maître d' to have a plate of assorted sandwiches and a pitcher of iced tea delivered to her cottage, and then strolled across the grounds. *So many wonderful things have happened since F.D. and I first came here*, she thought. She passed the cottage where they had spent their first three weeks in 1924, then so ramshackle that they could see the daylight through cracks in the walls. *What a difference!* She waved to four patients who were sitting on the front porch, engaged in a lively game of Parcheesi.

Back in 1924, FDR had given an interview to a reporter from the Atlanta *Journal* saying he planned to "swim my way back to health." And so he had, though he had never quite been able to walk unassisted. He gave up his quest when he had re-entered politics in 1928, winning election as governor of New York. *I didn't want him to run then*, Missy thought. *But thank God for the country he didn't listen to me—that time.*

My FBI badge is more persuasive than my gun with some people, Corey thought as he and Agent Rawlings headed back toward Warm Springs. Leo Woods had quickly lost his bluster and his wife had been thoroughly cowed after Corey flipped open his badge case and introduced the President's Secret Service agent.

Over glasses of the obligatory sweet iced tea in the living room—*How do Southerners drink this stuff?*—the couple had shared all they knew about Susan's disappearance and return. They made it very clear that they blamed Robert Biggs for "ruining" their daughter.

"That boy was so stuck on himself," Sharon Biggs said bitterly. "He was just using our Susan. Hauled her over to Phenix City and practically held her as a prisoner for six months. It's a miracle she got away."

"Did he take her against her will?" Corey asked.

The couple traded glances.

"Well, I'm not sure about that," Leo Biggs admitted. "He put a bunch of fool notions in her head, like he was going to take her out to California, so she could be a movie star. But she finally got tired of waiting and came on home." He hesitated. "I was awful hard on the girl, sent her to live with my sister. But I felt like she needed to learn a lesson, and Cleo was teaching it to her. And, of course, we wanted to make sure she wasn't, well, you know…"

"Pregnant?" Corey asked.

The Woods nodded, embarrassed.

"And she isn't?"

Mrs. Woods said softly, "No, she's not. We were about ready to take her back, and then we got the call from Cleo a few minutes ago that she had run off with a couple of women."

"Tell me again exactly what Cleo said," Corey ordered, taking out a note pad.

Mr. Woods took up the story. "She said the women were driving a maroon convertible with Georgia tags. Both of them were blonde, good-looking. One of them stayed in the car, but the other one, the one who said she was from a newspaper, was wearing a tight skirt." He laughed a little. "Cleo said you shoulda seen her try to get in that car once she aimed her shotgun."

Despite himself, Corey smiled. *Serves her right.*

"It sounds like the same woman who had been here earlier in the morning, trying to get me to talk about Susan," Mrs. Woods said. "Like I said, I wouldn't talk to her, and when she heard me calling the sheriff, she got out of here pretty quick. I don't know how she figured out Susan was at Cleo's."

"Mr. Woods, Mrs. Woods," Corey said, "I believe Susan may be an important witness in this case. I don't know what she saw the night Mr. Biggs died, but she may be able to confirm that she and Robert were in the room when the murder occurred. President and Mrs. Roosevelt are concerned that a miscarriage of justice may have been committed, and that an innocent woman will soon be put to death. Once we locate Susan, can we count on you to see that she does the right thing?"

Mr. Woods didn't hesitate. "If it means giving that rotten Robert Biggs what's coming to him, you sure can."

Passing through Greenville, Corey and Jim Rawlings again stopped at Melvin Jugg's office. The lawyer was once more engrossed in *The Case of the Sleepwalker's Niece,* and he turned white to the lips when he answered the knock to again find the law enforcement agents standing on his doorstep.

"Ever heard of the Mann Act?" Corey asked abruptly.

"The Mann Act?" Jugg said, casting about in his memory of those long afternoons drowsing over his uncle's law books.

"It makes it illegal to transport a woman across a state line for immoral purposes," Corey said. "We have good reason to believe that Robert did just that with Susan Woods after he killed his father. The death may well have been unintentional, but we need to find Robert Biggs, and the Mann Act enables the FBI to get involved in this case." He grinned suddenly. "Just wanted you to know, I'll be on this case until it's resolved."

CHAPTER 42

Greenville

Eula Clark had seen a lot in her lifetime, much of it sad, and she looked much older than her forty-eight years. Her husband had died of tuberculosis, and childhood illnesses had taken two of her seven children. A son had died in the Great War, and her youngest daughter had gone to prison for cutting her husband in a domestic dispute.

Things had finally seemed to be getting better, praise the Lord, when Nell was paroled and went to work in the Biggs household. Eula had come to live with her and her two grandchildren, Enoch and Delilah, keeping an eye on them while Nell worked. She and the children picked cotton in the fall, and Nell's remaining brother and sisters helped when they could. With that, the leftovers Nell brought from the Biggs's table, and a little assistance from New Deal programs, they got by.

Then had come that terrible night when Nell turned up on the doorstep, covered in blood and so hysterical Eula had trouble making out what she was saying. Nell had run into the woods to hide, but then the bloodhounds had come, and the trial was held, such that it was, and Eula doubted Enoch and Delilah would ever see their mother again.

Eula Clark thought she had seen everything—until that afternoon, when the First Lady of the United States came driving down the dirt road in a shiny blue car and parked outside their tarpaper shack. After that, it was like Santa Claus had arrived in May.

She was an extremely tall woman, Mrs. Roosevelt, towering over Eula, but her manner was so friendly and natural that Eula could not help but warm to her. And it helped that Eula had once lived in the same neighborhood as Daisy Bonner, who accompanied Mrs. Roosevelt. Daisy was carrying a tremendous basket of food, some of it fresh and fragrant and begging to be eaten, some of it canned to last them for some weeks. Enoch and Delilah could barely keep their eyes off the basket; they had been living on nothing much except cornbread and molasses for two weeks.

"How do you do?" the tall woman had said in her strange, high-pitched voice. "I believe you are the mother of Nell Gaines? I am Eleanor Roosevelt."

Collecting herself, Eula took the offered hand, introduced herself, and asked, "Would you like to come inside outta the sun?"

"Why, that would be lovely," Mrs. Roosevelt said. "It is uncommonly warm for May."

The strange little party went up the rickety steps and into the house, Eula quickly offering Mrs. Roosevelt the only chair, which she declined to accept.

"I have come to offer whatever assistance I can to you, and to your grandchildren," Mrs. Roosevelt said. "I also have come to tell you that the President and I, with the help of some of our friends, are trying very hard to reverse the conviction the courts gave Nell so that she can return to your home."

Eula was stunned. "Nell could be free?" she asked.

"We hope so," Mrs. Roosevelt said. "We're trying very hard to intervene before the..." She paused meaningfully.

"Enoch, Delilah, run outside," Eula said. When the children stood rooted to the floor, she said, "Go on, now."

"Perhaps they'd like a little snack?" Mrs. Roosevelt suggested. Reaching into the basket, she produced two drumsticks, crispy and still warm, and receiving an approving nod from Eula, gave one to each child. They scooted out of the door in seconds.

"I've brought along some clothes for them," she said. "Hand-me-downs, I'm afraid, it's the best I could do. They belonged to my oldest grandchildren, who wore them last time they visited the Little White House, but they outgrew them long ago."

"Yes'm," Eula said. "Thank you, ma'am."

"Now, as I was saying," Mrs. Roosevelt said. "We have some very able people trying to intervene for Nell, but I'd like you to do something as well."

"I'd do anything, ma'am," Eula said. "Anything to save my baby girl."

"I want you to pray, Mrs. Clark," Eleanor Roosevelt said earnestly. "I feel certain you are a woman of faith, but I want you to pray like you never have before."

"Yes'm," Eula said fervently. "Me, and my whole church, and my whole family. Prayer be a powerful thing."

"Yes, it is," Mrs. Roosevelt said softly. "I must be leaving. Thank you for your hospitality." She turned to go. "Oh, and one more thing. I'd like to make sweaters for your grandchildren, for the cool weather in the fall. Would you call them back in? I believe I have a tape measure here in my purse."

CHAPTER 43

Warm Springs

"So, what's it like to work with Bing Crosby?" Susan asked, squeezed between Ida and Joan on the front seat of the Hudson as the car headed south toward Warm Springs. "Is he as nice as he seems? I wanted to go see *Anything Goes* in January, but Robert wouldn't take me, he said he couldn't afford fifteen cents to go to the movies." Susan couldn't take her eyes off her famous driver.

"Oh, Bing is a lovely gentleman," Ida said. "Very kind, and fun to work with. I could listen to him sing all day."

"I worked with him once, too," Joan piped up.

"You did?" Susan asked, turning to the reporter. "You mean you're an actress too?"

"Well, I was," Joan said. "I was in his movie *She Loves Me Not* a couple of years ago."

Susan frowned. "I saw it, but I don't remember you. What was your character's name?"

"Well, I didn't have a title role, dear," Joan said, lighting a cigarette. "I was in a scene at the cabaret, sitting at a table next to a large potted palm. But I agree with Ida, Bing is a sweetheart."

Susan turned her full attention on Ida until they reached Warm Springs, peppering her with questions about her movies *Paris in Spring* ("Did you really go to Paris and climb up the Eye-full Tower?") and *Smart Girl*. As they neared the depot, Joan suggested Ida stop there so she could see if a telegram had arrived at the Western Union desk from Billy Bryce.

She hurried inside, pulling down her tight skirt to cover her knees.

"Oh, Miss Roswell, I'm sorry," Bob said, smiling at the pretty woman. "I just sent a messenger with the telegram to your cottage at the Foundation. He had a couple of other deliveries there, so I just handed him yours too."

"That's fine, Bob," Joan said. "Oh, and by the way, thanks for the excellent directions you gave me this morning. I found the Woods's house without any trouble at all." She sucked in a dimple and smiled at Bob, who almost wiggled in delight.

Missy used her key to let herself into the little cottage, quickly inhaling the heavy perfume of a gardenia bush by the door that was covered with white blossoms. Her cottage provided basic accommodations for two or three people: a bedroom with bath, living room, kitchen, and a sleeping porch with a separate toilet. *I remember how mad I was when I got the invoice from the builder,* she thought. *I felt that extra toilet was such an unneeded expense. I guess if I had to sleep on the porch, I would be glad for the convenience, though.*

She had been in the cottage only a few minutes when she heard a knock at the door. *Goodness, can that be lunch already?* But when she opened it, she found a young man from Western Union, who was riding an ancient blue bicycle.

"Oh! Miss LeHand," he said, recognizing her from previous visits to Warm Springs. "I'm sorry, I thought you would be staying at the Little White House."

"I am," Missy said. "But I own this cottage and just wanted to speak to the people who are renting it this week. Can I help you?"

"Sure," said the messenger. "I've got a telegram here for Miss Joan Roswell, but I also have one for you. I was going to take it over to the Little White House. This saves me a trip."

"I'm happy to sign for both," Missy said.

She laid Joan's telegram on a small table beside the couch, and folded hers, unread, in the pocket of her paisley print dress. "Thanks!" she said, fishing a quarter out of her purse to give the man a tip. He touched his fingers to his hat, mounted his bike and pedaled away, meeting a maroon Hudson convertible as it rolled into the yard. *I know that car*, Missy thought grimly. *And two of the people in it.*

Ida parked the Hudson under a flowering mimosa tree and the three women piled out, Susan still chattering and asking questions. But when Joan recognized the woman on the front porch, she froze. "Oh, hello, Missy," she said. "How nice of you to drop by."

Missy walked down the steps, extending her hand to Ida Lupino. "Good afternoon, Miss Lupino," she said. "I'm Marguerite LeHand, the President's private secretary. We are great fans of your movies. Imagine my surprise when I learned you had rented my cottage for your stay here."

"Oh!" Ida said, surprised. Then her acting skills kicked in and she smiled broadly. "What a pleasure," she said. "Tell the President I am a great fan of his also, both for starting this wonderful Foundation, and for the manner in which he is leading the country. I would love to campaign for him in the upcoming election."

"He'll be pleased to know it," Missy said. She cut her eyes to the right. "I was not aware that you knew our friend Joan here."

"We're fairly recently acquainted, dear," Joan said quickly. "In fact, we met on the train coming from Los Angeles. Miss Lupino convinced me to make a trip to Warm Springs to see for myself how the Birthday Ball money we raised is being used, and I must say I've been very impressed."

"Who is your young friend?" Missy asked, leveling her wide blue eyes on Susan Woods.

Before Joan could stop her, Susan piped up, "I'm Susan Woods. Do you really work for President Roosevelt? Gosh, that must be fun!"

"Indeed I do." Missy smiled. "Why don't we all go inside?" she said. "We have a lot to talk about."

CHAPTER 44

Warm Springs

"If you wouldn't mind, Jim," Corey said to his Secret Service counterpart, "would you drive by the hotel for a moment? I'd like to see if I have any messages there, then I'll go back to the Foundation and try to run down Miss LeHand."

Jim obliged, but had barely gotten the engine quiet when Corey came striding out of the three-story brick hotel. "Do you know where Missy LeHand's cottage is located?" he asked.

Jim nodded.

"Take me there, right away," he said. "Miss LeHand left me an urgent message to meet her there."

Ida had gotten a percolator of coffee going in the kitchen at about the time the sandwiches and iced tea arrived from the Foundation dining room. The four women gathered around the enamel-topped kitchen table, Susan ravenously devouring two sandwiches and downing a glass of tea in minutes, the other three eyeing each other speculatively.

When Susan had assuaged her immediate hunger, Missy said, "I understand you are Robert Biggs's girlfriend."

"Well, I used to be," Susan said, wiping her mouth with a paper napkin. "I don't know what I am now. He won't come home from Phenix City, says he's afraid for his life."

Missy raised her dark eyebrows. "Why is that?" she asked.

"He says Nell Gaines's people will kill him," she said matter-of-factly. "He says they'll all be mad about Nell being sentenced to die for killing Mr. Biggs and will come after him."

"And why would they do that?" Missy said.

"Well, it don't make much sense to me either," Susan said. "I mean, I was in the room over the garage when all this happened, and I heard some things, but it was dark, and I couldn't see much." She hesitated a minute, taking another swig of tea. "But I've had a long time to think about it, and it seems like Robert had a lot of blood on his hands to have just watched Nell kill his father. You know?"

About that time, there was a knock on the door and Joan jumped up to answer it. "Why Agent Wainwright," she said. "What a pleasant surprise! Will you join us, dear? We just sat down for lunch."

By three o'clock, Susan Woods's brain was almost overwhelmed by everything that had happened to her so far that day.

Rescued from Aunt Cleo's farm by Ida Lupino and an almost-famous actress! Served lunch by the secretary to the President of the United States! And now she had been interviewed by an FBI agent who was so handsome he could be a movie star himself, and he'd told her she was the key to solving an important case.

"Susan, are you listening to me?" Corey said, snapping his fingers in front of the girl's glazed eyes.

Susan jerked back to attention. "Yessir," she said. "It's just a lot to take in, all at once."

"I know it is, Susan, but I've got a very, very important question to ask you," Corey said. "It may be a little embarrassing, but I've got to know." He held Susan's

187

eyes with his. "Did you and Corey have sexual relations in Phenix City?"

Susan blushed bright red, hating that this good-looking man, who sounded just like an FBI man on "Gangbusters" and probably knew J. Edgar Hoover himself, should ask her such a question. But she swallowed and nodded her head. "Yessir," she said quietly. "The first night we got there." *And about every night after, too.*

Corey let out a long breath. "Thank you for your honesty, Susan," he said. "Let me ask you this: Would you be willing to testify to this in court?"

Susan's eyes got even wider. *Testify in court! How exciting! Heck, they might even make a picture about this whole case, and I could play myself in the movie!* "Yessir, I would," she assured Corey.

"Well, that enables me to be very involved in this case, and my next task will be to find Robert. That's where you can help me," Corey explained. "You said you were living in an apartment in Phenix City. Could you find it again?"

"Oh, yessir," she said. "I know exactly where it is. The address is 2806-A Fourth Avenue."

"Corey," Missy said.

The agent turned his eyes to the secretary. She was reading a telegram.

"I got this a little while ago from Betty Barnette at the farm prison," she said. "Nell Gaines is in labor."

CHAPTER 45

Phenix City

For Robert Biggs, things had changed—for the better—with Susan's departure. The slim wages he was earning stretched farther with just one mouth to feed and the furnished boarding house room he found on Seventeenth Avenue was more comfortable, closer to the mill, and cheaper than the apartment had been. Plus, Robert no longer had to put up with Susan's incessant chatter. Now when he came home in the evening after a long day in the hot, sticky picking house at the mill, Robert could wash, eat, and relax without having to constantly reply to her silly questions and pointless comments.

The relative freedom of his evenings gave him time to study the Bible or, late at night, when he had the energy, to tinker with the radio and pull in signals from The Cathedral of the Air, Sister Aimee Semple McPherson's radio ministry from California. Robert preferred Sister Aimee's hopeful, uplifting sermons and the fine music from her worship services to the hellfire and damnation tirades of some of the other radio preachers like Billy Sunday, who had, God rest his soul, gone to his just reward the previous fall. He also liked it that Sister Aimee admitted she wasn't perfect. After all, she'd been married three times.

Robert had swiped a thin piece of copper wire from a pile of junk at the mill, carried it back to his Seventeenth Avenue boarding house and attached it to his radio. His reception had improved dramatically and so now, more often than not, he could tune in Sister Aimee on Thursday and Saturday nights. Thursday nights were sometimes a challenge, as his long shift moving around five hundred-pound cotton bales sapped his strength. But, on Saturday nights, he could stay up as late as he liked; there was no working on Sunday.

Besides thrilling to the way Sister Aimee shared the Word, Robert admired the work being done by the minister and her congregation at the Angelus Temple. They'd set up a soup kitchen, a job service, a medical clinic, and a clothes closet for the thousands of Los Angelinos suffering through the Depression. He compared it to the piddling efforts of his mother and her church circle in Greenville, holding bake sales and bazaars to raise a few dollars to send to missionaries in China and other god-less places. Sometimes he fantasized that Sister Aimee was his real mother, and that his upbringing in Greenville was just all part of a bad dream. The only problem with Sister Aimee was that she believed whites and coloreds should worship together. *Well, that's California. She just ain't been around 'em like I have.*

Still, Robert pictured himself walking through the doors of the Angelus Temple, walking right up to Sister Aimee, and joining her ministry. Maybe she'd even adopt him! *Yes sir. I'm gonna save my money, study the Word, and go to California.*

After several weeks of saving what money he could, Robert realized that he would need another source of income before he could afford a bus ticket to California. It wasn't that the ticket was that expensive, it's just that once he hit the road, he'd have to have enough cash for food along the way and a place to stay once he got there. *Reckon Los Angeles is a more expensive place to live than Phenix City.*

There were a lot of ways to make money in Phenix City—if you were willing to take a chance. There was plenty of gambling down along Broad Street, and whoring and drinking too. Robert had even heard of some men who catered to the unholy sexual appetites of some of the soldiers from Fort Benning just across the river.

But none of that appealed to Robert, even if it did hold the promise for a fair amount of money in a short amount of time. No, the risks to body and soul were too great. Rather than indulge in sinfulness, Robert hit on a better plan. He'd sell the Buick.

Robert walked about a mile to and from work every day. It wasn't bad really and it saved a lot of money on gasoline and maintenance on the car—which, in truth, seemed out of place parked at a boarding house.

On Saturday afternoon, after the mill shut down for the weekend, Robert cleaned up and drove the car downtown. The place was already jumping with khaki-clad soldiers flowing in and out of the beer joints and dance halls as the sun dropped behind the tops of the buildings along Broad Street and the lights came on.

Robert pulled the shiny, blue Buick into the first used car lot he came to, killed the engine and climbed out. "What you got there, friend?" asked a fat man seated on a wooden stool next to the lot's small office.

"A Buick, for sale," Robert answered, looking the man over. His shirt was stretched tight across his belly, his neck was rolled over the sweat-stained collar of his shirt. He looked pretty old. Robert guessed he was fifty or so, maybe a little younger. Fat tended to age people faster.

"I can see it's a Buick, boy." The man laughed and struggled to his feet. He sauntered over to the car, circling it slowly, appraising it like a farmer would a prize bull. "Mighty nice. Looks practically new. How many miles you got on it?"

"Only seven thousand. It's a '34 model 47."

"So I see. Must've cost you quite a penny new," the man said, raising an eyebrow and sneaking a glance at Robert.

"Not me, my father."

"Why's he wanting to sell it?"

"He died. I'm wanting to sell it."

"Mmmm. You got the title to it, son?"

"Title?"

"Yeah. Legal proof of ownership."

"Sure." Robert reached back inside the car and pulled open the glove compartment. "Here you go." He handed over the official papers.

"Naw, son," the fat man said, looking up. "This is the registration. What I'm asking for is the title that shows this car belongs to you."

"Well, it's like I told you," Robert said. "It belonged to my father. He's dead. Now it belongs to me."

The fat man looked back at the papers in his hand. "You still live over in Greenville?"

"No. I live here now." *But not for long.*

The car dealer shook his head and handed the document back to Robert. "Can't help you, son, not without a title. This may be Phenix City, but I run a square business here."

Robert pouted his lips, reached out and took the registration from the man. "Thanks all the same." He climbed back in the car, pressed the starter and shifted into gear. He pulled back out on the street and headed south, paralleling the river.

"Denny's Dents" the sign read. "A Car for Every Budget." Robert drove onto the gravel lot and looked around. His Buick was far and away the classiest automobile in sight. Dusty and dented Fords and Chevys stood in an uneven row facing the street, interrupted only by an occasional Plymouth.

Robert climbed out of the car and was met almost immediately by a thin man wearing a half-sleeve shirt and a wide black neck tie. "How can I help you, sir?" he asked, breaking into a wide grin.

192

"I want to sell my car."

"Well, sir, you've come to the right place. Denny's the name and cars are my game." The man laughed and stuck out his hand. "That's surely a fine-looking automobile you got there. A 1934, right?" Denny began to circle the car.

"Right."

"A model 47?"

"Right."

"And you're wanting to sell it?"

"That's what I said."

"Well, it looks to be in fine shape." Denny stuck his head in through the driver's side and read the mileage on the odometer. He whistled. "Would you look at that? Practically new! Nothing wrong with, it is there?"

"No. I'm looking to go join the Army. Won't need it anymore."

"It belongs to you then?" Denny asked, still smiling.

"Yep."

"Well, all right then. I think we can do some business." Denny pulled a scratch pad from his pocket and jotted down some figures, tore the sheet off and handed it to Robert.

Robert felt his face flush, his temper rise. "A hundred fifty dollars? It's worth four times that much, maybe more." He crumpled the slip of paper and tossed it on the gravel. "You must think I'm some kind of idiot or something."

"No, friend. I don't think that at all," Denny said calmly, still smiling. "I just think this isn't really your car. I think I'll have to sell it off the books, which means extra risk for me. The good news for you is that I know how to handle these specialty transactions. Of course, you can try any of the other dealers in town if you want to go to the trouble." Denny's smile vanished. "Truth is, you'll end up right back here—if the law doesn't catch you first."

"It's not stolen, if that's what you think."

"I told you what I think. And I told you what I'd pay."

Robert dropped his eyes to the balled-up paper on the ground. When he looked back up, he said, "Cash."

CHAPTER 46

Warm Springs

Corey had let Agent Rawlings and his car go when he arrived at Missy's cottage, so the two returned to the Little White House on foot. It had been a hot, eventful day, but they were both excited and tense about what lay ahead: finding Robert Biggs before an unknown deadline expired for Nell Gaines.

It was almost four o'clock when they reached the President's small house. Enticing smells were starting to drift out of Daisy Bonner's kitchen, and they found President Roosevelt and Grace Tully on the back porch, Grace taking dictation in her lightning-fast stenography. Eleanor Roosevelt was with them, still knitting the moss-green sweater.

"Ho! Any news?" the President asked. Uncharacteristically, Eleanor dropped her knitting into her lap.

"Quite a lot, F.D.," Missy said. "We've had a breakthrough. Agent Wainwright spent the past two hours questioning Susan Woods."

"Oh, Agent Wainwright! How marvelous!" the First Lady said, a big smile on her face. "Please, sit down and tell us all about it. Would you like some tea or coffee?"

"Or something stronger?" the President prompted.

"It's not five o'clock yet, Franklin," Mrs. Roosevelt admonished. The daughter of an alcoholic, she did not enjoy drinking or being around drinkers.

"I think we're fine," Missy said. "We drank about a gallon of tea and coffee over at my cottage which, as Grace may have told you, has been harboring both Ida Lupino and our friend Joan Roswell."

Quickly, the two shared the details of their findings that day: Susan's revelations about Robert, Corey's meetings with the so-called defense attorney Melvin Jugg, and finally, the alarming telegram from Betty Barnette at the prison farm.

"Oh, no!" Mrs. Roosevelt said. "Oh, Franklin, I must go over there right way and make sure she is getting proper medical attention."

"I agree, Babs," FDR said. "Only this time, I want to make sure you get to see her." He turned to Grace Tully. "Grace, place a call to Governor Talmadge's office and let him know Mrs. Roosevelt is on her way to Milledgeville. Tell him she is to be allowed in to see Mrs. Gaines, no questions asked. Let me know if he gives you any guff and I'll talk to him personally."

"Right, Boss," Grace said, hurrying into the living room and the phone.

Mrs. Roosevelt stuffed her knitting into her bag and headed for the door, then paused to look at Corey Wainwright. "I don't suppose you have an extra set of handcuffs, do you?" she asked.

"No, ma'am," the agent replied, puzzled, "but I expect the Secret Service can come up with a set."

"Are you planning to make a citizen's arrest of the warden?" the President asked, incredulous.

"No, Franklin," Mrs. Roosevelt replied, "but as a last resort—and I do mean last—I plan to handcuff myself to Nell Gaines. I don't think even Governor Talmadge would try to electrocute the First Lady of the United States." She turned and entered the Little White House, calling for her secretary, Tommy Thompson, to accompany her. Even if Eleanor Roosevelt was going to prison, she still intended to file her *My Day* column.

"I'd like to think she was joking," the President said, "but I know I'd be wrong." He turned to Corey and Missy, "Now, so you won't think I've been lazing around all day, I want you to know about my own actions. I talked to my good friend Cason Calloway over in Hamilton this morning and he has found a very fine defense attorney from Atlanta, a fellow named Cornelius A. Bates III, who is willing to take on Mrs. Gaines's case. I spoke to him early this afternoon. It appears he's one of the few liberal Democrats in Georgia, and he especially enjoys fighting for the underdog." The President looked at his secretary and said, "Missy, he is the graduate of a little college in Boston near where you grew up."

"Would that be Harvard, F.D.?" Missy asked innocently.

The President laughed. "Yes, indeed. Not a contemporary of mine, but apparently quite outstanding. A protégé of our friend Felix Frankfurter." He lit a Camel and added nonchalantly, "Porcellian Club."

Missy laughed out loud. It had been one of the greatest disappointments of Franklin Roosevelt's life that he had been turned down for membership in the prestigious club, whose members wore gold fobs shaped like pigs on their watch chains. FDR had to content himself with collecting miniature porkers, which he displayed on the mantel of his bedroom at the White House.

"Was Mr. Bates familiar with the case?" Corey asked, unsure of the significance of the Porcellian Club.

"Yes, he'd followed it in the newspapers," the President said. "He was not aware of Mrs. Gaines's condition, however, and the fact that her defense attorney had not put up any witnesses bothered him a great deal. I can only imagine how bothered he will be to learn Mr. Jugg didn't even try to find Robert Biggs. I'll have another chat with him in the morning to get him up to speed."

FDR ground out his Camel in the ashtray attached to his wheelchair and looked from Corey to Missy. "So," he said, "I expect you will be getting a very early start in the morning and heading for Phenix City. It's not very far, is it?

"A little over an hour," Corey said.

"Well, I'll assign Agent Rawlings and his car to you again," the President said. "I suppose you will want to go as well, Missy?"

"Yes," Missy said. "We plan to get in touch with Susan's parents tonight and get their permission to take her with us, as she's familiar with the place Robert lived. They've promised their full cooperation, but I'm sure they will feel better if I go as her chaperone."

"What about the ladies who are renting your cottage?"

"Not invited," Corey said decisively.

"Good," FDR said. "No need to involve our lady reporter yet, with or without the lovely Miss Lupino." A clock pinged five times from the living room. "Ah, Children's Hour at last. How about a little sippy?"

CHAPTER 47

Warm Springs

Joan filed her story Wednesday night using the night letter, as Billy had instructed her in his telegram. It had the advantage of costing two-thirds the day rate, but wouldn't be delivered until the following business day, indicating Billy's low level of interest in her feature stories.

With all the excitement at the cottage that afternoon, she hadn't had the time to do the first-rate job she had promised her crusty editor but hoped she could keep him at bay long enough to get her big scoop about the involvement of the Roosevelts and Missy LeHand in the fight to save Nell Gaines.

POOLS, PARTIES PREPARE POLIO PATIENTS

By Joan Roswell, Special to the AP—Warm Springs, Georgia—Patients confined to wheel chairs or whose movements are restricted by crutches and canes would appear to be unlikely dance partners, but that's exactly what this reporter witnessed Tuesday evening at the Warm Springs Foundation's weekly square dance. More than a dozen polio victims suffering varying levels of infirmity circled, dosey-doed and wheeled to call of an authentic western-style square dance, just one way the staff and volunteers at the Foundation help patients look beyond their affliction and focus on their potential.

One Foundation volunteer is a familiar face: motion picture star Ida Lupino. Miss Lupino, coming off her critically-acclaimed performance in *Anything Goes*, is a dedicated contributor to the Foundation and its patients, spending part of her annual vacation working with the staff to ensure treatments and events—like the weekly square dance—go according to schedule. "It's one way I can help make things better for people suffering from this terrible disease," Miss Lupino told me recently during a break from her duties. "I worked with several Hollywood stars and studio executives last winter to host the President's Birthday Ball at the Roosevelt Hotel in Los Angeles. We raised over twenty thousand dollars and I wanted to follow that experience with another opportunity to look into the faces of some of the people those funds go to help."

Joan's story included her interview with Janice Howe, the physical therapist she had met at the pool, and a description of the soothing waters of the eponymous warm springs. It also included interviews with several patients, which Joan, unfortunately, had to fabricate because she had not found time to meet any real patients.

Billy will never know. And if he questions me, I'll just say I changed their names to protect their privacy!

Ida was surprised after Joan drove home from the depot that she had not returned Dr. Raper's damaged Hudson. That's when Joan divulged her plans for a trip to Phenix City the next day.

"But we can't!" Ida wailed. "We don't have permission to take his car to Alabama! He doesn't even know about the birdshot yet, and heaven knows what might happen in Phenix City!"

"We'll worry about that later," Joan declared. "They can snatch Susan Woods, but they're not going to shut me out of the hunt. I do all the leg work and uncover the key witness and Corey Wainwright swoops in and thinks he can just take over. Again! This is *my* story, and nobody is going to keep me from it, not you, or Mr. Corey Wainwright or President Franklin Delano Roosevelt himself!"

Ida didn't reply.

"So, are you coming or not?"

"I guess I'm coming," Ida said. "Just to keep an eye on that car!"

THURSDAY, MAY 21, 1936

CHAPTER 48

On the Road to Phenix City

"Missy, how much time do you think Nell has?" Corey asked just loud enough for Missy to hear. She was seated next to him on the back seat of the Lincoln phaeton that was now streaking down state Highway 85 toward Columbus. Jim Rawlings was behind the wheel with Susan perched on the front seat beside him. She would, Corey hoped, help them quickly find the apartment on Fourth Avenue once they crossed the river into Phenix City.

"God only knows, Corey. Mrs. Roosevelt called from Milledgeville about ten o'clock last night. She had gotten into the prison and was being allowed to sit with Nell. Apparently, Governor Talmadge is being cooperative for once."

"How long after the birth will they carry out the sentence? Do we have days—or just hours?"

Missy frowned. "That's another one for God," she said, crossing herself out of old Catholic habit. "But I've got a lot of faith in Mrs. Roosevelt too. I think she'll keep Nell safe for now, but we better wrap this up as quickly as we can."

Corey squeezed Missy's hand. She squeezed back —and didn't let go.

"Susan?" Missy said, leaning forward and shaking the girl gently by the shoulder. "Wake up, we're crossing the river." The car was approaching the bridge spanning the muddy Chattahoochee River that separated Georgia from Alabama.

Susan had had a difficult time sleeping the night before at Missy's cottage. The heady excitement of her escape, her new friendship with movie stars—Ida Lupino had loaned her some pajamas made of real silk! —and her involvement as the key witness in an FBI case had kept her tossing and turning for hours. But almost as soon as the car hit the road, the warm morning sun and the droning of the engine had put her to sleep.

Susan sat up, flexed her neck and shoulders, and looked out at the river below.

"Where do we go from here?" Corey asked from the back seat.

"I know the way," Susan said, the excitement returning and chasing away her sleepiness. "Once we get over the bridge, we turn right on Broad Street." Rawlings followed Susan's directions until he turned into a block of run-down apartments.

"Which building is it, Susan?" Corey asked.

"It's that one, the white one beside the street. We were on the second floor, Apartment A."

"All right. You ladies stay put. C'mon Jim." Corey and Rawlings climbed out of the car, buttoned their suit coats, and headed toward the apartment building.

"This is so exciting!" Susan said, her eyes wide with delight. "I wish I could be a fly on the wall when they break down the door!"

Missy rolled her eyes. "I think they'll probably just knock."

"Where to?" Ida asked as the Hudson rolled across the Thirteenth Street Bridge.

"Susan said 'Fourth.' I can't recall the street number. Let's stop and ask for directions."

Ida pulled into a filling station at the corner of Ninth Avenue and Thirteenth Street. "Fill 'er up, miss?" a young man asked. He wore a pale green shirt with a Texaco star patch on one breast and his name, "Fred," embroidered on the other.

"Thank you, no. We're from out of town and we're trying to find a friend's apartment. It's on Fourth Avenue."

"You're only off about three blocks," Fred said, leaning on the door of the snazzy convertible and eyeing its two beautiful occupants. He gave them quick instructions and said, "If you get to the railroad tracks, you've gone too far."

Ida thanked him and turned north on Ninth. "We're only a couple of minutes away."

CHAPTER 49

Phenix City

Corey knocked on the door to Apartment A as Jim Rawlings stood behind him and to the side. You never knew what would happen in a situation like this and Corey was grateful the President had offered a member of his protective detail for backup. Corey was about to knock a second time when he heard the shuffle of footsteps. The door opened, and Corey found himself staring into the sunken eyes of a young woman wearing a worn bathrobe.

"Quiet," she hissed, "or you'll wake the baby—and if you wake him, *you* change him, and *you* feed him!"

Corey held up his badge. "I'm special agent Corey Wainwright, FBI, and this is agent Jim Rawlings with the Secret Service. I'm sorry to bother you, ma'am, but we're looking for Robert Biggs. We believe he's been living in this apartment."

"Never heard of him."

Corey pocketed his credentials. "What's your name, ma'am?"

"Helen Kent."

"How long have you lived here, Mrs. Kent?"

"About a week. My husband is a sergeant over at the fort," she said, tossing her head in the general direction of the river. "We're waiting for housing on the post and living in this dump until something opens up."

Corey reached in his coat pocket and pulled out a snapshot Susan had contributed to the investigation. "Have you seen this man, Mrs. Kent?"

Kent stared at the photo a moment, then shook her head. "Nope. What's he done?"

"We'd just like to ask him a few questions." Corey returned the photograph to his pocket and withdrew a rectangular card. "If you do see him, Mrs. Kent, I'd appreciate it if you would contact me. You can call me collect at this number," he pointed to his office phone number, "and leave a message. Any information you can provide will be held in confidence and will be greatly appreciated."

"All right," Helen Kent said, taking the card and putting it in the pocket of her robe.

"Thank you, Mrs. Kent," Corey said with a tip of his hat. "Sorry to disturb you."

She disappeared back inside. As the door closed, a baby began to cry.

"We better get out of here fast!" Rawlings said with a smile.

"No soap," Corey said, pulling off his hat as he and Rawlings slid back into the car. "There's another tenant in the apartment now. Says she's never heard of or seen Robert Biggs."

"But that's where we lived. I promise!" Susan protested.

"I believe you, Susan. But Robert's not here now." Corey leaned forward, resting his arm on the seat back. "Where else did the two of you go? Any restaurants that you frequented, bars, any place that people would know you?"

"Robert was too cheap to go out to eat. And he don't drink either, except for Co-Cola. All he did was read books, go to work, and go to church on Sunday."

"Work? Where did he work?"

"At the mill."

"Susan, do you remember the name of the mill?" Missy asked.

"Oh, gosh, it was just 'the mill.' That's what he always called it."

Corey glanced up and caught Rawlings's eyes staring at him in the rear-view mirror. "Want to check with the local police, Agent Wainwright?"

"It seems like that would be the quickest way to find the mill," Missy said.

"No doubt. It's just that the local officials here in Phenix City don't have the most savory reputation." Corey turned his attention back to Susan. "Do you think you could remember the way to the mill?"

"Oh, I never been there. Robert would go to work and then he'd come home, but I never saw the place."

"So, you don't know where it is?"

"I just know that he walked that way," Susan said, pointing toward the west. "He said it was about a twenty-minute walk."

"That'd be about a mile," Rawlings said.

"I think you're right, Jim," Corey said, frowning. "I think we've got to go to the local police."

Rawlings cranked the car, pulled out of the apartment building's gravel lot, and head toward downtown.

"Stop!" Joan shouted. "There!" She pointed at the big black government car pulling out onto the street. "Quick! Pull into that driveway."

Ida whipped the wheel to the right and the Hudson bounced onto a rutted driveway beside a modest white frame house. She pulled all the way to the end of the drive, easing the car as close to the house as possible.

"I've got to tell you, Joan. For covert surveillance, a maroon Hudson with the top down is not the best choice."

"Uh oh!" Missy said with a groan as Rawlings turned onto Broad Street.

"What's wrong?" Corey asked with concern.

"We've got company."

"Who?"

"Our old friend, Joan. She's following us. She and Ida turned into the driveway we just passed."

"So help me… If she gets in the way, I'll arrest her. I swear!" Corey's face was flushed. "Step on it, Jim!"

CHAPTER 50

Phenix City

"Are you kidding?" the desk sergeant asked. Corey and Rawlings had located the police headquarters and gone inside. They were standing in front of a raised enclosure made of dark, heavy wood behind which sat the headquarters' gatekeeper. On the wall to the sergeant's right was a large map of the city, the river forming its eastern boundary. "There must be twenty or thirty mills around here, on both sides of the river."

"Well, the one we're looking for is about a mile away, within walking distance of downtown," Corey explained. "We're looking for this man." He showed the sergeant Robert's picture.

"Nice-looking boy. What's the beef?"

"Violation of the Mann Act." The sergeant laughed. Corey slipped the photo back into his pocket. "What's so funny, officer?"

The sergeant wiped his eyes. "Sorry. You'd have to be here on a payday Saturday night to understand. You could arrest half the soldiers in town."

"So you haven't seen our suspect?"

"No. I'm the booking officer. If we'd had any trouble with him, I'd remember."

"What about those mills?"

The sergeant stared at the ceiling for a moment and let out a sigh. "I've got three possibilities right off the top of my head. They'd have been within a mile of here, like you said."

Five minutes later, Corey and Rawlings were walking down the steps of police headquarters with a list in hand. When they got back to the car, Missy was gone.

"Where's Miss LeHand?" Corey asked Susan.

"Oh, she went over there." The girl pointed to the opposite side of the street.

Corey looked across the street to see Missy standing on the sidewalk next to a maroon convertible. *Very stealthy.*

"I'm warning you, Joan, time is running out for Nell Gaines and if you delay this investigation you may end up with blood on your hands. You too, Miss Lupino." Missy's temper was flaring.

"What's going on here?" Corey demanded, as he reached the three women.

"I was just advising our friends here that they would be wise to stay clear of our investigation."

"Sound advice," Corey said, shifting his gaze from Missy to Joan.

"Now, Corey, dear, where's the professional courtesy? You know we wouldn't dream of hindering your investigation," Joan said. "Why, you know I've always cooperated with you and the Bureau in every way." She paused. "Mr. Hoover knows it too. And besides, there's that pesky old First Amendment thing." She smiled.

Corey considered the symbiotic relationship that had—unfortunately—developed between his boss, J. Edgar Hoover, the powerful head of the FBI, and Joan Roswell, Hollywood gossip columnist and general pain-in-the-ass. Rather than waste time—and risk a dust-up with the Director—Corey hit on another strategy for dealing with these unwelcome interlopers.

Flashing a quick wink at Missy, Corey leaned on the door of the Hudson. "Get out your pen, Joan. Quickly!

Missy's right: we don't have much time. So we're going to have to work together."

"Together, dear?"

"Right." Corey looked down at the list of three mills. "I want you to go out to Payne's Hosiery Mill and ask around. See if they have a Robert Biggs on payroll. If the answer is no, ask if they've seen anybody matching his description."

"It would help if we had a picture, dear."

"Yeah, but I've only got one and while you're checking out Payne's, we'll be checking out some other mills. You'll just have to make do with your charms, Joan." Corey straightened up.

"I'm so glad you finally noticed, dear," Joan said, smiling and batting her eyelashes.

"What's the address?" Ida asked.

"210 Crawford. Drive out Fourteenth Street."

"How do we get in touch with you?" Ida asked.

"Meet us back here as soon as you can."

"How do we know you'll come back here, dear? How do we know you want just leave us out here all alone?"

Corey leaned over again, his eyes level with Joan's. "Same way I know you won't leave without reporting what you've found out, Joan. Professional courtesy."

"Mind telling me what you're up to?" Missy asked after Ida and Joan headed toward Fourteenth Street.

Corey shrugged. "Playing the odds. Beyond that, we've got three potential employers to cover and I want to do so as quickly as possible. C'mon," he said, taking Missy by the elbow as they re-crossed the street. "Susan said it took Robert twenty minutes to walk to work. Based on my calculations, which I admit I completed in a hurry, the Payne Hosiery Mill is more like a thirty-minute walk. So, I'm thinking it's the least likely of our candidates to be

Robert's employer. You and me and Rawlings and the girl are going to visit the other two mills. If my hunch is right, we'll find our man and Joan will find socks."

"I hope you don't mind, Joan," Ida said, setting the hand brake and killing the engine, "but I'm staying in the car. If somebody in there recognized me," she pointed to the long two-story, red brick factory building, "and it got back to the studio, I'd be in a real pickle trying to explain what I was doing in Phenix City, Alabama."

"I quite understand, dear," Joan replied, examining her face in the tiny mirror of her gold compact. "I'm sure I can handle this. Wait right here and I'll be back in a jiffy." Joan opened the car door and walked toward a door over which hung a sign stating "Office."

As she approached the building, Joan could hear the steady thrumming of heavy machinery and the whirring of powerful fans working to move the warm, moist air through the building and keep its interior temperature at least tolerable. Through the open windows of the office, Joan could hear the click-clack of typewriters and mechanical calculators.

Joan opened the screen door and stepped inside. Small fans stood on tops of filing cabinets, rotating slowly back and forth, ruffling papers and keeping flies on the move.

"Help you, miss?" a bored-looking middle-aged woman said, looking up from a desk behind a waist-high wooden rail.

"Yes, personnel please."

The woman pointed to her left. "Down this hallway, past the water cooler, on the left. You'll see a sign over the door."

"Thank you, dear." Joan followed the directions, passing down a dimly-lit hallway with a green linoleum floor until she came to the open doorway of the personnel office.

"Hello," Joan said with a smile, as she entered the office. There were two desks sitting perpendicular to the door and facing each other. Two plump, perspiring women looked up from their work.

"We only take applications on Wednesdays and Thursdays," the older of the two said before looking back at the work on her desk.

"Oh, no, dear. I'm not actually looking for a job. I'm looking for a person. My…little brother, Robert. We haven't heard from him in a while and, well, Mother is worried. She sent me to check up on him."

The older woman, the one who had spoken first, looked across at her office mate. "What's his name, honey?" the younger woman asked, scooting her chair back from her desk.

"Biggs, Robert Biggs. He's just the sweetest boy, and handsome? Makes all the ladies swoon. Do you know him, dear?"

"Nope. But I don't truck with the boys that work in the mill." The woman stood up and opened a metal filing cabinet standing in a row behind her desk. "Biggs, right?"

"That's right dear. Robert Biggs."

"Here we go." The woman pulled a folder from the cabinet and set it on her desk. She settled back into her chair and flipped open the file. "Robert Biggs. Been working here for nearly eight months. He works in the picking house."

"Can you direct me to the picking house?"

"Oh, listen, sister, you don't want to go in there. It's hot as he—hot as the dickens and dirty too. Let me call the foreman over there and see if your brother's working today."

"How kind!"

"Won't take but a minute." The woman picked up the black phone on her desk, dialed a zero and asked the switchboard to connect her. After a moment, she said, "Larry, it's Sheila. You got Robert Biggs working today? His sister is here in the office and wants to see him." Sheila listened for a moment then said, "All right, I'll tell her." Sheila hung up the phone and Joan leaned forward.

"He didn't show up for work today. Larry says that's unusual, that the kid's been very dependable."

"Oh, dear. I hope Robert's all right." Joan leaned over and placed her hands on Sheila's desk. "Does your file give his address, dear? I'll go check on him, make sure he's OK."

"Sure, sis." Sheila pulled a notepad toward her and jotted the address on the pad, ripped off the page, and handed it to Joan. "Seventeenth Avenue. Don't confuse that with Seventeenth Street. Lots of folks from out of town can't tell them apart."

Joan cocked her head and grinned. "And you could tell right away that I wasn't from around here, couldn't you? Amazing."

"Well," Sheila smiled, "it's sort of a gift of mine."

"Thank you so much, dear. I'll be sure to tell Robert how helpful you've been. Mother too."

With the address squeezed in her hand, Joan escaped from the mill's office as rapidly as decorum and her tight skirt would allow. She climbed back into the car, a satisfied smile on her face.

"Find him?"

"Almost. He didn't come to work this morning, but his address is 1087 Seventeenth Avenue. It can't be far."

CHAPTER 51

Phenix City

By the time Joan and Ida pulled out to search for Robert's address, Corey and Missy had already struck out at one mill and were on their way to the next.

"I'm getting a bad feeling about this," Missy said, leaning closer to Corey in the back seat and speaking so only he could hear her.

"Don't despair," Corey said as he reached over again to give her hand a squeeze. "We're the FBI. We always get our man."

Missy liked sitting in the back seat with the handsome agent. She wished it was just the two of them on the case, that Rawlings and Susan were back in Warm Springs. In fact, Missy wished they were all back in Warm Springs and that this whole, awful case was behind them, that Nell Gaines was safe and out of prison and able to care for her new baby as well as her other children. *What a tragedy!*

Joan walked up the steps to the front porch of the large house on Seventeenth Avenue. A small sign hung horizontally from one of the porch's columns: "Room to Let." Joan knocked, peering through the screen door at the darkened interior. "Hello!" she called. "Is anyone home?"

A door on the right of the center hall opened and an older woman stepped out. "I'm Mrs. Carter. This is my home. Are you here about a room? I just had one open up."

Joan hesitated for a moment, then said, "Yes. May I see it?"

Mrs. Carter unhooked the screen door and said, "Please come in, Miss—"

"Roswell. Joan Roswell."

"Where are you from, Miss Roswell?"

"From Atlanta. I'm here on an assignment for my company and I need a clean, hospitable, and decent place to stay."

"Follow me and I'll show you the room." Mrs. Carter turned right to go up the stairs. "What company do you work for?"

"*Southeastern Textile Report*. I'm doing a feature on the Payne Mill. Sheila at the office there suggested I check with you about accommodations. She said there were some other mill employees also living here."

"There were, yes."

Joan paused on the top step. "Were?"

"Yes. We had a very nice young man living here and working there. Rather quiet, and so handsome. Nice Christian boy." Mrs. Carter turned to her left at the top of the stairs and opened a door facing the landing. "This was his room, in fact. He settled his rent and left just this morning."

"What a coincidence. Do you recall his name?"

"Of course. We're all like family here. His name was Robert, Robert Biggs."

"Now what?" Missy asked, as she and Corey, Rawlings, and Susan sat in the car waiting to rendezvous with Ida and Joan. They'd come up empty at both of the textile plants. No one had heard of Robert Biggs and no one recognized his picture.

"We wait for Joan to show and then we check the next closest mills to see if Biggs is working there."

"What if our girl doesn't show back up?"

"Speak for yourself," Corey snorted. "She's not my girl. But don't worry. She'll show." *I hope.*

Ten minutes later, a relieved Corey watched as Ida pulled the Hudson to the curb in front of the government car. Corey and Missy climbed out of the back seat and walked to the passenger side of the convertible where Joan sat with a smug grin on her face.

"Do you want the good news or the bad news?" Joan asked.

"How about you just tell me what you found out, Joan."

"Now, Corey, dear, be patient and be a gentleman. After all, we're working as a team. And I'm pleased to report that Robert Biggs has been working at the Payne Mill."

"Did you actually see him?" Missy asked.

"No, dear. He wasn't there. He didn't come to work this morning."

"Did they—" Joan held up her hand, interrupting Missy.

"He also settled his rent with the boarding house where he's been living on Seventeenth Avenue, dear." Joan smiled. "He left this morning about eleven o'clock, but not until after he'd made his bed, cleaned the room thoroughly and packed up all his things. According to his landlady, the only thing he left was an old Philco radio."

Corey stepped back for a moment, rubbing his square chin. "He left his radio, huh?"

"That's what the lady said."

"What does that mean?" Missy asked, looking from Joan to Corey.

"It means he isn't traveling by car. Come on," he said, again taking Missy by the arm and heading back toward Rawlings and the car. "Follow us, Ida!"

"Where are we going this time?" Missy asked, hurrying to keep up with Corey's longer stride.

"Back to police headquarters."

"No, the tracks run just north of town, but if you want passenger service, you have to go across to Columbus. That's where the station is," the desk sergeant explained.

"How about a bus terminal?"

"Same-o, same-o. Columbus."

"Any idea when the trains depart?"

"There's a morning train and an afternoon train. I'm guessing the morning train isn't much interest to you at this time of day. The afternoon train leaves at 3:25 headed to Atlanta."

Corey was busy making notes on a pocket-sized pad. He stopped to glance at his watch. "How close is the Columbus depot?"

"Five minutes, if you catch the lights."

"That doesn't leave us much time. Thanks, sarge!" Corey called over his shoulder as he pushed through the headquarters' doors.

Rawlings's feet were busy pumping the clutch and pressing the gas as the big Lincoln's engine screamed. At the first red light, Rawlings slowed the car and then shot through a gap in the oncoming traffic as horns blared and tires screeched.

"They're not keeping up," Rawlings said, watching the rear-view mirror as Ida and Joan fell farther behind.

"Don't worry about them! I sent them to the bus station. There's no guarantee Biggs is going by train. If he's tight on funds, bus travel is a lot cheaper."

"But you don't think he's going by bus?" Missy asked.

"Nope. I'm playing another hunch, Missy. I'm betting he left that radio because it's too big to carry around. That means he's not driving a car. If he's not driving a car, logic suggests that he sold the one he had. So, I'm guessing he's got a pocketful of money."

"Sounds like a brilliant deduction, Holmes," Missy said with a laugh.

"Hope this hunch plays out better than my last one."

Joan hated bus stations. The exhaust fumes from the buses were overpowering and the ladies' room was never clean. She sighed as she looked around the dank, dirty waiting room filling up with soldiers and a great unwashed tribe of farm workers and other manual laborers about to board a Greyhound for someplace more exciting. *Which would be just about anywhere.*

Joan had been pleased with herself. *I can run those FBI boys a pretty close race.* She was betting—hoping, really—that Robert Biggs was escaping by wheel rather than by rail. *Hoover will fall all over himself if I crack another case for Corey Wainwright.*

Joan sat on the end of one of the long wooden benches and pulled a Chesterfield from her purse. *Nothing to do but wait and watch.*

CHAPTER 52

Phenix City

"Missy, you and Susan stick together and stay out of sight. If Robert is here and he sees Susan, he'll get spooked." Having reached the Columbus train station, Corey was giving the team last-minute instructions. "According to the station master, that's the train." Corey gestured toward the locomotive sitting next to the red brick station's passenger apron building up steam. "Jim, take another look at his picture. He's five foot ten, about a hundred sixty-five pounds with red hair and blue eyes. Right, Susan?"

"Right," Susan said, smiling up at the FBI man. Corey smiled back.

"So, Jim's position is over there on the south end of the passenger platform. Missy, you and Susan take the north end, but stay behind some baggage or a post or something. I don't want him to see Susan before we see him."

"Where will you be?" Missy asked.

"I'm going to be reading a newspaper right over there at the gate through which all the passengers go to reach the train. If anybody sees Robert, go to the first railroad official you can find, show him your credentials and have him hold the train. And then come and find me. If I see him first, I'll stretch and hold my paper over my head. If I do that, everybody but Susan rally on me." Corey turned to the young woman, who seemed tired and listless. "Susan, whatever happens, stay out of sight. Understand?"

"Yes sir."

"All right. Everybody, take your positions. The train is due to leave in five minutes. Robert, if he's taking that train," Corey motioned toward the cars with a tip of his head, "will probably board at the last possible minute."

"Now boarding at track number one for Opelika, Auburn, Tuskegee, Montgomery..." the towns rolled off the tongue of the public address announcer so fast that Joan couldn't keep track. Several of the travelers in the waiting room stood and collected their baggage and then shuffled out into the parking lot. Joan shut her eyes and tried to picture in her mind the photograph Velma Biggs had shown her. She had to keep Robert's picture in her mind so she would recognize him if by some miracle he showed up to catch a bus. *That is if he isn't already gone!*

Joan shifted on the hard, wooden bench as a young man in blue work dungarees walked over to the red Coca-Cola machine and dropped in a nickel. He pulled out a cold bottle and turned. Joan saw his face. *Nope, not him.*

Corey stole a look at his watch. Three minutes until the train was set to depart. So far, no one matching Robert's description had come through the gate. Corey shifted his gaze toward the far end of the platform. He could see Missy leaning against a post, her eyes scanning the crowd of travelers. He looked over his shoulder. Jim had also picked up a newspaper and was using it to shield his watchful eyes.

"Ladies and gentlemen, all aboard, all aboard for Jordan City, Gentian, Flat Rock, Midland..." the announcement of the station's loudspeaker droned on with all the towns slurring together until finally the announcer said, "annnnd Atlanta. All aboard track number one."

If it's going to happen, it's going to happen now.

A businessman in a suit, carrying a small leather satchel, jogged through the gate, slowing only to show the agent his ticket. "Have a good trip, sir!" the agent said with a smile. Immediately behind the businessman came a woman holding the hand of a little girl. Corey guessed she was six or seven.

"Can we still make the train?" the woman asked, worry in her voice.

"Yes ma'am," the agent assured her. "Do you need help with any bags?"

"No, these are all we've got." She nodded toward the small bags in their hands. The agent waved to a porter who stepped over to help them aboard. Corey watched as they stepped up onto the train. From behind him, a whistle blew. He turned to see a black-suited conductor waving a red flag. The porters, one standing at the stairs leading to each of the train's cars, picked up the small steps they had placed on the platform and began to pull themselves aboard. The locomotive belched and clanked as the train began to move, imperceptibly at first.

Corey turned back to the gate just as the ticket agent waved through a slender young man.

Robert Biggs!

Corey stretched the newspaper above his head, knowing that the others would have no time to reach him before the train pulled out. He dropped the paper to the ground as Biggs pulled himself aboard the accelerating train. Corey sprinted toward the last car, caught the hand rail at its back end, ran alongside for several strides and hauled himself aboard. He turned and looked back to see Rawlings, Missy, and Susan all staring wide-eyed and open-mouthed as the train left them behind.

"Quick!" Missy exclaimed, turning from the receding train toward Jim Rawlings. "Get the car. Susan, go with Agent Rawlings."

"What about you?" Susan asked.

"I'm going to find out where the next stop is. I'll meet you out front! Hurry!"

CHAPTER 53

On the Train

The train continued to accelerate as Corey opened the door at the end of the carriage. He had seen Robert Biggs climb aboard the next car in line, so he hurried down the center aisle as quickly as the rocking of the train along the tracks would allow.

Corey passed by the restroom at the end of the carriage and pushed through the door leading to the opening between the two carriages. Here the clatter of the iron wheels on the rails was louder and the wind buffeting between the cars threatened to snatch off his fedora. He grabbed the brim with one hand as he opened the door to the next car.

Easy now. Don't let him see you looking for him. Corey pulled the door behind him as he stepped into the next car. He was momentarily disoriented when he found all the passengers' couches facing him. He lowered his eyes and began to walk up the aisle, steadying himself with the backs of the seats as he passed. A pair of businessmen occupied the seats on his left. A mother and two young girls sat on the right. Beyond them, the members of what appeared to be a farm family sat on both sides of the aisle, the mother wearing a hand-made flower-print dress, the father in a starched pair of faded blue denim overalls, his face clean-shaven.

Corey passed the farm family and paused, leaning over as if to peer out the window as the countryside glided by. When he stood back up, he caught a glimpse of Robert Biggs. The boy sat in the last aisle seat on the left, just ahead, a seat from which he had a commanding view of the rest of the carriage. He was dressed in a white, long-sleeve cotton shirt and blue pants. He had an open book in his lap, but his eyes were focused on the aisle. Corey, who avoided eye contact, would have preferred to claim a seat nearby from which he could watch the boy and plan his next move but all the other seats were facing away from Biggs. Corey's best option was to claim the vacant seat immediately across the aisle from the boy and wait until the train reached its next stop. Then he could arrest Biggs and hustle him off the train.

When he reached the last row of seats, Corey sidled in to the seat directly across the narrow aisle from Biggs. He took off his hat and held it in his lap. It took all of his concentration not to stare at the boy. Instead, he alternated looks out the window with a careful inspection of the grosgrain ribbon band of his hat.

The door behind him opened with a loud clattering and the rush of air. A blue-suited conductor wearing a watch on a chain, a silver name badge that read LLOYD and the round cap of the Southern Railway appeared from over Corey's shoulder, placed his hand on the back of Biggs's seat and said, "Ticket, please."

Biggs surrendered his ticket without comment. The conductor punched it and handed it back with a quick, "Thank you," then turned to Corey.

"Ticket, please."

Corey looked up and, hidden from Biggs's view by the body of the conductor, laid a finger across his lips. He reached into his pocket and pulled out the leather wallet containing his badge and FBI credentials. As the conductor's eyes widened, Corey jerked his head back toward the door between the cars through which the railroad official had just come.

"Of course, sir," Conductor Lloyd nodded, squeezing his puncher as if he had used it on Corey's nonexistent ticket. He stepped aside to allow Corey to climb out of his seat. Biggs looked up. Corey exited the car, followed by the conductor. They crossed the shifting platform above the couplings and entered the next carriage.

"Thank you for your discretion," Corey began as soon as the door closed behind them. They were standing just outside the restrooms at the end of the carriage. "The young man sitting directly across the aisle from me is wanted for questioning by the FBI. How far is it to the next station?"

The conductor, his mind still trying to catch up with what his eyes were seeing and his ears hearing, hesitated for a moment. "Well, Jordan City is next, but it's just a flag stop. If there's nobody getting on, we won't even slow down much. Then, after that is Gentian, also a flag stop. The first scheduled stop is Flat Rock."

"How far?"

"Ten miles from Columbus. Our scheduled arrival time is 3:46 pm. If we don't get flagged at either of those first two stops, we typically arrive a couple of minutes ahead of schedule."

Corey rubbed his jaw. "All right. Well, you just go about your duties. When we get to Flat Rock, I'll make my move. You make sure the train stays put until I get the suspect off. Clear?"

"Yes sir, whatever you say."

"All right. You go ahead. I'll follow behind you."

The conductor nodded his head and exited the carriage, crossing back over the couplings and into the car he and Corey had left only moments before. Through the small windows in the doors at the end of either carriage, Corey watched Lloyd make his way down the aisle, taking and punching tickets. Corey didn't want to give Biggs any reason to think he and the conductor were in concert, so he waited another minute or so before returning to the carriage and taking his seat. Corey took a deep breath and did a double take.

Robert Biggs's seat was empty.

Missy hurried back through the gate and up to the ticket counter in the lobby of the station.

"Where's the next stop?" she asked a clerk wearing a green-shaded visor.

"The next stop, miss?"

"Yes, yes for the train that just left, the Atlanta train." Missy gripped the edge of the counter, fighting to control her anxiety. Corey was on that train—without any back up—and with a likely killer.

"Here's a copy of the complete timetable, miss." The clerk leaned across the counter and motioned to a metal rack stuffed with yellow pamphlets bearing the Southern Railway banner. "You'll find all the stops along with—"

"Thank you so much!" Missy cried, grabbing a folder and dashing toward the front of the station where Agent Rawlings and Susan were already waiting in the big Lincoln. Missy jumped into the front seat, unfolding the pamphlet as she did so.

"Which way?" Rawlings asked.

"Toward Gentian!" she gasped.

"Where's that?"

Susan piped up from the back seat. "Oh, that's on the edge of town. Turn right here and then the next right and go til you hit Talbotton Road and go right again."

Missy turned in the front seat to give the young passenger a smile. "You seem to know your way around."

"Well, Mama and me used to come to Columbus every year to do my back-to-school shopping. I guess some of it just rubbed off on me."

"You're being a big help, Susan." Missy turned her attention back to the driver. "It says here that the first two stops are only flag stops. I doubt we can get to either in time to wave down the train. The first scheduled station isn't until Flat Rock. Do you know how to get there?"

"No, but there's a Georgia map in the glove box."

Missy opened the compartment and took out a Texaco road map of the state of Georgia. Her eyes raced across the map, quickly finding Columbus and, with Susan's assistance, Flat Rock. "Here it is," she said pointing with her finger. "According to the timetable, the train will arrive there at 3:46, which gives us," she glanced at her watch, "about nine minutes."

Rawlings pressed on the gas and the big car shot forward. Missy looked at her watch again. *It's going to be close!*

Corey fought back a momentary panic. *Think, think!* The train hadn't stopped; it was still chugging along. Biggs couldn't have gotten off without leaping toward a very uncertain landing. And why would he have jumped to start with? Biggs wouldn't have recognized Corey as a law man. Having gotten on the train, following whatever plan he'd devised, why would he abandon it now?

Corey stood at the head of the aisle, his eyes sweeping back and forth over the seat backs in front of him. Maybe he'd changed seats. Up ahead, the conductor checked the last passenger's ticket. Corey caught the conductor's eye and raised his hands in front of him. *Where did he go?* Conductor Lloyd shrugged and shook his head.

Corey pressed his lips together and took a step toward the conductor. *Maybe the kid changed cars.* Then he froze. Robert Biggs exited the rest room and began walking toward him.

Jim Rawlings had challenged every traffic regulation in the books. He had rolled through stop signs, run red lights, crossed the double yellow lines to pass slower cars, and exceeded every posted speed limit—and they were still three minutes from Flat Rock.

"Listen!" Susan squealed from the back seat. "I hear it!"

Missy heard the steam whistle as a train approached a crossing. "Oh, we've got to catch up with them!" The big Lincoln barreled around a curve. Ahead was a railroad crossing, its red lights flashing, the last car of a train sliding out of view behind the trees.

"Think that's it?" Rawlings asked, his question nearly drowned out by the roar of the car's engine as he pressed the gas to the floor.

"I'm betting on it!" Missy shouted as the car shot across the tracks.

Corey had quickly reclaimed his seat, hoping that he hadn't done anything to make the boy suspicious. Biggs returned to his seat, book in hand, and stared out the window.

The train began to slow. At the far end of the car, the conductor pulled his watch from his pocket and checked the time. "Flat Rock!" he called out. "Pulling into Flat Rock!"

"Where you headed?" Corey asked, leaning across the aisle and smiling.

"Atlanta," Biggs replied.

"Me too. How about that. You got some family there?"

"No."

The carriage jerked as the train slowed and the couplings banged together. The train was clearly approaching its stop. Corey looked to the far end of the car and nodded at the conductor, who nodded back.

"Where you going from Atlanta?"

"Washington, or maybe New York," the young man replied without making eye contact. The train stopped. The woman with the two young daughters stood, collected their things and walked up the aisle toward the door just beyond Corey. Corey leaned away from the aisle to give them clearance. As the girls passed, Biggs quickly stood and followed behind them.

Corey hesitated for just a moment. *This isn't Atlanta, kid.* He watched as Biggs followed the mother and daughters out the door and down the steps to the ground. Corey glanced back at the conductor who had turned his attention to greeting the three new passengers boarding at Flat Rock. Corey peered out the window. Biggs was walking away from the train, heading south along the tracks.

Corey set his hat on his head and pushed through the door onto the coupling platform, then down the steps. He reached the ground in time to hear a shrill whistle and see the station agent waving a red flag toward the locomotive. "All aboard!" the man cried.

Corey looked around but didn't see Biggs. *Where'd he go?* Corey walked toward the back of the train. The locomotive huffed, belching black smoke, its powerful wheels straining against the track as the train began to move again. Corey looked south along the tracks. Nothing.

"Hey! Hey!" It was Conductor Lloyd, standing in the doorway of the last carriage. He waved at Corey, beckoning him. "He got back on!"

Corey raced for the last carriage, reaching his fastest pace in three strides. He stretched out his hand for the iron rail of the train's steps but couldn't hold on. He tried again, but the train was accelerating as it reached the end of the passenger apron. Corey lunged—and missed— but a powerful hand grabbed his wrist and pulled him upward. Corey's hand closed around the iron rail, his feet found purchase on the bottom step and he looked up to the smiling face of the conductor.

"You almost missed your train, sir."

"Again!" Corey gasped.

The black smoke of the departing train could be seen above the trees as the big car bumped over the tracks. "Where to?" Rawlings asked, frowning at their near miss.

"Stay on Highway 85. It'll take us to Midland. It's only about three miles," Missy said. "We can catch them this time. We won't be going through any towns between here and there and you can accelerate faster than that train!"

CHAPTER 54

On the Train

"Thanks for your help!" Corey said to Conductor Lloyd, once he caught his breath. The train was gaining speed now. From up ahead, he heard its whistle blast as it approached a crossroads. He started to push past the conductor, but the man placed his hand on Corey's sleeve.

"Take some advice?"

Corey paused. "Sure."

"Well, apparently that boy got spooked. If he saw you get off and then sees you back on the train, he's likely to take off again. My advice is that you wait at the end of this carriage. I'll go on through just like I normally do. If he tries to go through to the next car, I'll make up an excuse to stop him. If he comes this way, you'll be waiting on him. Next stop is only about three minutes away. I'll block the far door and you close on him from this direction. He'll be squeezed in the middle."

Corey didn't have much time to consider the plan before it had to be put in motion. "All right. But don't take chances. He could be dangerous."

Conductor Lloyd laughed. "This is the railroad, sir," he said, producing a set of brass knuckles from one pocket and a pair of handcuffs from the other. "We're used to all kinds of customers."

Thank goodness! Missy thought as the Lincoln pulled up to the Midland railroad crossing. No logging trucks, no cattle crossings, and no school buses had interfered with their white-knuckle race from Flat Rock to

Midland. Agent Rawlings had reached seventy miles per hour at one point, scaring Missy, but delighting Susan who kept squealing, "Faster!" Now, Rawlings pulled the Lincoln to a stop near the tracks, its engine clicking and popping as it began to cool down. From down the tracks to the south, Missy could hear the chugging of the approaching train.

"Good work, Jim!" she said, patting him on the shoulder. "Susan, you stay in the car. I'll hang towards the back of the train, Jim, you take the front. Keep your eyes peeled for Corey and follow his instructions."

Rawlings and Missy got out of the car and approached the track as the train appeared from between the rows of tall pine trees lining the roadbed.

Corey waited just inside the door of the last carriage on the train as it glided to a smooth stop. Corey stepped out onto the coupling platform and peered through the window into the next car. The aisle was clear. Apparently, no one was getting off the train at Midland. He took a deep breath, opened the door and immediately made eye contact with Robert Biggs at the far end of the car.

Uh oh.

Biggs jumped to his feet and spun toward the door behind him. Corey broke into a run—at least as much of one as the narrow aisle allowed. Biggs attempted to push through the door, but, true to his word, Conductor Lloyd had blocked it with his body from the outside. Biggs, the former football player, lowered his shoulder and hit the door with all the strength and skill he'd once employed to punch through his opponent's line. He knocked the conductor backward, causing him to stumble against the railing of the coupling platform, but Lloyd was used to rough customers. Regaining his balance, he socked Biggs in the jaw with the brass knuckles and the boy went down in a heap. There was no resistance as he and Corey handcuffed his hands behind his back.

"Not bad for an old man, eh?" Lloyd said. "What was that kid, a linebacker?"

"No, just a quarterback," Corey said with a grin. "Nice work, Mr. Lloyd!"

The conductor got to his feet and pulled the emergency cord summoning the engineer. By the time he had gotten to the last car, Missy, Rawlings and Susan were standing outside as well, along with a pretty sizeable crowd from the two cars.

"What happened here?" the engineer said, hands on hips. "We've got a schedule to keep."

"Hold on," Corey said, presenting his FBI badge for inspection. "We've got a crime scene here. Your conductor has been assaulted. You can't leave the scene without an investigation being completed and statements taken."

"Where did the assault happen?" the engineer asked, looking from the G-man to the slender, young man in the handcuffs, who was starting to regain consciousness.

"Right here," Corey replied.

"Good. Then we'll take the scene of the crime with us to Atlanta. I'll have a railroad detective meet us at Warm Springs."

"Perfect," Corey said with a smile. He stepped over the supine Robert Biggs and hung out the door to speak to Missy, Rawlings and Susan. "All under control," he said to them. "Meet us at the Warm Springs Depot."

With no stops to make in between Midland and Warm Springs, Jim Rawlings had Missy, Susan, and the Lincoln waiting on the train when it pulled into the station just after five o'clock. Missy—and Susan—smiled when they saw Corey escort the manacled Robert Biggs down the steps and finally off the train for good.

"Did you finish all your statements?" Missy asked.

"Yes. Mr. Lloyd, the conductor, opted not to press local charges, but I had him write a statement about his assistance anyway. We may file additional charges against Mr. Biggs here," Corey said nodding toward his prisoner.

"Additional to what? You haven't told me what I've been charged with," Robert whined. His jaw was swollen and purple from the impact with Lloyd's brass knuckles.

Corey turned to face Biggs. "Robert Biggs, you are charged with violation of the Mann Act. You have the right to consult an attorney and any statements you make can be used to prosecute you."

"What the heck is the Mann Act?"

"It is also known as the White Slave Traffic Act of 1910," Corey said in his most severe voice. "You are charged with violating this act when you drove a young woman over a state line for the purpose of sexual congress."

Robert's mouth hung open. "You mean Susan?" he asked, dumbfounded.

Susan, avoiding eye contact with Robert, whispered in Missy's ear, "What does sexual congress mean?"

By seven o'clock, Joan Roswell was bored and hungry. Throughout the long, hot afternoon, she'd made occasional trips out to the parking lot where Ida was sitting in the Hudson reading Joan's advance copy of *Gone with the Wind*, occasionally making notes in the margins about scenes she'd like to rehearse.

"He's not here," Joan huffed, as the sun touched the upper stories of the west-facing buildings. "He's not here and he's not going to be here. That boy's gone, long gone. Corey Wainwright and Missy LeHand have forgotten all about us. Wait till I tell Hoover about this!"

"Oh c'mon, Joan. They wouldn't forget about us. They owe you too much. You practically broke the case open by finding Susan Woods. I'm no expert, but I'd say that was a nifty piece of detective work. Here, run some dialogue with me. I'll play Scarlett and you play Rhett Butler. Can you do a Southern accent?"

"Ah you kiddin'?" Joan groused. "After a week around this place, Ah'll be lucky if Ah can lose it!"

CHAPTER 55

Warm Springs

"Oh my gosh!" Missy exclaimed, sitting bolt upright. She and Corey Wainwright were on the back porch of the Little White House with the President.

Following their arrival back in Warm Springs, Corey and Biggs by train, the rest by car, Missy had accompanied Corey to the county jail in Greenville where the FBI agent had remanded Robert Biggs to the custody of the sheriff pending arraignment on federal charges.

They had returned to the Little White House and found the President and Grace Tully on the back porch, enjoying cocktails and toasting the birth of Nell Gaines's healthy baby girl. The President quickly put his martini shaker back into action for the newcomers. "Eleanor called a little while ago," he said. "Both mother and child are doing well, and she plans to stay on for a few more days. She'll be delighted to know there's a good chance Nell will be exonerated."

Over cold drinks, Missy and Corey had shared the account of the manhunt and chase, giving plenty of credit to the fearless conductor on the train.

"Well done, well done!" the President had said at the conclusion, clapping his hands. "What did Joan Roswell say when she found out she had sat at the bus station all afternoon for nothing?"

That's when Missy exclaimed, jumped to her feet and ran back into the house.

"Missy!" the President called, turning in his chair. "Where on earth are you going?"

"To call the bus station in Columbus!"

"Mr. President, thank you for your hospitality," Corey said, shaking Franklin Roosevelt's hand as he prepared to leave later that evening. "I very much enjoyed the good meal and the company even more so. What did you say that dish is called?"

"Country Captain," the President said, calling out to Daisy Bonner, "You've won another convert, Daisy!" The cook came through the pantry and smiled at the compliment. "You can try all you want to, Mr. President," she said. "I ain't givin' out my secret recipe."

Roosevelt guffawed. "A lady of discretion! Good for you, Daisy!" He turned back to Corey. "It's a treat for me to hear from soldiers on the front-lines of life and to learn about the good work being done by the Bureau," said the President, whose favorite leisure reading was crime fiction. Corey had shared details about some of the FBI's most wanted men and women and anecdotes—always favorable—about his boss Hoover. "I hope to see you again soon. Missy, ask Jim Rawlings to drive Corey back to the hotel, would you?"

"Of course. I'll show you out." Missy escorted Corey through the house and out into the cool night air where the crickets and tree frogs were engaged in an endless contest to determine which group could make more noise.

"Quite a fellow, your boss," Corey said, as Missy slipped her hand into the agent's.

"He is," she agreed, leaning her cheek against his shoulder. "And he took a real liking to you. He can see right through phonies." Corey chuckled, drawing a sideways glance from Missy. "What?"

"I'm sure he enjoyed some of my stories, particularly the ones about San Francisco, but if he likes me, I think it has more to do with the company I'm keeping."

"Flirt," Missy said.

"Guilty," Corey whispered as he leaned over and kissed her. For a moment, all the night sounds receded, and the only thing Missy could hear was the pulsing of her heart. When Corey pulled back, he had a smile on his face. "That was even better than dessert."

"Why, Agent Wainwright! What liberties you take!"

"All for the good of the country, ma'am." Corey tipped Missy's chin up with his forefinger. "I wish our jobs didn't keep us so darn busy. I'd like to see you more often when we get back to Washington."

"Want a little help with that wish?" Missy asked.

"What do you mean?"

Missy reached into her pocket and removed a folded dinner napkin. "Daisy slipped me this," she said, laughing. She unwrapped the napkin, producing a wishbone from the chicken Daisy had used in the Country Captain. "She knows how superstitious we Irish are. Make a wish and pull."

Corey grinned and grasped one side of the wishbone, Missy the other. Just then they heard a twig snap on the lawn. It was Agent Rawlings.

"Oh, Jim," Missy said, palming the wishbone. "I was just about to come looking for you to take Agent Wainwright back to the hotel. He's had quite a day!"

CHAPTER 56

MY DAY
By Eleanor Roosevelt

Millegeville, Georgia—When my husband was governor of New York, he often sent me to tour public institutions, such as prisons and lunatic asylums, and report back to him. He was never satisfied with what I saw on guided tours, but insisted I go on my own into the kitchens and lift the lids on the pots to see what was being served to the inmates. In this way, we were able to address serious problems.

It is unfortunate that I cannot be as influential here in Georgia, where I have been visiting the Georgia State Prison in Milledgeville. If I were the governor here, I should be ashamed for anyone to see this place.

Never have I seen an institution that offers less hope for rehabilitation. The dormitories, especially those of the colored women, are unfit for habitation—rat-infested and filthy, with inadequate sanitary facilities. The women are fed scant rations that enable them to barely hold body and soul together, while they work long hours under the hot sun. Prisoners are not offered any classes that would fit them for suitable employment upon their release, except that involving a hoe and a gunny sack.

I am spending time with a young woman who had the misfortune to give birth in the infirmary here. Her child is beautiful, and I am so touched that she has been named for me and for my husband's secretary, Miss LeHand. All I can say is that poor little Eleanor Marguerite and her mother face a very bleak future, and my heart aches for them. Prison should certainly be a place of punishment for bad deeds, but our Constitution prohibits "cruel and unusual punishment." It is my belief that such conditions apply here in Milledgeville.

I have now presented the facts to Governor Talmadge and hope he will make his own inspection. Or better yet, send his wife!

FRIDAY, MAY 22, 1936

CHAPTER 57

Warm Springs

Corey Wainwright checked the time again. He'd been told to be ready and waiting in front of the Hotel Warm Springs by eight-thirty Thursday morning. It was eight-twenty-five and Corey was standing with his hat in his hand enjoying the cooler morning air. It was almost as if the sun was waiting for the little town to come fully awake before it decided to climb any higher.

Corey wasn't sure what to expect, only that he was to accompany Mr. Cornelius A. Bates III on a visit to Greenville to see the district attorney who had prosecuted the case against Nell Gaines. He'd never met Bates before, never even heard of him until yesterday when the President said the Atlanta lawyer was taking the case. From the conversation at the Little White House, Corey figured the guy must be pretty bright, but it would take more than just smarts to get the Gaines case reopened. It would take political acumen, a little luck, color-blind justice, and a legal adversary with an open mind—none of which had been in evidence so far during Corey's Southern sojourn.

Corey looked down the street toward the rumble of a big engine. A gun-metal gray Packard sedan with a long hood and wide, whitewall tires pulled up in front of him. A chauffeur wearing a blue suit, matching cap, black tie, and spotless white shirt hopped out of the car.

"Agent Wainwright?" the chauffeur asked, stepping around to the passenger side and opening the rear door.

Corey nodded and climbed into the car. "Good morning," he said to the occupant of the spacious back seat.

"Good morning, Agent Wainwright," the man said, offering his hand. The hand was soft, but muscular. *Like a rock wrapped in velvet*, Corey thought. "I'm Cornelius A. Bates III. Thank you for your punctuality. It's a mark of courtesy that one doesn't always encounter, but which I greatly value."

"Nice to meet you, Mr. Bates." Corey noticed copies of the Atlanta *Constitution* and the *Wall Street Journal*, both neatly folded, resting on the seat. "You must have had to leave Atlanta pretty early to get to Warm Springs by eight-thirty."

"Indeed. Kevin and I were rolling at 6 a.m., but the early departure gave me a chance to read the latest news and the time to stop at this wonderful little diner in Fayetteville where they serve fresh eggs and bacon with biscuits and honey." The chauffeur was back in his seat and the big Packard began to move again. Bates chuckled. "For a breakfast like that, I'd leave early every day. Of course, leaving in the morning darkness has another advantage too."

"What's that?"

"You get on your way ahead of the traffic. Atlanta has a quarter of a million residents, and it seems like every one of them has a car, though I know that's not possible. Still, Atlanta traffic has got to be the worst in the South, maybe even the country!"

"Have you been to Washington lately?" Corey asked with a laugh.

"Point well taken," Bates said, smiling. "Tell me, Agent Wainwright, how you came to be mixed up in this whole sordid Gaines affair. Pardon the pun."

Corey proceeded to fill in the gaps of Bates's cursory knowledge of the case, beginning with his summons to Mr. Hoover's office and immediate dispatch to Warm Springs just a few days earlier. He shared a synopsis of the trial transcript and the utter lack of effort from Mrs.

Gaines's court-appointed defense attorney. As he talked, he appraised his companion. Cornelius Bates was in his early forties, with a mane of wavy dark brown hair streaked with gray that was a little too long to conform with the fashion of the day. He had brown eyes and a full face. He was neither fat nor thin and his three-piece cream-colored linen suit was impeccably tailored. He wore gold cuff links, a red tie decorated with blue diamonds, and a white silk shirt. His gold watch chain was adorned with a small gold key and a tiny porcine fob. A Panama hat sat beside him on the seat.

"Yesterday, we were finally able to apprehend the younger Biggs," Corey said. "He's in the county jail awaiting arraignment on federal charges."

The attorney frowned. "What charges? Everything in play would seem to be a state or local offense."

"We've got him for violation of the Mann Act."

"The Mann Act!" Bates snorted. "You federal boys trot that old nag out of the barn so often I'm surprised she can still run. I suppose you'd be willing to drop the federal charges in exchange for his cooperation on the Gaines case?"

"Yes sir. I think that's a safe assumption."

"So, you have some legal leverage with the elusive Mr. Biggs." Bates stared out the window as the car passed a field of two-foot high corn. "What we need is leverage with the D.A."

CHAPTER 58

Greenville

The Meriwether County Courthouse was the most imposing structure in town, sitting as it did in the middle of a central square. Red brick in the classical revival style, it had been built just after the turn of the century and sported clocks on four faces on the eight-sided cupola that capped the two-story building. Kevin steered the Packard to a halt in front of the columned west entrance to the building. He got out of the car and opened the rear door on Bates's side.

"Thank you, Kevin. I suspect we'll be here about an hour, maybe a little longer."

"Very good, sir."

Corey hadn't waited for his door to be opened for him. By the time Kevin turned his way, the agent was already standing on the curb beside Bates.

"Shall we?" Bates said with a quick nod toward the courthouse entrance. As they walked up the wide sidewalk, Bates continued, "What do you know about Mr. Osburn, the district attorney?"

"Nothing. I'm in unfamiliar territory here. I've never had any dealings at all with the judicial system of the State of Georgia."

"Quite a bit in federal court I'm sure."

"Yes sir."

"Good. Well, let me take the lead with Osburn. If there are some specifics that you feel may be material to our discussion, please speak up. And don't be offended if I appear to monopolize our side of the conversation. Osburn has a good reputation, but many of the officials in our smaller towns become resentful at what they view as federal interference in local affairs." Bates chuckled and leaned toward Corey as they walked up the courthouse steps. "Many of them feel the same way about city folks from Atlanta!"

The district attorney's suite of offices was on the second floor, on the opposite corner from the courtroom. Bates presented himself and Corey to the secretary in the outer office who escorted them down the hall to a closed door, the upper half of which was composed of frosted glass on which was painted:

MICHAEL J. OSBURN
District Attorney

The secretary knocked on the door and was greeted with a muffled reply. She pushed the door open a crack and announced the two visitors. Another muffled response and she pushed the door fully open and stepped aside, nodding to Bates and Corey.

Michael Osburn was an ordinary-looking man with very short gray hair. He had sharp features dominated by intelligent brown eyes which peered out from behind wire-rimmed glasses. Corey judged that the trim attorney was in his late forties.

"It's not often that we have such distinguished visitors," Osburn said with a smile as he stepped around his desk to greet his guests. "Would you like some coffee?"

"No, thank you," Bates replied as Corey scanned the surroundings.

"Mr. Wainwright?"

"No, thanks," Corey said, continuing to scan the office. He noted the desk with neatly stacked file folders next to an even row of sharpened pencils. Behind the desk, flanking a dark wooden credenza stood an American and a Georgia flag, and on the wall a framed diploma from the

University of Georgia School of Law. On top of the credenza were several photographs, one of which appeared to be of Osburn and his family, another, an older picture of Osburn in a naval uniform.

"Have a seat," Osburn said pointing to a pair of wooden arm chairs with red leather seats. He wore a crisply starched white shirt and a red-and-black striped tie. His light tan suit jacket was hanging on a hook on the back of his office door.

"First of all," Bates said, sliding forward to the edge of his seat, "thank you for taking the time to see us. I can only imagine how busy you are."

"Always happy to assist one of our profession's more prominent members," Osburn said with a smile that didn't quite reach all the way to his eyes.

"I'll get right to the point. We're here about the Gaines trial. Last year, Nell Gaines was found guilty of the murder of her employer, a Mr. Wilton Biggs."

Osburn nodded. "Of course. I remember it well. Rather sensational case for our little town. What's your interest in the case?" he asked, a challenge in his voice. "You're rather far afield from Atlanta."

"Only that justice be served," Bates replied with a slight smile.

"The good people of Meriwether County are confident in the verdict that was returned, and the sentence pronounced." Osburn's voice now held a definite edge.

"As they have every right to be based on the evidence that was known at the time."

"At the time?"

"Yes," Bates said. "Yesterday, Agent Wainwright arrested Robert Biggs. He's in the county jail. He's charged with violation of the Mann Act."

Osburn snorted. "Susan Woods?"

"Yes sir."

"It's a small town. Word spreads pretty quickly." Osburn nudged one of the pencils on his desk back into place. "What's this got to do with the Gaines case and with my office?"

Bates cleared his throat, leaned forward just slightly and fixed his host with a steady gaze. "Nell Gaines claims Robert Biggs, and Susan Woods too for that matter, were present when Wilton Biggs was killed. In fact, she says that Robert Biggs killed his father, not her."

Osburn stared at Bates without saying a word, picked up one of his pencils and toyed with it, thumping the eraser softly on the desk. "You have a reputation as a brilliant advocate, Mr. Bates. As for you, Agent Wainwright, I have only the highest regard for the FBI. But I'm sure both of you can understand why I put little credence in the post-conviction claims of a colored woman sitting on death row for murdering a white man. One would expect a claim like that, if true, to have come out at her trial. It's a little late in the day for that kind of thing, isn't it?"

"Mr. Osburn, please don't take offense at this, but not all our fellow members of the Georgia Bar maintain the same high standards set by you and your office," Bates said smoothly.

"You mean Melvin Jugg? Judge Johnson tosses Melvin cases that are either hopeless or can't be fouled up. Preferably both."

Bates leaned back in his seat. "Yes. Only this time he got a case that wasn't hopeless and had plenty of room to be fouled up. Nell Gaines says she told Jugg that the younger Biggs and Miss Woods were present at the crime scene. As he didn't do anything with that information, neither Robert nor Susan has ever made a formal statement about the case, about what they saw, heard, and did. In fact, they disappeared immediately after the murder and

Mr. Jugg made no effort whatsoever to find them." He paused, delicately clearing his throat.

"I'm listening," Osburn said. He had stopped tapping the pencil.

"If they were there, then maybe they can shed some light on what really happened. A woman's life is in the balance, Mr. Osburn. A woman with two small children, who has just given birth to a third who may well be the child of Wilton Biggs. Discovery of this suppressed evidence surely merits an interview with Susan Woods and Robert Biggs." Bates paused. "And a stay of the execution of Nell Gaines."

Osburn leaned back in his leather chair, pressing his hands together and bringing them up to his lips. "You don't ask for much, do you, Mr. Bates?"

"Young Biggs is in custody, Mr. Osburn. Maybe it comes to nothing. Maybe Nell Gaines is making all this up to save her guilty skin. Maybe not. The legal profession in the State of Georgia is a rather small community. You were a summa cum laude graduate of University of Georgia School of Law and chose to return to your home town to serve the people here. The book on Michael Osburn is that he believes in the law and wants to see justice done."

"I thank you for the compliment, Mr. Bates, but this isn't an Atlanta case and it's not a federal case. It's a local case and—"

"I am sure the case of the Scottsboro boys is still fresh in your mind, Mr. Osburn," Bates said.

Osburn sighed. "I don't think there's a district attorney in the South who is not reminded regularly of the Scottsboro trial," he said. The notorious case, in which nine young black men had been convicted of rape on flimsy evidence in Alabama, had been appealed to the U.S. Supreme Court, which had ordered a new trial because the defendants had inadequate legal counsel.

"Well, I don't think we want to be made an example of here in Georgia, as were the good people of Alabama," Bates continued. "But it goes farther than that. I suspect," he paused to shake his head again, "no, I *believe*, that you, like me, like Agent Wainwright here, are more concerned with seeing that justice is done than with simple expediency. This isn't about doing the popular thing. It's not about getting reelected or keeping clear of the U.S. Supreme Court. This is about doing the right thing. It's about making sure the system—imperfect as it is—protects the innocent and punishes the guilty. It's about living up to the high ethical standards that are part of what attracted us to the bar in the first place. We're only asking you to take an extra look. That's not too much to ask when a woman's life, a mother's life, is on the line, is it?"

Osburn stared at his guest. "No, Mr. Bates. I reckon it's not."

CHAPTER 59

Warm Springs

Joan walked up to Georgia Hall, hoping she could catch Dr. Raper before he began to see patients. She found him in the cafeteria, just finishing his breakfast.

"Oh, hello, Dr. Raper!" she cooed, sucking in her cheek to form a dimple. "How are you this very beautiful morning?"

"I'm fine, Miss Roswell," the young doctor said. "Have a seat and join me in a last cup of coffee. Where's Miss Lupino this morning?"

"She decided to have breakfast at the cottage before she begins her therapy session," Joan improvised. "Dr. Raper, you've been so awfully kind to let Ida and me use your car this week. I wonder if I could ask a teensy-weensy favor?"

Dr. Raper looked a bit wary, but said, "Of course, if I can."

"Well," Joan said, "Ida has been such a darling this week, sharing her cottage with me and helping me with my article on the Warm Springs Foundation, I wanted to go shopping for a little thank-you gift. But I don't think I'll find anything suitable in Warm Springs, so I was thinking of driving up to Greenville. Could I possibly use your car, just for the morning?"

Dr. Raper hesitated for just a second. "I think that would be fine," he said, "though I do want it back early this afternoon. I have a date this evening, and I wanted to get it washed before I pick her up."

"Of course," Joan said automatically. *You could get it washed by then, but you sure can't get the paint touched up or the windshield replaced.* The last bit of damage had occurred on the road home from Phenix City, when they had an unfortunate encounter with a gravel truck. She batted her eyes. "Who is your date? Anyone I know?"

Dr. Raper grinned. "In fact, you interviewed her for your story. Janice Howe, the prettiest physio on the campus."

"Ooooh!" Joan squealed. "She is a lovely girl! Aren't you the lucky one!"

Dr. Raper chuckled. "To be honest, the ratio of women to men here is so high that the Hunchback of Notre Dame could probably get a date, but I do feel pretty lucky."

Joan stood and gave the nice young doctor a peck on the cheek. "Thank you so much, Dr. Raper. I'll have the car back to you before lunch, I promise."

Joan covered the ten or so miles to Greenville while the sun was still fairly low in the morning sky, before the day had had a chance to turn hot. She'd enjoyed the cool breeze in her hair as she peered through the cracked windshield. *When I strike it big, I'm going to buy a car like this one and drive all over Hollywood with the top down!*

As she drove, she turned over the story she was building in her mind: "Justice Served Southern Style." It had the elements of an award-winning series: the in-depth features that would address the crime, replete with the taboo sexual angles; the trial and wrongful conviction; the race issue; the damage to the families involved; and ultimately—she hoped—the just resolution of the entire matter. Of course, that last part had yet to play out. It seemed to Joan that catching Robert Biggs was a large step in the right direction, but that freeing Nell Gaines still depended on extracting a confession from the actual killer of Wilton Biggs. What a tangled web!

Her plan this morning was to catch Velma Biggs before she left her house for her volunteer work at the Foundation. Joan remembered from their earlier interview how much more at ease—and talkative—Velma had been at home than on the Foundation's grounds. She was eager to capture Velma's reaction to the return of her son; she imagined the woman would be pleased that her baby was safe, if not exactly ecstatic that he'd returned to his hometown cuffed and charged with a federal crime.

Joan pulled into the gravel driveway just as Velma emerged from the side door of the house. She had her purse on her arm and keys in her hand as Joan braked to a halt just behind Velma's Chevrolet.

Joan put on her friendly smile and stepped from the Hudson. "Good morning, dear!" she called out, pen and pad in hand, ready for an impromptu interview.

Velma stopped in her tracks and stared at Joan, the color draining from her fleshy face. "You evil woman!" she spat. "You got my boy arrested and thrown in jail. How could you do that to me? And after you pretended to be my friend! 'I'm a good listener,' you said. You she-devil!"

Velma's face was changing from pale to flushed as her anger magnified. She slowly advanced on Joan, shouting at the top of her lungs.

"You caused all my problems! You just had to go and find that little tramp, didn't you? That low-down little slut! She tempted my boy, just like Eve with Adam! She's no better than a common harlot, leading my boy to sin and ruin. And you... you," Velma pointed her finger in Joan's face, "if you're not off my property by the time I count to three, I'll throw you off myself!"

"Now, Velma, dear," Joan said, retreating a step. "I understand you're upset. That's only natural, dear, with your son in jail." Velma let out a mournful sound. "But the good news is that Robert's alive and safe. You don't have to be fearful for him anymore."

"Don't have to be fearful? He's in jail, charged with a federal crime, you idiot. One!" Velma began to count. "And it's your fault! You had to stick your nose into other people's business. You couldn't leave bad enough alone. You had to have your precious little story for your gossip-mongering, city folks who go to work in offices and never put in a real day's labor in their lives. Two!"

"Calm down, Velma, and give me your side of the story!" Joan shouted, hoping to shock the older woman into gaining control of her emotions.

"Don't tell me what to do! Three!" Velma lunged forward, swinging her purse and catching Joan on the side of her head. The reporter's pen and pad flew from her hand as she was knocked off balance. "Get out of here, you witch!" Velma shoved Joan with both her hands, sending the reporter sprawling on the dew-wet grass beside the driveway. She pulled back her leg to kick Joan, then stopped. An eerie smile replaced the mask of anger on Velma's face. She turned and stalked to the Chevrolet, climbing in as Joan scrambled to her feet.

Joan brushed herself off. She'd torn the elbow of her blouse in the fall and her stockings were a mess, but she was otherwise unhurt. She bent over to retrieve her pad and pen and heard Velma's car crank to life. *I can take a hint. Especially when it's accompanied by violence.* Joan started toward the driver's side of the Hudson just as Velma shifted into gear. She popped the Chevy's clutch and the car lurched backward, slamming into Dr. Raper's Hudson with a sickening crunch of metal.

Joan gaped at the damage as Velma put the Chevrolet into first gear and pulled forward. *Holy... I've got to get out of here. And I've got to get this car out of here!* Joan dashed for the driver's side door.

Velma shifted into reverse again and hit the gas, sending the Chevy's rear bumper into the grill of the Hudson. Another loud crash was accompanied by the scattering of debris as one of the Hudson's headlights shattered. While Velma drove forward again, Joan dove behind the wheel, turned the key and pressed the starter. The Hudson's engine coughed to life. Velma reversed again, angling her path to hit the other headlight. Joan was addled under the pressure, lifting her foot off the clutch too quickly. The engine coughed and died, but not before the car jumped backwards, spoiling Velma's aim. As Velma pulled forward again, Joan restarted the Hudson and this time managed to reach the street, before shifting into first gear and spattering gravel as the Hudson squealed away.

She's gone batty, Joan thought, staring in the rear-view mirror as the battered back end of the Chevrolet stopped at the end of the driveway. *Completely batty! Oh, Lord, what am I going to tell poor Dr. Raper?*

"Think he'll do it?" Corey asked as he and Bates walked along the oak-shaded sidewalk surrounding the courthouse.

Bates shrugged. He held his coat thrown over one shoulder, a concession to the mounting midday heat. "Maybe yes, maybe no. Whatever course he chooses, he'll have to make his decision soon. Gaines's execution won't long be delayed."

"What's our next step?"

"In a perfect world, we'd wait on Mr. Osburn to do the right thing and everything would work out just fine."

"We wait?" Corey pulled up short. Bates stopped and turned to face him.

"In a perfect world, yes. But, of course, we live in a world of mortals and miscreants. While we await the good Mr. Osburn's next move, we continue to move our pieces around the board as well. We don't have the power and machinery of the state behind us. We can't stay the execution, commute the sentence, overturn the conviction, but we're not without weapons."

"Such as?"

"First off, we need to determine if lawyer Jugg took any statement from Gaines and if so, does it still exist. We could use such a statement to allege ineffective assistance of counsel and request a new trial. The problem there is time. We haven't got much. We also interview Woods and Biggs. We've got to know what happened above the garage. You, Agent Wainwright, are the key to Biggs. He's your prisoner. I'd appreciate the opportunity to participate in your questioning of Biggs, in an unofficial capacity, of course."

"Unofficially, no problem," Corey agreed at once.

Bates wiped his forehead with his linen handkerchief. "And then, we use the press. The problem, of course, is that in this corner of Dixie, a sympathetic press is often hard to come by. We need someone who will at least appear to be impartial, someone with access to the wire services."

"I might know just the person," Corey said, a grin tugging at the corner of his mouth.

CHAPTER 60

Warm Springs

"A favor, dear? From me?"

"That's right. Mr. Bates and I have a small request to make." Corey had introduced the Atlanta lawyer to Joan after they'd arrived back at Warm Springs. Now, Joan's green eyes were flashing between the two men, the handsome FBI agent and the rich-looking lawyer. *What a pleasing variety.*

"Why, Corey Wainwright," Joan said, cocking her head to the side and smiling, "you know I'm always willing to do you a favor."

Corey shot a glance toward Bates, smiled, and said, "I told you Miss Roswell would help."

"In return for exclusive access to the suspects, witnesses, and the history of your involvement in the case." Joan held her smile while she reached into her purse for a Chesterfield. She pulled it out and inserted it into her ebony cigarette holder and stuck it in her mouth.

"Allow me," Bates said smoothly, pulling a gold lighter from his pocket.

"How chivalrous!" The lighter flared and Joan puffed. She took a long, refreshing drag, leaned back and exhaled. "Do we have an agreement?"

Bates looked at Corey and raised his eyebrows. Corey swallowed and nodded. "Yes. And I'll make sure that Mr. Hoover understands how you've once again assisted the Bureau."

"Wonderful, dear." Joan's eyes played between the two men. "Let's get started."

By mid-afternoon, Corey, Joan, and Bates were back in Greenville, sitting in the Diner on the Square at a booth near the back of the restaurant. Lunch was over and the lawyers, clerks, and others having business before the county court had returned to the courthouse across the street leaving the diner empty except for the three out-of-towners.

"Here's how I'd like this to work," Bates said, setting his bell-shaped Coke glass back on the table. "Agent Wainwright does the questioning. He's in charge. He makes his Mann Act case, which shouldn't be too tough based on what the girl has already told us. Then, he starts asking questions about the murder. Miss Roswell," Bates paused, looking across the table.

"Joan, dear."

"Joan. You're our stenographer. You take good notes, which you get to share, but we leave the questioning to Agent Wainwright."

"And what about you, dear?" Joan asked.

"Hopefully, I can sit and listen. I won't ask a question if I don't have to." Bates pulled the watch from his vest pocket and flipped open its lid. "Two forty-five." He placed fifty cents on the table and stood, retrieving his coat from a hook on the side of the booth. "Let's go."

CHAPTER 61

Greenville

Corey Wainwright, Cornelius Bates, and Joan Roswell stood in the corridor until Robert Biggs was escorted into the interview room by a deputy. There was only one such room in the Meriwether County Jail and it was small. Corey had had to borrow two straight-backed, cane-bottom chairs from outside the courtroom on the second floor for his companions. Only hard work by an eight-inch oscillating fan mounted high in the corner of the room made the space bearable. The open, ground-level window set into the upper third of the wall provided natural light and, despite the bars covering it, let in some fresh air as well.

"You can remove his handcuffs," Corey said curtly. The deputy did so, then placed his hand on Biggs's shoulder and guided him to the uncomfortable-looking chair on the opposite side of the narrow wooden table.

"I'll be outside in the hallway, cap'n," the deputy said, pulling the door closed behind him.

Corey nodded to the others and they took their seats. Corey took his time, removing his coat and draping it across the back of his chair. He had had to check his Bureau-issue pistol with the sheriff, but his black leather shoulder holster was a stark reminder of his authority.

"In case you've forgotten, Mr. Biggs, I'm Special Agent Wainwright of the Federal Bureau of Investigation. You're charged with violation of the White Slave Traffic Act of 1910, more commonly known as the Mann Act. As

I told you yesterday, you have the right to an attorney. Now, I'd like to ask you some questions."

Robert Biggs stared across the table at the FBI man. "Who are these other people?"

"Friends."

"Mine," Robert asked, pausing, "or yours?"

"Did you drive your family's Buick across the Chattahoochee River into Phenix City, Alabama on September tenth of last year?"

"Yes. There's nothing wrong with that is there? This is still a free country, isn't it? A man can go where he wants to, can't he?"

"Were you alone?"

"Why do you ask?"

"Susan Woods says that you drove her across the state line into Alabama on September tenth. Is she telling the truth?"

"Sure," Robert answered looking away from his questioner and staring out the barred window.

"How long were you in Alabama?"

"Until yesterday when you arrested me on the train." Robert turned his attention back to the FBI man and smirked. "Don't you remember?"

"And how long was Susan Woods with you?"

"She left around the middle of March."

"Did you live together between your arrival in Phenix City and her departure?"

"Of course."

"Where did you reside?"

"At first, we lived in a motor court. Then we moved into an apartment."

"This was the apartment on Fourth Avenue?"

"That's right."

"And did you and Miss Woods, during the time you lived together, engage in sexual relations?"

The silence in the room was marred only by the scratching of Joan's pen across her pad.

"A gentleman never answers a question like that," Robert said finally, shaking his head, his eyes fixed on his questioner.

"Don't mistake yourself for a gentleman, Mr. Biggs. Answer my question."

"I will not."

"Susan Woods says that you had sexual relations. Numerous times. Are you saying she's a liar?"

"I have never known Susan to lie."

"Not even about going to the picture show on the night of September tenth with you?"

"We did go to the show."

"But you didn't stay. You left and went to your house. Isn't that right?"

"Susan told you this?"

"Yes. She said that the two of you went upstairs to the room above the garage. Is that a truthful statement, or has the trustworthy Miss Woods begun to spin yarns?"

"I told you, Susan doesn't lie."

"Well, that's interesting, because Susan told us that you attacked your father with a big knife of some kind," Corey said. She hadn't really said that, not exactly, but Biggs didn't know that and since he'd vouched twice now for her veracity, Corey risked taking a little liberty with what the girl had really said.

Robert dropped his eyes to his folded hands resting on the table top.

"True or false, Mr. Biggs?"

"What difference does it make? He's dead. You aren't going to bring him back. Nobody is."

"It matters because an innocent woman has a date with the electric chair."

"Nell? She's not innocent." Biggs sneered, his countenance darkened with anger.

"So, you're saying that Susan is lying, that Nell Gaines killed your father?" Corey's voice rose in tenor.

"I'm just saying that she's not innocent."

Corey leaned forward, his palms on the table, his voice quiet now. "But she's innocent of killing your father, isn't she, son?"

"Why should I help you?" Robert asked, his voice catching in his throat.

"Nell Gaines didn't kill your father. She knows that, and he knows that, God rest his soul. But you're the only person who can actually unravel this unholy mess, Robert. You're the only one who can set things right again, the only one who can save an innocent woman's life."

Robert sat quietly, as if contemplating his response, then spat out his words: "That black whore led my father to his judgement. If she hadn't bewitched him, he'd still be alive today."

"But she didn't kill him, did she, son?" Robert stared at the table. "She wouldn't have killed the father of her new daughter, would she?"

Robert's head jerked up as if it were mounted on a spring. "What?"

"You didn't know?" Corey asked, with feigned surprise. "You didn't know she was pregnant?"

"Nell?"

"Yes. She just gave birth to a baby girl—your half-sister—in prison. And now that little baby, who truly *is* innocent, is about to be deprived of her mother all because of you. Imagine what that child's life will be like without her mother, Robert. Her father's already gone. Of course, she'll have a big brother, but he's likely to be locked away serving ten years in a federal prison—unless you cooperate with us, son." Corey watched Biggs's face. "What d'ya say Robert?" he said softly. "You're a Christian man. Do the right thing."

From behind him, Corey heard Cornelius Bates clear his throat. "Thou shalt not bear false witness," he said. "Exodus, chapter 20, verse 16."

Robert's eyes darted to Bates's, then back to Corey's. Joan's pen stopped scratching on the page. Everyone waited for the next person to speak.

CHAPTER 62

Greenville

"No sir, no sir," Michael Osburn insisted into the telephone, "I haven't had any contact from anyone at the White House. The closest I got to that was an FBI agent who came along with Bates." Osburn listened for a moment then replied, "Robert Biggs was his arrest." Another pause. "They brought up the Scottsboro case." He held the phone away from his ear as the governor let loose with some loud and colorful language.

Osburn had closed the door of his office and instructed his secretary to hold all his calls after Cornelius Bates III and Corey Wainwright had left. He had needed time to think. By then, he was already resolved to what he had to do. The harder question was how to do it, what careful words he should choose and what logic he should employ when he called Atlanta. He'd spent an hour thinking through the conversation he was now having.

"No, sir, I'm not saying she's innocent. That's not what I'm saying. I haven't said anything like that and I'm not going to, at least not until I have a chance to question all the witnesses myself." He listened again. "That's exactly what I intend to do, sir. My—our—reputation for justice is at risk here. We can't leave this kind of thing up to the incompetent public defenders of the world. Why, if the Yankee press ever got hold of this and we hadn't taken prudent steps we'd end up with the Department of Justice crawling all over Georgia, just like in Alabama. It'd be the worst federal incursion since Sherman."

Osburn picked up the phone base and stood as close to his desktop fan as he could, enjoying the cooling sensation of the air blowing over his damp forehead. "A stay. That's all I'm asking for, sir. Give me a week—or just give me three days—but give me a chance to see if there's something to this story that Cornelius Bates is telling. Give me a chance to find out what, if anything, Mrs. Gaines's lawyer hid from the court. What's the worst that could happen?" Osburn answered his own question. "The worst that can happen is that we delay the execution by a few days. Even in that situation, we—you—get credit for being diligent and thoughtful and for going the extra mile to ensure justice is served. And if we find that she didn't kill Biggs, well, then we avoid an unjust execution that none of us want—and maybe save our souls a little grief as well."

Osburn stopped talking. He'd presented his most eloquent case for doing what he considered right. Now it was up to Governor Eugene Talmadge to make his decision.

"In light of this startling new evidence, we're calling on Governor Talmadge to stay the execution of Nell Gaines. We're calling on District Attorney Osburn to reopen the case. The people of Meriwether County deserve to know the full facts of this case and they—and Nell Gaines—demand a system of justice that protects the innocent and serves the best interests of all the people." It was late afternoon when Cornelius A. Bates III stood on the top step of the courthouse looking down at the reporters who had gathered for his hastily-called press conference. He wasn't concerned that only two had shown up. While one was from the *Vindicator*, the county's hometown paper and was unlikely to make much of the story, the other reporter was Joan Roswell, and Cornelius Bates knew where her sympathies lay.

"I'll be happy to answer your questions."

"How'd you get onto this case?" the *Vindicator* editor asked, his pencil poised above a lined pad.

"Various contacts of mine informed me that there were some startling irregularities in Mrs. Gaines's case. When I reviewed the trial transcript, I was horrified that any Georgian should be subjected to such inadequate legal defense." The last thing Bates intended was to invoke the name of Franklin Roosevelt and touch off an internecine conflict among Georgia Democrats.

"How come none of these claims came out at the trial?"

"Even the most cursory review of the trial record reveals the stunning incompetence of Mrs. Gaines's defense." Bates hated to go after a fellow member of the bar, but his response was calculated to enflame passions about the case and as a result, generate as much attention as possible. With the national reach of the article Joan would write, Governor Talmadge would soon begin to interpret that attention as pressure—and it was Talmadge who had to make the next move.

"You think the governor will intervene?" the *Vindicator* editor asked.

"We are well acquainted with Governor Talmadge's long-standing commitment to a just and fair judiciary and to seeing that it serves all Georgians. I am personally confident that the governor will carefully consider the merits of this case and will employ the full authority of his office to redress this miscarriage of justice."

"What if he doesn't?" Joan asked, drawing a look from the local reporter.

"Then an innocent woman will soon be executed for the crime of another, and three innocent children, including a tiny baby, will be deprived of their mother."

SATURDAY, MAY 23, 1936

CHAPTER 63

NEW EVIDENCE POINTS TO INNOCENCE
Young Mother Awaiting Electric Chair Has Cause for Hope

By Joan Roswell, Special to the AP—Greenville, Georgia—The arrest of the son of a murder victim in this small west Georgia town has surfaced doubts about the conviction of the murderess awaiting execution in Georgia's electric chair.

Robert Biggs, the eighteen-year-old son of Wilton Biggs, a prominent local businessman found hacked to death by a machete last September, was arrested two days ago on federal charges unrelated to his father's murder. In statements made to authorities following his arrest, the younger Biggs, who disappeared on the night of his father's death, admitted that he was present at the time and place of the murder.

Twenty-eight-year-old Nell Gaines, a Negro woman working as a domestic servant for the Biggs family, was charged with the crime, convicted, and sentenced to die in Georgia's electric chair. Her execution was delayed only by the death-row birth of her child, whom some in this rural Georgia community speculate is, in fact, the daughter of the murdered Wilton Biggs.

Not bad, not bad at all, Cornelius Bates thought with a smile as he reread the article that had appeared in that morning's Atlanta *Constitution*. The article in the Meriwether *Vindicator* had been relegated to the bottom corner of an inside page, but Joan's story was front page in the more prestigious—and widely read—Atlanta paper. And the wire service by-line meant it was likely to get additional play all over the country. Mrs. Roosevelt's *My Day* column would also focus the spotlight on the deplorable conditions at the prison farm. *That'll keep the pressure on Talmadge.* Bates took a sip of his coffee and chuckled.

CALL ME ASAP STOP

Joan reread the terse telegram from Billy Bryce. She'd been pleased to read her wire service story about the Biggs case on the front page of the South's most prominent newspaper. Billy would have been proud too. He probably wanted to congratulate her personally. Maybe he'd even wire her some money—not that she'd been a spendthrift on this trip! Between Sam's generosity on the train and Ida's at Warm Springs, Joan still had nearly half of her travel advance. And now she'd use a nickel to call Billy—collect.

Joan slipped the nickel into the slot of the phone in the wood paneled booth in the lobby of Georgia Hall. It was past midday, that meant that Billy would just be arriving in his Los Angeles office.

"Collect call to Billy Bryce at the *Standard* in Los Angeles," Joan told the operator, then gave her the number. She waited while the call was placed, watching patients and their families wander through the high-ceilinged corridors on their way to therapy sessions, craft classes, or the spring-fed pools.

"Los Angeles *Standard*," came a voice from the distant end of a long tunnel.

"Collect call for Billy Bryce from Joan Roswell. Will you accept the charges?"

"One moment, please."

Joan listened to the pops of static along the transcontinental phone line. After a couple of minutes, Billy finally picked up the phone and accepted the call.

"Hello, dear!" Joan sang out, a smile in her voice. "The Atlanta *Constitution* ran my story on page one. Did you know?"

Billy's silence was the first clue that he wasn't as enamored with her story as she was. "I send you at considerable expense all the way across the country and you're covering local news. This is a Los Angeles paper, Joan. You remember Los Angeles, don't you? Home of the motion picture industry, which when last I checked was your beat. Know how many stories I've seen from you on the motion picture industry since you left town? One."

"Now dear, that's not quite fair," Joan replied. The best way to handle Billy was to go on the offensive. "The stories on the polio Foundation here have had a Hollywood connection."

"A very tenuous connection, Joan, and one which I might suggest has outlived whatever usefulness it might have once enjoyed. I might also suggest that it's time to end your little vacation and get back to work. Mr. Marcengill is questioning why our 'ace' Hollywood reporter is getting scooped on an almost daily basis by Louella Parsons." Horace Marcengill was the owner and publisher of the *Standard*.

"I've been doing some of my best work ever!"

"I'm not criticizing the quality of your work," Billy snapped from two thousand miles away, "I'm criticizing the focus of your reporting. You were supposed to interview what's-her-name about her new book and then come back to work, not go gallivanting across Georgia covering local stories. We've got local news all over the place out here. If I wanted you to cover local stories, I'd have sent you out to Santa Monica. Now get on that train and get back to work!"

Before Joan could snap off a response, she heard a *click* and the line went dead. Joan replaced the receiver. She could put Billy off, but not for long. If she stretched this trip out for more than another day or so, she ran the risk of getting back to the *Standard* to find herself out of a job. *Whatever is going to happen needs to happen fast.*

CHAPTER 64

Atlanta

"Leave her out of it," Keeler Heath said, wiping the sweat from his forehead with a damp white handkerchief.

"Leave her out of it?" Governor Eugene Talmadge asked, turning from the open window of his office to face his secretary and political advisor. It was an unseasonably warm day, and the governor, as usual when not seeing anyone in the office, was in shirtsleeves with his trademark red galluses holding up his pants. He stared scornfully at his aide through his over-sized round glasses. "She's central to the whole case, the whole issue. She's the one about to be fried. I pay you for advice and that's the best you got?"

Talmadge passed a hand through his lank dark hair. A thin smile played at the governor's mouth but it was a cynical smile, not one prompted by the humor of the situation. "I got a nigra woman sitting down there in Milledgeville on death row. She's convicted of killing a white man—a prominent supporter of mine, at that. I've already had to put off the execution once because she let herself get knocked up—and that's when she's already got two other brats that she can't take care of. Then I get a call from this Osburn fellow who's all the sudden developed a bleeding heart for the coloreds and wants to reopen the case. And now the newspapers are picking up the story. Next thing you know I'll have nine justices in black robes breathing down my neck."

The afternoon *Journal* had run an edited version of the story that had appeared in that morning's *Constitution*.

Talmadge turned back to the window, looking out over the park-like grounds of Capitol Square. "You're a big help, Keeler, a real big help," he shot over his shoulder.

"Hear what I'm saying," the younger man said, shifting uncomfortably from foot to foot. "Make the issue about justice for the widow or justice for the deceased. Leave the nigra woman out of it. Sign the order for the stay and then release a statement to the press." Heath closed his eyes and began to dictate in a sonorous voice. "'In the interest of justice for the family of my dear friend whatever-his-name-was…'"

"Biggs, Wilton Biggs."

"'…I have directed the district attorney to reopen the investigation into the murder of Mr. Biggs to ensure that justice is served, and his widow is comforted…' Somethin' like that. You don't mention Gaines at all. See? She's just a minor player in the vast drama of life in the governor's office. Make the saintly Mrs. Biggs the focus for the public. If it delays the execution for a day or a week or a month, who cares? That nigra ain't going nowhere." Heath leaned forward now and looked toward the governor. "And if by some miracle, Osburn determines that she didn't do it, then you're positioned as the champion of justice for all, not just the rich, but the poor and the downtrodden."

"Even the Negroes?" Talmadge turned slowly from the window.

Heath pursed his lips. They locked eyes for a minute.

Talmadge stepped over to his desk. He leaned over and flipped the switch on his intercom. "Zeke? Come in here and bring a notepad."

"Yes sir."

Talmadge looked up at Heath and winked. "I might just keep you around for another day, son."

CHAPTER 65

Milledgeville

"Stay of execution?" said Warden Carlson, staring at the handset of his phone in disbelief. "For how long?"

"We don't know. Could be permanent. The district attorney is reopening the case," said Keeler Heath. "Wilton Biggs's son Robert is in the Meriwether County Jail on some federal charge, and they're interviewing him about what happened the night of the murder. Apparently, he was at the scene. It sounds like Miz Gaines's counsel did a pretty sorry job with her defense and may have suppressed some evidence that would exonerate her."

The warden swore under his breath. "Well, keep me in touch," he growled. "She's in the infirmary with her brat, with Mrs. Roosevelt guarding her like a mother hen."

"The governor is well aware of that," Heath said acidly. "He reads her *My Day* column, along with half the rest of the people in the country. He wasn't very happy about the one about the conditions at your prison farm."

Carlson was silent. "I wasn't either," he finally said. "Good-bye, sir."

He slammed down the phone and sat staring at it for a few minutes, drumming his thick fingers on the scarred desk. If that can of worms was reopened, all kind of things might come crawling out, like the sweetheart deal he'd made with Biggs that got him Nell Gaines as a cook in the first place. *And a dozen others just like it. Time to take some action to put the lid back on the can.*

Carlson strode out of his office, pausing by Betty Barnette's desk. "I'm taking off for the rest of the day," he said to his secretary. "If anyone calls, just tell 'em I've gone home sick."

"Yessir," Betty said. "I hope you feel better tomorrow, sir."

"Oh, I will," the warden said with a smirk. "I'm sure I will be feeling much better tomorrow."

CHAPTER 66

Milledgeville

"It's such a shame that I didn't have an extra set of needles," Mrs. Roosevelt said, "but I think I can at least get you started on your first knitting lessons with these pencils."

She was sitting in a straight-backed chair beside Nelle Gaines's bed in the infirmary, the new baby sleeping peacefully in a peach basket beside her feet. Nell, looking much better, was holding a pair of sharpened yellow pencils in her hands and looking closely at the First Lady's knitting needles. "Now, let's cast on," Eleanor began, demonstrating with her own needles and a ball of yarn.

At that moment, Tommy Thompson burst into the room. "Mrs. Roosevelt!" she said urgently, "we've got company coming. A bunch of men—and they are wearing Klan robes!"

Nell moaned and dropped her pencils. "Oh, sweet Jesus," she cried, "they've come to get me. Quick, Miz Roosevelt, we got to hide the baby!"

"An excellent suggestion, Nell," the First Lady said, calmly rising to her feet. "Tommy, please take the baby and hide in the closet. Nell, move over so I can sit beside you."

Tommy grabbed the handle of the peach basket and scurried into a supply closet at the far end of the infirmary, closing the door behind her. Eleanor seated herself beside Nell on the bed, her left arm around the younger woman's shoulders. The stamping of feet grew louder, along with some language that made Mrs. Roosevelt wince.

When the door burst open to admit a group of men in white hoods and robes, they were met by the sight of the First Lady of the United States, calmly pointing a .22 caliber Smith & Wesson revolver at them. "Good evening, gentlemen," Mrs. Roosevelt said. "It's kind of you to pay a call, but I'm afraid visiting hours are over. Mrs. Gaines and her baby need their sleep."

The men were struck silent. Finally, one of them spoke up. "Hey, Carlson, you didn't tell us Mrs. Roosevelt was still here!"

"Yeah," said another, shoving his hand against the shoulder of the Klansman at the front of the crowd. "It's one thing to lynch a prisoner who's already goin' to the chair, but we could get into a lot of trouble for threatening the First Lady."

"What are you afraid of?" Carlson said angrily from under his hood. "She's just an interfering Yankee who has no business sticking her nose into our affairs. I say—

"Gentlemen," Mrs. Roosevelt interrupted, "I may be an 'interfering Yankee,' but I do know how to use this gun. And I'm not hiding under a sheet. Who put you up to this?"

"He did," a short, rotund man said, yanking the hood off Carlson's head. He then pulled off his own hood. "I'm sorry, Mrs. Roosevelt," he said. "There's not even a Klan around here any more. I had to dig through my grandfather's trunks for an hour to find this suit. We didn't know you were still here. Carlson got us all riled up, said we needed to get down here and show this n—uh, colored woman some Southern justice."

"Well, she seems to have gotten plenty of that already," Mrs. Roosevelt said tartly, rising from the bed. "Did he happen to tell you the governor has issued a stay of execution while her case is reopened?"

"Well, no," said the short man sheepishly. "He just said this thing was dragging on too long, and we needed to take things into our own hands. I guess we jumped the gun a little."

"Well, then," Mrs. Roosevelt said pleasantly. "May I ask you now to give us all some privacy, so Mrs. Gaines can nurse her baby and get to sleep? I'm sure you will want to return to your own homes."

"C'mon, Carlson," said the short man, grabbing the warden by the arm. The others shuffled out of the room after them. A man at the rear muttered, "My wife is gonna kill me when she finds out what I done to one of her bedsheets."

SUNDAY, MAY 24, 1936

CHAPTER 67

FIRST LADY HOLDS OFF KLANSMEN AT PRISON
Shots Fired as Mrs. Roosevelt Thwarts Lynching

By Joan Roswell, Special to the AP—Warm Springs, Georgia—Eleanor Roosevelt, demonstrating a lust for adventure more often associated with her famous uncle Theodore than with her role as First Lady, last night held off an armed mob of Ku Klux Klansmen at the Georgia State Prison in Milledgeville. Mrs. Roosevelt faced down approximately thirty hooded men armed with shotguns and hunting rifles who had come to the prison to lynch Nell Gaines, the Negro woman many observers now believe was falsely accused, tried, and convicted in the murder last year of her abusive employer, a prominent white businessman.

In an exclusive interview with this reporter, Mrs. Roosevelt downplayed her role in this unfolding drama, saying only that she was "confident the good people of Georgia will see that justice is served in this case." The execution of Mrs. Gaines, who was convicted last November, was delayed by Governor Eugene Talmadge when he learned that the condemned was with child. The baby, a girl, was delivered on Thursday, and the wheels of justice had begun to turn once again toward Mrs. Gaines's date with the Georgia electric chair. But, as previously reported, new evidence casting doubt on Mrs. Gaines's guilt recently surfaced, prompting

Governor Talmadge to issue a temporary stay of the execution.

That stay prompted last night's assault at the prison. As she was keeping vigil with the accused and her baby, Mrs. Roosevelt was alerted to the approach of the Klansmen by her secretary. Sources tell this reporter that the First Lady brandished her pistol and fired warning shots over the heads of her adversaries and then challenged the "first man who wants to die" to step forward.

"I was so scared I almost died right then and there," Mrs. Gaines admitted. "But Mrs. Roosevelt, she stood up to those men and, God bless her, they backed down just like a dog that's been swatted on the nose. She saved me and my baby."

"Sometimes our simple presence in a difficult situation is what makes the difference," Mrs. Roosevelt said modestly. Georgia authorities are investigating the incident. FBI director J. Edgar Hoover has volunteered the "full resources of the Bureau" to assist state officials.

Billy Bryce held the editor's copy of Joan's dispatch between ink-stained fingers and shook his head slowly. *She's got nine lives and she always lands on her feet.* He'd been within a day of firing his wayward reporter, but this scoop—not to mention the rare personal visit it had prompted from Mr. Marcengill, the *Standard's* publisher—had secured her job for the foreseeable future. *She'll be asking for more money now.* Billy initialed the draft and hollered, "Copy boy!"

Kelly Durham and Kathryn Smith

MONDAY, MAY 25, 1936

CHAPTER 68

Greenville

"Biggs!" the jailer shouted, startling Robert. "Stand up and come over here." The fat, khaki-uniformed man was standing in front of Robert's barred cell, a pair of heavy black manacles in his chubby hands. "Hold your hands out," the man commanded, as he passed the cuffs through the bars. "Put these on. You've got a visitor."

"Who is it?" Robert asked as he clamped the cold iron around his wrists. He held his cuffs up next to the bars, so the jailer could lock them.

"You'll see. Step back." The jailer selected a long round key from the ring on his belt and unlocked the cell door. "Alright, let's go." The deputy grasped Robert's upper arm and guided him along the corridor and up the narrow stairs to the interview room, the same room where he'd talked to the G-man and the lawyer from Atlanta, Mr. Bates.

The deputy pushed the door open to reveal a pasty-faced young man wearing a yellow seersucker suit and mopping his brow with a stained handkerchief.

"Who are you?" Robert asked as the jailer pushed him onto the wooden chair across the narrow table from the sweating man.

"I'm your attorney," the man said, offering a weak handshake.

"Mr. Gardner's the attorney my father always used."

"Well, yes, that's so, but—"

"I want to talk with my mother. Why isn't she here? I can't understand why she hasn't come to see me yet. She'd know to call Mr. Gardner."

"Well, right, but see there's a problem with all that," the attorney stammered.

"What kind of problem?" Robert stared at the attorney who refused to make eye contact with his younger client.

"Well, it's your mother, see? She's had some health problems."

Robert felt a slug of ice push through his heart. He gulped. "Is she all right?"

"Well, now she's going to be fine, just fine, but she's getting some badly needed rest. These last few months have been very hard on her. I'm sure you can understand that, Robert. Is it all right if I call you Robert?"

Robert shifted his gaze toward the window. "You better tell me what's wrong with her before I wrap this chain around your neck." He held up his manacles and rattled them.

"Now, don't, don't get upset," the attorney said, holding up both hands in a "stop" sign. "Your mother's in the hospital. She's getting the best of care." Robert rattled the chain again. "She's been admitted to the state mental hospital at Milledgeville," the attorney, whose face had gone even paler, croaked. "I'm sure she'll be fine in a couple of weeks."

"A couple of weeks?"

"Months?"

Robert shook his head angrily. "What do you want, anyway?"

"Like I said, I'm your lawyer, appointed by the court since your mother is unable to make decisions in her present condition. And, if you'll calm down for a few minutes, I'll share that I actually bring some good news."

"Good news?"

"Well, yes, good and bad, really."

"Go on."

"Well, the district attorney, Mr. Osburn, is charging you with manslaughter in the death of your father. It seems that Mrs. Gaines's and Miss Woods's statements leave you as the only credible suspect and since you have refused to deny your involvement, you're the last man standing, so to speak." Robert stared blankly at the attorney who continued to perspire. "I'm sure I can get you a reduced sentence if you cooperate with the D.A. That's my recommendation, by the way. Plead guilty, show remorse, behave, and you'll probably be out of prison in five years or so."

"That's the good news?" Robert asked, gritting his teeth, his nostrils flaring.

"Good? My heavens, no. That's the bad news."

"What's the good news, then Clarence Darrow?"

"The feds have agreed to drop the Mann Act charges." The attorney smiled for the first time. "And you don't have to call me 'Darrow.' My name is Melvin Jugg."

CHAPTER 69

Warm Springs

It was the last night at the Little White House before the Roosevelts and their staff headed back to Washington on the train and guests had come to dinner. Gathered around the table with the President and First Lady were Missy and Grace, Corey Wainwright, and Cornelius Bates, who had returned from Atlanta for the special occasion. Mrs. Roosevelt had also invited Ida Lupino and Joan Roswell to join them.

As they dug into Daisy Bonner's smothered pork chops, collard greens, black-eyed peas and fresh corn on the cob, the President rolled his eyes. "Oh, Daisy," he hollered toward the kitchen, "how I will miss your cooking when I return to Washington!"

Daisy walked through the butler's pantry, smiling. "Mr. President," she said simply, "you appreciate my cooking better than anyone."

"Now, Franklin," Eleanor admonished once Daisy had left the dining room, "you know Mrs. Nesbitt and her cooks do their best."

"Yes," he said. "She does her best to see they overcook or undercook any dish so it's almost inedible."

"Let's talk about our good news," Missy said tactfully, hoping to avoid another row about the White House cuisine. "So much has happened in the past two days it makes my head swim! I always thought the wheels of justice turned slowly. Not this time."

"Sometimes Lady Justice surprises us," agreed Cornelius Bates. "The D.A. really put a scare into Robert by sending Melvin Jugg down to the jail to see him. Five minutes after he'd left, Robert offered to make a full confession if they'd just give him a competent attorney. The charge of manslaughter was totally appropriate, to my way of thinking. He certainly didn't mean to kill his father."

"No," Mrs. Roosevelt said frostily. "He meant to kill Nell Gaines, and his father just got in the way. I am not sure young Robert feels any remorse for what he did."

"I agree, dear," Joan said, taking a sip of the sweet iced tea in her glass and nodding to Eleanor. "I managed to get an exclusive interview with him at the jail, and he didn't seem the least bit sorry for what he did."

"Five years in prison might give him some time to reflect on his actions," Corey said. "I wonder if he and Nell will pass on the road to Milledgeville?"

That brought smiles to everyone around the table. Joan's articles had created such a stir of sympathy for Nell that Governor Talmadge had expedited her release, and she was scheduled to come home and rejoin her mother and children the following day.

Ida Lupino, who had been given the place of honor beside her fellow polio survivor, favored FDR with her dazzling smile. "Mr. President, did you have something to do with Nell being offered a parole position at the Warm Springs Foundation?"

"No, no, I can't take credit for that one," the President laughed, eyes twinkling at the pretty starlet. "That would all be the doing of my missus." He turned his great head to his wife and held up his iced tea glass in salute. "When she puts her mind to, there's no stopping her."

"To Mrs. Roosevelt!" cried Grace Tully, and they all raised their glasses.

"I thought it was the best solution all around," Mrs. Roosevelt said modestly. "Nell's excellent cooking skills will be put to good use, she'll get away from Greenville, which has such unpleasant memories for her, and her children can attend the new school being built for them here in Warm Springs."

"I know you were working on getting a better school for the colored children here," Missy said to FDR. "When will it open?"

"Next spring," the President said. "They've decided to name it the Eleanor Roosevelt School."

"Very appropriate!" Mr. Bates said. "I understand you were a teacher for some years, in New York, Mrs. Roosevelt?"

"Yes," the First Lady said. "I adored teaching and still miss it very much."

The conversation turned to other subjects then, and over banana pudding and coffee, they shared their plans for the next day. Ida would be staying on for another week of therapy, Corey would be returning on the train with the Roosevelt party, and Cornelius Bates would depart for Atlanta in his chauffeur-driven Packard.

"What a coincidence, dear," Joan said, batting her eyes at the distinguished attorney. "I'll be heading to Atlanta as well, to catch the afternoon train back west, though I suppose I shall have to ride that poky milk train from Warm Springs that takes forever to get there."

"I would be delighted to offer you a ride," the attorney said, eyeing the attractive reporter appreciatively. "I'll be traveling alone and would be happy to have a charming companion such as yourself."

"How chivalrous! I accept!" Joan said quickly.

"We'll be at your cottage at 10 a.m. sharp," Bates said. "Plenty of time to enjoy a good lunch once we reach Atlanta."

Corey had been invited to stay in the guest cottage behind the Little White House that night, and after dinner he and Missy lingered on the porch of the President's home. They listened to the sounds of the crickets and tree frogs for a few moments, and then he pulled a small white box from his pocket.

"I've got a little gift for you," he said. "It isn't much, but it caught my eye when I walked past the window of a jewelry store in Greenville the other day."

Missy smiled and opened the box. Inside was a tiny gold charm shaped like a wishbone. "Oh, Corey, how darling!" she said. "Thank you. I'll add it to my bracelet as soon as I get back to Washington. You know, we never did pull that wishbone Daisy gave us to see who got their wish."

"We don't need to," he said, tipping up her chin with his finger. "I think we have the same wish."

Kelly Durham and Kathryn Smith

TUESDAY, MAY 26, 1936

CHAPTER 70

Atlanta

Joan Roswell stepped from the big Packard at the Spring Street entrance to Atlanta's Terminal Station. A rare morning thunderstorm had cooled off the blisteringly hot day and steam was rising from the asphalt and the sidewalks. Taxis were pulling up to and away from the curb as excited or weary travelers hefted their bags or tipped a Red Cap. From inside the terminal loudspeakers rattled as train departures and arrivals were announced. Cornelius Bates walked around the back end of his car while his chauffeur lifted Joan's suitcases from the trunk.

"I can't remember a more charming ride through the country," the wealthy lawyer said, smiling broadly. "I was fascinated by your stories and enchanted by your company." He lifted Joan's hand to his lips while staring into her beautiful green eyes.

"You're the charmer, Cornelius. And so gallant— offering me a luxurious ride instead of making me sit with the rural unwashed on that train!" Joan shifted the strap of the heavy bag on her shoulder.

"It was my pleasure, Joan. Next time I'm out to the west coast, I may just give you a call."

"If you ever come out to California, dear, you'd better give me a call, or my feelings will be irrevocably wounded." Joan flashed her eyes and smiled, and Bates thought he'd never seen a prettier woman, certainly never shared his car with one. "Thank you again, dear, for the ride and also for helping that poor woman escape with her life."

Bates looked around at the large expanse of the station's front, at the dozens of people scurrying here and there. "You know," he said, looking back at Joan, "sometimes I forget that I went into the law to help people. Sometimes I get so caught up in the arcane minutiae and the drive to win the case that I lose consciousness of the humanity involved. Mrs. Gaines was a good reminder for me."

Joan leaned forward, patted him on the chest and kissed his cheek. "Thank you for what you did. It made a wonderful story and this tiny little bit of humanity is grateful."

"Beg your pardon, Miss Roswell," the chauffeur said, approaching from the direction of the terminal. "Your bags are being loaded. Here are your claim stubs."

Joan favored the young man with a smile. "Thank you, dear." She turned back to Bates. "Well, I guess it's back on the tracks for me." She placed her hand on the sleeve of his coat. "Do please call me when you come west." She turned and headed into the terminal.

Cornelius Bates watched as Joan strode into the crowd and it closed around her.

It was slightly cooler under the train station's canopies, but the air was thick with humidity and the bustle of porters, passengers, and people of every sort flowing to and from the trackside platforms, searching for the right train or an arriving loved one.

Joan checked her ticket as she threaded her way through the milling crowd. Her train was leaving from Track Three in ten minutes. She would like to have waited another week, to have returned to Los Angeles as Ida's traveling companion—Ida who could afford a stateroom but who could not afford to offend Joan and would therefore have offered to share her accommodations.

Despite the popularity of her articles about the Gaines case, despite her growing readership, Billy had ordered her back to Los Angeles— "BACK TO WORK," he had cabled—as though she hadn't been working all along. And he had not offered any additional travel money, so she would be sitting in coach again.

Of course, Billy's telegram hadn't been the only one she'd received. She'd also gotten a wire from the managing editor at the Associated Press, complimenting her on the Gaines articles. Billy didn't know that yet. Joan would play that card when the timing was right. But for now, it was three nights on the train. *I just hope I don't wind up next to any kids!*

Joan reached Track Three and approached the closest carriage, ticket in hand. She offered it to the conductor at the bottom of the steps. "Welcome aboard, miss," he said with a smile. "Turn left through this first carriage. Your seat is about halfway along in the second car you come to."

Joan smiled and pulled herself up onto the iron staircase.

"Joan! Hey! Joan!"

She turned to find a young man loping toward the train. It was Sam! *What a stroke of luck! Private compartment, here I come!*

Joan waited at the top of the steps as Sam presented his ticket and received directions from the conductor. He bounded up the steps with an eager grin.

"Hello, you handsome thing!" Joan said, turning her cheek up toward Sam. He hesitated for only a moment before kissing her and she quickly linked her arm through his. "How was your conference, dear? I can't wait to hear all about it!"

Sam smiled as they headed into the carriage and along its narrow aisle. "It was swell. How was your trip? Did you meet that author lady?"

"Oh, my trip was most rewarding, dear. I'll tell you all about it if you invite me to dinner." Joan cocked her head to one side and smiled. Sam's lopsided grin faltered, then slid off his face. "What's the matter, dear?"

"Well, I uh, sort of miscalculated my per diem and travel allowance."

"But, dear, you're an accountant."

"True, but even accountants make mistakes, especially junior ones."

"Well, then," Joan said, lifting her face and catching Sam's eyes, "I'll buy your dinner. It's the least I can do to repay your kindnesses to me on our trip east." *And you can make it up to me with a nice, soft bed afterwards*, she thought.

They crossed the platform between the carriages as a whistle blew on the platform and a voice shouted, "All aboard for Anniston, Birmingham, Montgomery, Pensaco—" The door closed behind them.

"Where's your compartment, dear?" Joan asked looking up at Sam. "I'll meet you there at seven and we'll go to the dining car."

The tips of Sam's ears turned red. "I, uh, I'm actually traveling coach this leg of the trip." He paused. "Actually, all the way to California. In fact, that's my seat right there." He pointed to the chair next to the window.

"How lovely," Joan said, only partially masking her disappointment. "We may not travel in luxury, dear, but at least we'll be traveling together." She stood in the aisle as Sam climbed into his seat, then sat down beside him.

Sam smiled. "I read your articles in the newspaper. Tell me all about what happened in Warm Springs."

"I'm sorry, dear," Joan said, reaching down into her bag and extracting a large manuscript. "'That author lady' gave me a preview copy of her book, and I'm afraid I'll be spending every minute reading it, so I can write a follow-up story as soon as I get back to L.A."

She opened the book and began to read, "Scarlett O'Hara was not beautiful, but men seldom realized it when caught by her charm as the Tarleton twins were."

Sam sighed and looked out the window.

EPILOGUE

Saturday, May 30, 1936
Washington, D. C.

It was a beautiful, sunny Saturday, and Missy was clearing her desk in preparation for a mid-afternoon departure with the President for Annapolis, Maryland. There they would board the presidential yacht SS *Potomac* for a leisurely overnight trip. Two of FDR's favorite speech writers, Sam Rosenman and Stanley High, would be aboard, and as a special favor the President had suggested Missy invite Corey Wainwright along as her guest. "Just a little thank you for the excellent work he did in Warm Springs," he had said with a wink. Missy smiled in anticipation and the color rose in her cheeks. She was looking forward to the weekend ahead with the handsome and attentive special agent. She had even managed to get her jeweler to attach the wishbone charm to her bracelet in record time, so she could wear it. *I wonder if he'll notice?*

Missy's thoughts were interrupted by a shout from the Oval Office, which connected directly to hers. She jumped to her feet.

"Yes, F.D.?" she asked from the doorway.

"Missy!" the President called out. "What's this all about?"

Missy quickly crossed the room and walked behind his massive desk, cluttered with ashtrays and miniature donkeys, to look over his shoulder. The President was reviewing a typed letter on stationery from the Warm Springs Foundation.

"It's something about damages to an automobile," the President said, passing the letter to his secretary. "Dr.

Raper sent us an itemized repair bill, says the car was used on 'White House business.' Good lord! 'Cracked windshield, crushed fender and bumper, repaint job due to birdshot.' What in the world is he talking about?"

Missy clenched her jaw. *That Joan Roswell!*

HISTORICAL NOTES

ELEANOR ROOSEVELT GOES TO PRISON is a work of fiction, though many of the characters were real people, used fictitiously, of course. These include the Roosevelts, Missy, Grace Tully, Malvina "Tommy" Thompson, Ida Lupino. Dr. Stuart Raper and his wife-to-be, Janice Howe, Daisy Bonner, and Governor Eugene Talmadge. The case of Nell Gaines is based on a true miscarriage of justice in Georgia, the execution in the electric chair of Lena Baker in 1945. Baker was convicted of the murder of her employer, Ernest Knight, who had held her as a sex slave in his gristmill. She shot him in self-defense during a struggle and turned herself in to authorities. Like Nell Gaines, Lena Baker was tried by a judge who kept two loaded guns in sight when he was on the bench and an all-male, all-white jury. The domestic parole program that put Nell in the employ of the Biggs family was also a feature of Georgia's prison system. In fact, in the 1970s a woman named Mary Fitzpatrick was paroled into domestic service at the governor's mansion, where she served as the nanny of Gov. Jimmy Carter's daughter, Amy.

Eleanor Roosevelt toured many prisons, both as First Lady of New York and First Lady of the United States, and was an outspoken proponent of reform. She particularly admired the work of Mary B. Harris, who ran the federal women's prison in Alderson, West Virginia. That prison focused on training women for careers rather than punishment, and its inmates lived in cottages rather than in cellblocks. Among its celebrity inmates over the years were blues singer Billie Holiday; Kathryn Kelly, wife and partner-in-crime of "Machin Gun" Kelly; and domestic diva Martha Stewart.

President Roosevelt loved his time in Warm Springs, which he customarily visited in the spring and fall during his presidency. Mrs. Roosevelt was not a fan and usually delegated hostess duties to Missy LeHand while she stayed in Washington or traveled elsewhere. There was no visit by the president in May 1936, and Ida Lupino was never a patient there, though she did, indeed, suffer from polio. Lupino did not get the role of Scarlett O'Hara, of course – that went to her fellow Brit Vivien Leigh — but she had a long and successful career in Hollywood, becoming a director of both films and television programs. Among her films was *Never Fear* in 1949, about a young dancer stricken with polio who finds the hope to go on with her life at an institution similar to the Warm Springs Foundation.

If you would like to learn more about the history on which this book is based, we recommend:

- *The Man He Became: How FDR Defied Polio to Win the Presidency* by James Tobin, Simon & Schuster, 2013

- *Southern Daughter: The Life of Margaret Mitchell* by Darden Asbury Pyron, Oxford University Press, 1991

- *The Gatekeeper: Missy LeHand, FDR and the Untold Story of the Partnership that Defined a Presidency* by Kathryn Smith, Touchstone, 2016

- *Ida Lupino: Beyond the Camera* by Mary Ann Anderson with Ida Lupino, BearManor Media, 2018

ABOUT THE AUTHORS

Kelly Durham and Kathryn Smith attended D.W. Daniel High School near Clemson, South Carolina together, but didn't become friends until more than forty years later when Kathryn began editing some of Kelly's novels. This is their third collaboration.

Kelly lives in Clemson with his wife, Yvonne. They are the parents of Mary Kate, Addison, and Callie, and also provide for their dog, George Marshall. A graduate of Clemson University, Kelly served four years in the U.S. Army with assignments in Arizona and Germany before returning to Clemson and entering private business. Kelly is also the author of THE WAR WIDOW,

Eleanor Roosevelt Goes to Prison

BERLIN CALLING, WADE'S WAR, THE RELUCTANT COPILOT, THE MOVIE STAR AND ME, HOLLYWOOD STARLET, TEMPORARY ALLIANCE and UNFORESEEN COMPLICATIONS. Visit his website, www.kellydurham.com, or contact him at kelly@kellydurham.com.

Kathryn lives in Anderson, South Carolina with her husband, Leo. They are the parents of two grown children and the grandparents of four small children. A graduate of the University of Georgia, Kathryn worked as a daily newspaper reporter and editor before entering nonprofit management work in Anderson. She is the author of the only biography of Marguerite LeHand, THE GATEKEEPER: MISSY LEHAND, FDR, AND THE UNTOLD STORY OF THE PARTNERSHIP THAT DEFINED A PRESIDENCY (Touchstone, 2016) as well as A NECESSARY WAR, a collection of interviews with World War II veterans. Her next biography, GERTIE: THE FABULOUS LIFE OF GERTRUDE SANFORD LEGENDRE, will be published this September by Evening Post Books. Kathryn speaks widely on Missy LeHand, sometimes impersonating her in period costume. Visit her website, www.kathrynsmithwords.com, and the Missy LeHand page on Facebook.

ABOUT THE COVER ARTIST

Jed Bugini-Smith, a native of South Carolina and a high school mate of the authors, moved to Italy after a long and successful career as a senior creative leader in marketing. Today, Jed focuses his talents on personal expression and embraces writing, painting, and photography with equal passion. His blog, ItalyWise.com, which has developed a loyal following, chronicles his transition to becoming an American expat in Italy. Jed shares insights and advice about managing a multitude of logistics, as well as writing about navigating a host of mental and emotional challenges that come with making such a monumental life change.

An accomplished painter, Jed is a Signature Member of the prestigious National Watercolor Society.

Kelly Durham and Kathryn Smith

Made in the USA
Columbia, SC
17 February 2019